WAHIDA CLARK PRESENTS:

LUST NOW, CRY LATER

A Novel
by
Tahanee

Wahida Clark Presents Publishing

60 Evergreen Place

Suite 904A

East Orange, New Jersey 07018

1(866)-910-6920

www.wclarkpublishing.com

Library of Congress Cataloging-In-Publication Data:

Tahanee

Lust Now Cry Later

ISBN 13-digit 9781947732292   (paper)

ISBN 13-digit 9781947732315 (ebook)

ISBN 13-digit 9781947732308 (Hardcover)

LCCN: 2018906371

1. Sex - 2. Domestic violence - 3. Washington DC - 4. African American- HIV - 5.Homosexuality - 6. Violence - 7. Relationships - 8. New Jersey – 9. Suspends

Cover design and layout by Nuance Art, LLC

Book design by $weet & Tasty Visual Arts

www.artdiggs.com

Edited by Linda Wilson

Proofreader Rosalind Hamilton

Dedication

This book is dedicated to those who struggle with finding the true meaning of "self-love." May the Creator give you the strength, knowledge, and confidence you deserve in order to love your beautiful selves.

Acknowledgments

First and foremost, "All Praises Be to Allah," the beneficent and merciful. I would like to thank my mother, Delores Jones Sayyid, for her words of encouragement and for telling me to, "Never give up on my dreams." My father, Abdul Latif Sayyid, whom I received the gift of writing from and knowledge of Islam, my sisters, Amirrah and Nyla, and most of all, Samiyyah Sayyid for the support, constructive criticism, and wonderful ideas!

Thank you to the rest of my extended family members and friends for the continuous support throughout this long, highly anticipated journey. Rest in peace to magnificent Uncle, Charles Cranford III, my beautiful cousin, Latoya Shantel Cranford, Aunt, Louise Patton, and soulmate, Dave Thomas and the rest of my family and friends who have passed on to paradise; may your beautiful souls rest in peace with our Creator for eternity! A very special thank you to my aunt and uncle, Helen and Alvin McCain for all of their love, support and thoughtful acts of kindness; I love you both! The entire Cranford family; you guys mean the world to me, thank you Shelly Bolling, for being a positive motivator throughout this journey; may Allah continue to reward you! The talented Queen of Street Fiction herself, Wahida Clark! I thank you for giving me the opportunity to share my story with the world; may the blessings of Allah be bestowed upon you. Thank you to Dr. Maxine Thompson and Linda Norswether-Wilson for their literary assistance, and Nuance Art for a magnificent book cover and last by not least, the entire team at *Everything Girls Love* magazine.

July 24, 2002
Prologue

"Well, looks like it's just you and me, kiddo." Sdia's Great Uncle George winked, closing the door behind him. Walking past her, he reached down and pinched her on her buttocks.

Eight-year-old Sdia quickly grabbed her behind and frowned. She let out a yelp. "Ouch!" *That wasn't nice!* she thought.

"Come on over here and let me see how big you've grown." Uncle George chuckled, tickled by her reaction. He placed one hand over his semi-erect penis and reclined in the seat with the other. "I'm waiting," he sang.

Sdia looked down at the faux wood floor, rather confused as to what was going on. She leaned both feet to the side, occasionally bringing them in and out as her dress followed the rhythm, swaying back and forth. Something just didn't feel right. *I wish Mommy could have taken me to work with her, instead of leaving me here with Uncle George. I hope she comes back soon!*

"Come on now," he teased, pulling on a piece of cotton that had seeped from out of the arm of the chair. "Don't tell me you're shy. I saw you over there earlier, dancing to the sound of the wind chimes, or as you say, *dingles*. I know you didn't come all the way to Maryland from DC to stand in a corner." He seductively twirled the cotton around his long triangular-shaped fingernails and smiled.

Sdia's eyes remained glued to the floor as she continued

1

to balance her weight on both ankles.

"I don't bite." He gave a low belly laugh. "Come here." He motioned with his index finger, studying her every movement. Sdia began to fidget with her fingers. *What is going on? Uncle George is looking at me. I'm not going to look up; I don't want to look at him!*

"Those sure are some pretty shoes," he said, referring to the light pink jellies she wore.

She abruptly stopped titling her ankles and looked at her shoes. Her chapped lips slowly parted. "My mommy bought them," she whispered, slowly raising her eyes from the floor until they were greeted by her Uncle George's joker-like smile.

"You're going to mess up those beautiful shoes by tilting your feet like that. You wouldn't want to mess up those shoes, now—would you?"

"No," she mumbled.

"Exactly." George nodded, leaning forward and squinting. "I like your dress. Are those roses?"

Sdia looked down at her dress. "These aren't roses; they're sunflowers." Her voice broke off into a whine.

"No. Those are roses."

"Nuh-uuuhn," she sang, shaking her head no.

"Uh-huuhn," he mocked, nodding yes.

Sdia gave him a blank gaze.

"Those are rosy rose roses." Uncle George spoke with his tongue partially exposed, imitating Donald Duck.

Sdia giggled. "Uncle George. These are sunflowers." She pointed to one of the flowers on her dress. "Roses are red."

"Maybe you're right. You know Uncle George can't see that well." He squinted. "Can you come a little closer so that I can get a better look?" His eyes widened.

Bashfully, Sdia looked down.

"Come on. It's okay, sweetie," he promised.

Sdia slowly raised her head, and bit by bit, cautiously walked toward him; the old wooden floors squeaked beneath her feet.

"That's right. Come on and sit right here." He excitedly motioned her to sit on his lap. "Hurry, hurry, hurry," he squealed, fanning both hands wildly as if he'd touched a hot surface. Sdia held out her small hand and placed it into his.

George quickly pulled her down onto his lap, positioning her buttocks on top of his penis. Sdia quickly jumped up and looked down at her uncle's lap. *What was that? What did I just sit on?* "I want Mommy," Sdia blurted out with a frown.

"Your mama's at work. She won't be back till later this evening," he reminded her, pulling her closer, until they were face to face.

"I tell you what? How about you sit in the big red chair?" He smiled, revealing a mouthful of brown teeth.

Sdia scrunched up her nose as the stench of decaying teeth and rotten egg hit her directly in the face. *Uncle George's breath smells like doo-doo.*

He stood, placed both hands under her arms, and lifted her into the chair. The ridged, torn pieces of leather clawed at her arms and legs, leaving unpleasant long white scratches as he scooted her backward. "Woo wee! You sho' is heavy," he grunted, standing straight up and dusting

3

his hands together. Slowly he kneeled down to adjust the seat back until it couldn't go any further. "Comfy?" he asked, taking a step back with his hands in his pocket. Sdia stared down at the flowers on her dress.

"I swear you look just like your mama when she was younger," he said, gazing down at her. "You know she used to love to come and visit me when she was younger. Do you know what her favorite game was?" George squatted beside her as a gust of hot air and the scent of Old Spice rushed her nostrils. "I'll give you a hint. The itsy bitsy spider ..." he began to sing, giving her a quick wink. "Came up the water spout ..." His warm, wrinkled fingers glided across her thighs ..."Down came the rain and washed the spider out."

I want my mommy. I want to go home! Sweat beads formed on Sdia's back and the back of her thighs. She squirmed in the chair as the warm leather latched onto her skin. *I want to get up! I don't like this!* She stretched her neck far back, poked out her chest and clenched the tattered arms of the chair, trying to pull herself up.

"Just relax!" George said, placing his hand on her chest and shoving her back. She fell backward and quickly closed her eyes. *I want my mommy!* Her uncle continued to run his fingers up her thighs, his breathing grew heavier; the hot air from his mouth and nose landed on her knee caps, sending chills up her spine.

She then tried focusing on the wind chimes jingling in the far distance. *The dingles! The dingles are dancing. One-two-three, one-two-three.* George meticulously moved her panties aside and stroked her vagina with the back of his index finger. Sdia's eyes widened as she gripped onto the arms of the chair. She nervously began to scratch at the rips in the couch, pulling and scrabbling at cotton.

"I want my mommy!" she whined.

George frantically popped his head up and removed his hand from under her dress. "I told your ass your mama is working. She won't be back till later!" he said coldly, staring her in the eyes.

Sdia quickly looked down. She set her eyes on one of the sunflowers on her dress. *Don't blink, Sdia. Whatever you do, don't blink!* she coached herself as her eyes began to water.

"What the hell is wrong with you!" George shouted. Sdia gulped. "You know damn well your mama is at work!"

She took a deep breath as her bottom lip quivered. The longer she stared at the sunflower on her dress, the more her eyes tingled and filled with tears, causing the flower to transform into a blurry spot. Sdia bulged her eyes to avoid the tears from spilling. She clawed her fingernails into the arms of the couch, pulling and tugging at the loose pieces of cotton.

"Don't you go ripping that cotton out my chair!" George said, reaching up and snatching both of her hands from the arms of the chair.

Chapter 1

Sixteen years later . . .

"People act like they're doing God a favor by coming to church!" Pastor Jones shouted into the microphone. "But what you fail to realize is that God doesn't need you; you need God!" he stated boldly as he grabbed the microphone from its holder and walked down the stairs. "You see, that's the problem with folks these days. They think they're too good for God! Well, let me tell you ... You ain't nothing without God!"

Sdia sat in the third row at Mount Calvary Baptist Church, shaking her head from side to side. *Feels like Pastor is talking to me! I needed to be here today to hear the Word.* She watched Pastor Jones as he made his way across the stage, removed the small white handkerchief from his suit jacket, and wiped his forehead. "God created you, and what do you do to show your appreciation?" His voice cracked. "I'll tell you what you do; you turn around and worship another human being. You show your gratitude by putting all your trust, love, and time into man, when all you need to do is call on your Lord and Savior, Jesus Christ!" he concluded, high-pitched.

"Man didn't wake you up this morning; man didn't save you in your time of need; man didn't send his only begotten son to forgive you for your sins; God did!" He stomped and jumped around in circles at the altar as the congregation stood to their feet and rejoiced with praise, shouting, "Hallelujah!"

Sdia lifted her head toward the ceiling and closed her eyes. "Hallelujah! Hallelujah! Hallelujah!" she sobbed as

tears slowly fell from her eyes. Whimpers emerged from
the pit of her stomach causing her body to jerk. *Please
help me God. Please heal my heart Father-God. Please!*
Her heart pounded in her chest; if she wanted she could
have counted each beat. "Thank you Jesus. Thank you
Father-God. Thank you Lord!" The pastor softly chanted
into the microphone, and the organ played on cue as a
young, slender gentleman emerged from the choir singing
"I Need You Now" by Smokey Norful. Tears continued to
spill from her eyes soaking her cheeks. Her eyes remained
closed as her body rocked from side to side rhythmically
with the organ. Her weeps were masked by the choir
sending her back in time seven months ago . . .

"Just let me explain," Sean had said, running behind
Sdia as she stormed ahead of him toward the restaurant's
exit.

"Explain what?" Sdia yelled. "There ain't shit you can
tell me!"

"I swear she's lying! Please believe me. She must be
drunk or something," he pleaded, reaching for her arm. "I
don't know what she's talking about!"

"Yeah, okay," she screamed, snatching her arm away
and barging through the exit doors.

"I swear to God she's lying!" Sean said, now practically
on her heels.

"Excuse me, sir?" their waiter called, running behind
them. "Your receipt and change," he said, holding out their
receipt and two crisp twenties.

"Keep the change." Sean waved without turning back.

Sdia's feet padded on the wet concrete as she quickly
ran across the congested Manhattan streets. The cold
winter rain lightly fell from the sky, frizzing her freshly

straightened hair. "Shit. I need a taxi," she murmured, holding her clutch above her head with one hand and flagging down a taxi with the other.

"Sdia!" Sean called out as he ran across the street toward her. "Where are you going?"

"Stay the fuck away from me!" she shouted, turning and slapping him across the face with her purse, catching the attention of a pedestrian.

Sean grabbed her by the arm. "I swear on my dead grandmother I don't know what she's talking about!" he screeched. "I don't even know who that is."

"Get the fuck off me!" Sdia shouted, pulling away.

"Calm down. You're making a scene." Sean nervously looked around; the last thing he wanted was to catch the attention of a NYPD officer.

"I don't give a shit!" Sdia reached up, clawing his chin and lips with her stiletto-shaped fingernails. "You're full of shit!" She violently shoved him in the face; Sean's head jerked back. "Stay away from me!" she roared.

"You're bugging out." He slowly released her grip.

"*I'm* bugging out?" She quickly charged him like a bull. "How the fuck am I the one bugging out when you're the one who had some random broad who clearly knows you, approaching you while we're out celebrating our so-called anniversary and saying 'Oooh, I'm telling!'"

Sean took a deep breath, placed both hands his hands in his pocket, and looked down at the wet pavement.

Sdia balled up her fist and began pacing back and forth. "I swear to God I should punch you in your face! I gotta get out of here!"

"I'm telling you that I don't know what that crazy bitch

is talking about. She was probably drunk or something. First of all, did you see that bitch's lace front? The fucking hairline was on her forehead! How the fuck are you going to believe a bitch as black as tar wearing a cheap ass fake wig? I swear on my dead grandmother . . . I don't know why she would say that. Baby, please!" He grabbed her by the hand and softly kissed it. "I love you, and I would never do anything to hurt you or put our relationship in jeopardy!"

Sdia looked down at the ground. "Sean, please do not lie to me." He gently stroked both of her thighs.

"Baby, I'm not. Look, it's raining, it's cold, and we're both getting wet. Let's go home and put all of this behind us," he said, pulling her closer.

Slowly, Sdia raised her head and placed both hands on the side of his face. "Sean, look me in the eyes and tell me the truth."

Gently, he took her hands into his own and kissed them. "I love you, and you mean the world to me. Let's just go back to my place and—" Screeching tires approached, and he quickly glanced over to the street. "Oh shit!" he shouted, pushing Sdia aside.

"Sean?" Sdia called out into the darkness. He shooed her away as he ran toward the black 2019 Honda Civic, recklessly pulling up onto the curb. "Sean!" Sdia shouted.

"What the fuck is going on!" a female shouted as the driver's door burst open.

"Let me explain," Sean replied, as the woman emerged wearing a Pink Victoria's Secret sweat suit, brown leather jacket, and brown suede UGGS. Honey-complexioned and about five-five, with very wide hips and thighs. Her hair was cut short; she slightly favored Halle Berry.

9

"Tina, calm down and let me explain." Sean's voice trembled as he rushed around to the driver's side.

"No, fuck that! You said it was over between y'all!" the woman shouted, pointing to Sdi.

"Tina, please just get back in the car," he begged, holding the woman by her shoulders and shoving her into the car.

Slowly, Sdia approached the vehicle. "What the hell is going on?" She moved her neck from side to side for a better view of the female, but the open driver's door made it impossible for her to get a full view.

"Sdia, stay over there!" Sean demanded, with his hand out.

"I wish she would come over here!" Tina snarled. "I'ma bust her ass."

"Sean, who is this hoodrat?" Sdia frowned.

"Hoodrat?" Tina roared. "Oh, hell no! Let me go! Let me go!" she said, wildly waving her arms, trying to break free from Sean's grip.

"Calm the fuck down!" Sean grabbed her by the arms. Get in the motherfucking car!" He violently shoved her back into the car, reached across her body, and snatched the keys from the ignition. "And don't get out!" he said, slamming the door.

Sdia placed her hand over heart. "Oh my God!" she said, hunching over as dinner from that evening resurfaced, exploding from her mouth and nose.

Sean quickly ran over, "Sdia, you okay?" he asked, kneeling. He gently rubbed her back with one hand and wiped the tears from his eyes with the other. Sdia sobbed uncontrollably as the rain fell ruthlessly from the sky onto the pavement, diluting her vomit. She weakly moved the vomited splattered pieces of hair from the side of her mouth.

"Get the fuck off of me, Sean!" she shouted, pulling away as he remained lowered toward the ground. "Stay the fuck away from me!"

"Baby, I'm sorry." Sean sniffled as tears spilled from his eyes. "I-I gotta go," he said, fumbling with the car keys, twirling them around his index finger.

**

The jingling of the church's tambourine snapped Sdia back into reality. *I can't believe he left me!* Tears rolled down the side of her cheeks and into her ears.

"That's right, praise Him! Let it out and praise Him!" the elderly woman sitting beside her said. She tilted her head back and joined Sdia. "Thank you, Lord!" she shouted, staring at the ceiling. "Hallelujah!" she hollered, taking Sdia by the hand as tears fell from her own eyes.

Sdia opened her eyes, scrunched her nose, and looked at the woman. "Excuse me," she said, respectfully pulling her hand away.

The woman peeked at Sdia from the corner of her eyes. "Are you okay, dear?" she asked, opening both eyes.

With the back of her hand, Sdia wiped her eyes. "Yes. I just need some fresh air."

"Pardon me." Her voice cracked as she rose to her feet. "Excuse me." She made her way through the crowded aisles with her head hung low.

Sdia fanned her hand in front of her face. *God forgive me, but I gotta get out of here.*

"Excuse me," she said, briskly walking past an usher.

She forcefully pushed the heavy metal double doors open, and the thick, hot, muggy air instantly latched onto her skin. She let out a sigh of relief that no one was outside of the church. She took advantage of the opportunity and permitted the welled up tears to freely roll down her cheeks. She bent down to remove the four-inch Gucci sandals from her feet and placed them under her right arm. *I just want to go home*, she thought as she quickly walked across the crowded parking lot, licking the falling salty tears from the top of her lip.

"Asshole!" she said, jerking the car door open and tossing her shoes into the backseat. "Son-of-a- bitch gonna break up with me!" she whimpered while starting the ignition. "Two and a half years of my life down the fucking drain! I should block my number and call his ass." She snatched her iPhone from her purse and looked at the blank screen and hesitantly dialed his number. *Let go and let God*, she remembered the pastor's words. She paused and glanced out of the window. *What's wrong with me? It's 7:45 in the morning, and I'm sitting in the car when I should be in church. I left service early because of him?* She looked down at her phone and let out a deep sigh. "I know exactly who to call," she said, deleting the numbers on her screen.

"Hello?" her mother Sharon answered groggily.

"I miss him," Sdia quickly blurted out.

"Shouldn't you be in church?" Sharon asked.

"Yeah, I should be, but this is really annoying me."

"Sdia, we can talk about this tomorrow when you get here. You really need to be in church."

"I don't understand how he could do this."

"Didn't you hear what I just said?"

"Yeah, I hear you, but I'm not thinking about service right now! I came outside to call you, Ma, not to talk about church."

"Look!" Sharon raised her tone. "God is more important than some nigga. See, you already have me yelling. And I don't want to awake your father," she whispered.

"Sorry, Ma."

"Mmm hmm," Sharon replied.

"Ma, I'm sad. Say something to make me feel better."

"Sdia, you can't keep on tormenting yourself over his decision. Besides, hasn't it been almost a year since you two broke up? You need to let it go!" Sharon whispered.

"No, it hasn't been a year! It's only been seven months, two weeks, and five days."

"Okay, okay, don't kill me," Sharon replied in her normal tone, noticing the chord she struck."

"I just don't get it, Ma." Sdia sighed.

"Why do I have to keep telling you the same thing? You have so much going for yourself. You're—"

"Smart, beautiful, and independent. I can have any man I want. Why do I allow that loser to occupy so much space in my brain? Right, Ma?" A beat passed between them. "Thanks for the typical pep talk. Well, if I'm all of those things, why did he cheat? Why doesn't he see those qualities in me?" Sdia asked, a blink away from more tears.

"Because maybe they're not for him to see. What's important is that you see those things!" Sharon sighed. "I am getting so tired of telling you the same thing, Dia. If you don't see these things in yourself, then no man is going to treat you the way you deserve to be treated!"

"I know, Ma. I know. It's just that I really wish I could get even with him!"

"What did I tell you, Dia? You don't have to worry about hurting anyone because people don't get away with doing shit. Remember, only hurt people hurt people, and his day is coming."

"They're probably having sex right now as we speak," Sdia added.

"So what if they are! Who gives a shit? I wouldn't want him touching me, especially after he slept with someone else."

"I don't want him to touch me!" Sdia lied.

"Good. There's no sense in sitting there making yourself depressed over something that is clearly out of your control!"

"I know, but—" Sdia replied.

"Listen," Sharon interrupted. "If it's meant for you and Sean to be together and God knows I pray it isn't; it will be!" She paused. "The only thing you should be worried about is getting back in that church and preparing for your trip tomorrow; anything else is minute, especially a damn man—a lying, cheating one at that!"

"I know, Ma."

"I'm glad you know. Now get your tail back in that church; you're on the Lord's time, and I need to start breakfast!"

"Okay, I love you, Ma."

"Uh-huh, love you too. I swear you gotta get it together, girl. I can't keep telling you the same thing over and over again. Anyway, call me when service is over."

Sdia placed her phone back into her purse and grabbed her shoes from the backseat. *Let go and let God* she thought, as she stepped from her vehicle and back into the blazing sun. She slowly walked up the small path leading to the church and up the steep stairs. Once inside she looked around until she spotted the elderly woman she had been sitting next to and maneuvered her way back to her seat.

"Are you okay dear?" the woman asked. Sdia nodded and looked up at the image of Jesus on the stained glass ceiling.

I'm not gonna let you fight Tina! Sdia, she's pregnant with my baby! Sean's words resonated in her head. *Wait ... what! Pregnant? Baby?* Sdia didn't fight back her tears this time. Instead she allowed them to flow.

"That's right, baby. Let it out. Just let go and let God," the elderly woman whispered.

I still can't believe he has a baby now! Sdia thought.

Chapter 2

"Dammit!" Sdia shouted. "Six-thirty in the fucking morning, and I'm not in the mood for this shit!" The softness of the signature pink and white striped Victoria Secret comforter felt amazing against her skin, and coolness of the room made her curse herself for promising her mother she would drive up to Washington, DC for Memorial Day. Sdia buried face into the comforter. The fresh, light, sweet, citrus aroma made her smile. *Oh my God! Those Downy Unstoppables give me life! I could lay here and do this all day.* Sdia rarely got the chance to sleep in on the weekdays and since the holiday fell on a Monday, she would have gotten the chance to watch all of her favorite shows as opposed to recording them. This was her second week working as a writer for *Reach* magazine and her first time living alone. Moving to New Jersey had been a big step for her, considering the fact she was born and raised in Washington, DC. Sdia sat up and stretched, feeling rejuvenated.

"Look at this mess," she said, looking around at all the boxes in her bedroom that she hadn't unpacked. The thought of opening them and finding a home for her belongings made her sick to her stomach. Instead of spending some useful time at home unpacking, she had to drive all the way to DC. *I know this barbecue is going to be boring as hell. Ain't nobody gonna be there, but me, Mommy, Dad, and Charmaine.* Her bare feet sank into the fluffy beige carpet as she dragged herself out of bed.

Sdia stood in front of her bedroom mirror naked while oiling her body. She turned around and looked at her voluptuous round ass. *These Instagram bitches gettin' injections and jeopardizing their lives to have an ass like this!* Her ass was one of her most favorite assets. "Too bad I can't share this amazing body with anyone. Damn, I've been celibate for a while." She reminisced about the last time she'd had sex, which was approximately seven months ago. She hated long distance relationships, but she figured once she graduated from Mary Washington, she and Sean would get engaged and find a place together in Jersey since it was only a half-hour away from where they both worked, but Sean had other plans that didn't include her. Just before their life together was about to begin, she found out about his infidelity with his co-worker, Tina. Her stomach knotted up as she thought about the last time she had seen Sean.

"I love you and I would never do anything to hurt you, or put our relationship in jeopardy!" What a fucking liar!

All Sdia could do at the time was cry. She had never had her heart broken.

"And now this mother-fucker has the nerve to be a father!"

Sdia grabbed one of the many workbooks from her bookshelf and opened it:

Chapter Five

Learning to love yourself is the first step to gaining real self-esteem.

She smiled and continued reading:

Every day, look at yourself in the mirror and remind yourself of how wonderful and valuable you are.

Sdia closed the book and sighed. "I am a wonderful person and of great value!" she said apathetically.

She looked down at the floor and sighed. "Who am I fooling?" Suddenly, she spotted a small black spider scurrying across the carpet. The hairs on her arm stood up.

♪ *The itsy bitsy spider ran up the water spout.*

Down came the rain and washed the spider out. ♪

"UGH!" Flashbacks of her uncle's fingertips running across her thighs gave her the willies. "Fuck!" she shouted, vigorously rubbing both legs. *I should've told someone!* The entire incident replayed in her mind.

Uncle George can't see that well. What is that? Peach fuzz? I'm a fucking pervert, but don't tell your mama.

"Blah, blah, fucking blah!" she mocked. "Burn in hell! I hope he is burning in hell!" Sdia said devilishly while gritting her teeth.

George died from lung cancer over six years ago. She didn't see much of him before his death, and she couldn't have been happier. At his funeral, she watched her family members huddle over the cherrywood coffin he lay in and said their goodbyes.

"Dia, do you want to come up with me?" her mother Sharon had asked as she dabbed her cheeks with the soiled Kleenex she had balled in her hand.

"No, Ma." Sdia looked at her mother and shook her head no. As a child she was subjected to his decrepit face for three years, without a choice, a say so or option, but not today! Today she had a choice. Fuck no, I don't want to see that ugly son-of-a-bitch!

"I'll go up with you, babe," Sdia's father, Thomas replied, escorting his wife to the casket.

Sdia dabbed her nose with the klenex. "One day. One day I have go to tell them what he did to me chiled." She looked down

The warm spring air pushed her mind to the present. The soothing breeze felt great against her skin. Sdia took a deep breath and looked up.

"Life isn't that bad," she mumbled.

"Good morning, sunshine," a voice called from the balcony behind her. Sdia turned and glanced up.

"Good morning, Ms. Wallace. How are you?" she asked in her most polite, innocent voice—the one she used when she spoke to her elders.

"I'm doing just fine. Just out here watering my babies," Ms. Wallace replied in her southern accent. She stood two apartments up on her small balcony.

"Well, enjoy your day, Ms. Wallace."

"Where are you going so early?" Ms. Wallace asked.

Oh boy, here we go. Sdia slowly spun around to face her. "I'm headed home for a family barbecue. I'll be back tonight or early tomorrow morning."

"Cooking out? Y'all going to have chicken?" Ms. Wallace asked enthusiastically.

"I don't know, more than likely we will," Sdia replied, perplexed.

"Can you bring me back a plate, suga?"

Sdia smiled. "Uh, a plate? Um okay." *I can't believe she just asked me to bring her back a damn plate. She hardly speaks to me, and two days ago she called the cops on me for playing my music too loud.*

"Thanks, baby. If you can, try to bring me two plates, that way I don't have to cook." Ms. Wallace chuckled.

Sdia nodded.

"Oh, and one more thing, suga … The next time you decide to play your music all loud and what not, make sure it isn't a bunch of cursing! I don't see how you call yourself going to church to praise the Lord, but then come home and play that filth!"

Sdia turned and walked to her car. She knew if she stayed a minute longer, she would laugh in Ms. Wallace's face, and then curse her out. Then more than likely, she would feel bad about it later. Sdia was raised to respect her elders at all times. *However, sometimes people need to be put in their place, and maybe it's time to let my mother know a thing or two about her beloved uncle,* she thought as she hopped into her car and sped off.

After forty-five minutes of driving, Sdia was almost at the end of the New Jersey turnpike when she decided to stop to get gas, a snack, and to use the restroom. After paying for her gas, she got into her car and drove to the rest area. The moment she got out of her car, she snapped her fingers. *Damn, I was supposed to call my mother!* She dialed home with one hand and locked the car door with the other. A navy blue 8 series BMW coupe with tinted windows and shiny chrome rims pulled up next to her. She looked up at the driver as the window began to slowly roll down. She was greeted by a man with a dark-brown complexion. His round button eyes had the most beautiful, long eyelashes she'd ever seen. The dark waves in his hair and diamond studs in both ears sexified his appearance. Sdia looked at the diamond-face watch that securely hugged his wrist as his tattooed arm hung from out of the window. He reciprocated the stare.

Chapter 3

"What do you want for dinner, babe?" Carl Adler asked as he breathed heavily, trying his best to keep up with his wife Natalya, who was now opening the car door.

"I don't know, and by the looks of it, eating should be the last thing your fat ass wants do!" she shouted.

"Don't start your shit with me, Natalya!"

"Whatever. Can you hurry up? It's hot out here!"

Natalya started the ignition and watched in disgust as her 260-pound husband wobbled to the car. She thought about how she would have been gone, if it weren't for his money. She stopped trying to convince herself that she loved him. Heck, she wasn't even sure she liked him, but she had to take the bitter with the sweet.

She pounded on the horn. "Hurry up!"

Natalya couldn't deny that she was blessed. She was a thirty-five-year-old housewife with a beautiful three-level home, a four-car garage that held three cars of her own, two walk-in closets of her own, and a bank account that held $58,562.19, and that was just her checking account. She had everything a woman could ask for. Carl was fourteen years her senior and a well-respected executive in the District of Columbia.

"Whew, it's hot as hell out there!" Carl stated as he opened the passenger side door, entering butt first.

Natalya noticed the sweat streak down the crack of his khaki shorts. Grimacing, she rolled her eyes and without a second thought, put the car in reverse.

"Damn, Natalya!" Carl shouted as his right leg hung out

21

of the car.

"I told you to hurry up," she replied with a smirk. She pressed her foot on the brake and waited for him to position himself in the car.

"I don't understand you. You act like you hate me," he stated as he lifted his right thigh into the car. He turned and waited for her response, but instead, she stared emotionless through the rearview mirror. Carl turned and glared out of the window. *Is his fat ass really crying?* Natalya thought as her husband wiped his eyes with the back of his right hand.

* * *

"I don't think so, bitch. These niggas be on some other shit and mama don't have time to be raising no man." Will laughed. He had no problem calling his close friends and co-workers out their name; it was a form of endearment and they didn't shy away from showing the same affection in return.

"Bitch, you have all the time in the world. I've seen you raise quite a few," his co-worker, Ryan replied.

"Exactly! That's why I won't be doing it again. Anyway, are you gonna spot me or what? I want to get one more set in before my next client arrives."

"Yeah, yeah." Ryan waved him off. "You're probably fucking that one too." He grabbed his towel from his locker. "I'll be by the leg press when you're ready," he said, before exiting.

"Okay."

Will jogged over to his locker and removed his gym bag. "Hmm," he said, fumbling through the assortment of lubricants and condoms. "Sheesh!" He sucked his teeth and picked up a handful of condoms that were in the way. He walked over to the trashcan and tossed them inside. Upon returning to his bag, he picked a random lubricant, stuffed the gym bag back into the locker and hurriedly walked through the locker room toward the janitor's closet, peeking under each bathroom stall along the way. Satisfied that he was alone, he slowly stepped into the dark closet. The gap underneath the door provided him just enough light to make his way around the small space. Will removed the Axe body spray from his back pocket and generously sprayed the air, but the stench of mildew and musk overpowered. "Fuck it." He shrugged. Just then, he heard a familiar voice humming Niki Minaj's song, "Good Form." Will looked at his watch and smiled, anxiously removing his gym shorts and Polo boxer briefs. He assumed the position and bent over with his ass cheeks spread apart.

The door to the janitor's closet slowly crept open and in walked Stello, his four o'clock appointment.

"You know what to do," Stello said, with his dick in his hand. Will rushed over to him and dropped down to his knees. He greedily rammed Stello's limp dick into his mouth, tightly wrapped both lips around it and slowly let them slide up and down his tool, leaving a large trail of saliva with every stroke until warm semen exploded into the back of his throat.

Chapter 4

Got-damn, she's fine! She probably has a man. Somebody that fine has to be taken. Either that, or she has a bunch of niggas in her DM. Sdia rolled her eyes before walking away.

"Excuse me, miss?" He called out. *I know this bitch ain't trying to ignore me!*

"Yes?" she asked, turning to face him.

"Can I talk to you for a minute?" he asked as he got out of the car, dressed in all black.

"I'm really in a rush," Sdia replied, annoyed.

"Well, that makes two of us," he joked.

He couldn't deny that not only was she perfect in height with a nice body, but she also spoke well. As he approached her, he noticed how attractive and well-groomed she was; she was absolutely breathtaking.

"So what's your name?" he asked.

"Michelle," Sdia replied quickly.

"Hmm, Michelle?" he asked suspiciously, as if he knew she was lying.

"Yeah, Michelle, why?" she asked, defensively.

"So if your name is Michelle, then why does this say, Sdia?" He reached in his pocket and pulled out her credit card, looking down at it to verify his pronunciation.

"Oh, shit!" Sdia shouted, wide-eyed while reaching in her wallet. "Where did you find that?"

"You dropped it back there!" He laughed at her expression and pointed toward the service area.

"Thanks," she replied nonchalantly, noticing how amused he was by her reaction.

"No problem." He chuckled. "I figured you would need that." She snatched the credit card from his hand and walked away.

"Have a good one," he called out, trying to hide his embarrassment.

"Wow!" he said under his breath, "She's fucking gorgeous!"

He loved her reaction. He was turned on by her rudeness, and how she treated him as if he were an average guy. It was rare that he came in contact with women who had that sassy attitude; most of the time they fell at his feet, but not her. It was something about her that caught his attention. He decided that he had to use the restroom and followed her.

* * *

Natalya opened her desert-sand brown, cat-like eyes. It was a little after nine in the morning, and they had just gone to bed only two hours ago. She forgot where she was for a moment, until she looked over at Lamar, her husband's assistant. *Morris Chestnut has nothing on him. I can't believe how experienced he is at the age of twenty-two!* Natalya struggled to her feet, and grabbed a towel from the floor to cover her naked body. She looked around the room and smiled. It looked like a tornado had hit. She stumbled over the bottle of Bollinger that sat on the floor next to a box of condoms. She picked up the champagne bottle and guzzled what was left, before kicking it under the bed.

"Damn, we did it again!" she said, bending back down to pick up the box of condoms.

25

This was the third time they hadn't used protection, and she wasn't taking any form of birth control. She and Carl didn't have any children, and as far as she was concerned, they weren't.

I can't believe I spent the night out again. She glanced over at Lamar's naked body and smiled devilishly. *But then again, good black dick makes you do some crazy things!*

Natalya walked over to the dresser and removed her wedding ring from her finger; she hated showering with her ring and having to pick the small pieces of soap from her diamonds afterward. She picked up her phone; her stomach dropped when she saw the name "Carl," and the number seventeen, under missed calls.

"Desperate. He called seventeen times!" she murmured as she shook her head. *Maybe I'll call him back, but that depends on how I feel after I take a shower and go another round with my boy toy!* she thought, placing the phone back onto the dresser and heading to the bathroom.

As the hot water hit her back, she closed her eyes and thought of a lie she'd tell Carl. She couldn't use the excuse that she was too intoxicated to drive and stayed at her best friend Abby's, because Abby was in the hospital. And she couldn't say that she'd gotten arrested and spent the night in jail, because she had used that lie three weeks ago.

Suddenly, her concentration was broken as the shower curtain flung open. Lamar stood there naked, biting his bottom lip. Natalya gazed up and down at his cocoa brown naked body—perfect! He had the curliest hair she had ever seen. His goatee looked as if it were drawn with a fine point pen—each line straight and sharp. His lips were full and succulent. He licked them and smiled, revealing a deep dimple on his right cheek. His dark-brown, almond-shaped eyes reciprocated the stare. Her eyes moved down to his muscular chest, past his rippled six-pack, where the words, "pray for me," rested, accompanied by a pair of praying hands. Her eyes continued to survey his body until she reached the prize. His penis stood erect and at attention.

Damn, that has got to be at least nine inches! she thought.

She reached her soap-covered hand out and began to conceal it with lather, slowly moving her hand up and down. Lamar stepped into the shower, all the while planting tender kisses on her neck and cuffing her behind with both hands. Natalya continued to stroke his endowed manhood, feeling her vagina secreting. Lamar began to pant heavily as he inserted his middle finger into her. Natalya's divine womanhood clamped his finger tightly as he gently pushed it in and out. She moaned while licking and nibbling on his right ear. Lamar quickly snatched her hand from his penis, slowly removed his finger from her vagina, and directed her to turn around. Natalya complied and placed both hands on the shower wall. He gently separated both her legs and slowly inserted his penis. She moaned while softly rocking her body back and forth, keeping up with his rhythm. Lamar cuffed her breasts as his tongue slithered across the back of her neck.

"You feel so good, I swear," he breathlessly whispered in her ear as he continued to wind his hips in a circular motion, moving in and out of her.

"Lamar, Lamar . . . Oh, my, oh ..." Natalya panted.

She trembled reaching climax. Lamar pushed himself deeper inside, being sure to hit every corner and angle. She closed her eyes as her uterus began to throb.

"I'm coming! I'm coming!" she sang.

Lamar quickened his pace, placing shorter and faster humps onto her. "Oh, shit, oh, shit," he grunted, and before he knew it, he was relieving himself. Satiated, Lamar removed his penis and stared down at his feet; he knew he should have pulled out, but he just couldn't help himself.

"Natalya, I'm so sorry!" he explained.

Natalya turned, lifted his chin, and smiled. As much as she wanted to, she couldn't get upset. She had enjoyed every minute of it.

"Next time," she said, kissing his forehead.

* * *

Natalya took a seat on the mint-green sofa of the West Inn & Suites Hotel, while Lamar checked out at the front desk. She looked up at the huge crystal chandelier. "Nice." She nodded. Her phone softly vibrated in her purse. "This bastard doesn't know when to stop!" Enraged, she removed her phone from her purse and looked at the screen, but to her surprise it was her mother, Phyllis. Natalya clenched her jaw, "Fucking bitch!" she mumbled ignoring the call. They had never been close, in fact, she couldn't recall her mother ever calling her by her name as a child; it was always "Bitch."

Chapter 5

Lamar couldn't help but notice Natalya in deep thought. He loved how she looked when she was concentrating, but what he loved most of all was her dark chocolate complexion and her soft baby skin. He fantasized about the night before and how amazing she was. Chills shot up his spine as he thought about her thick thighs securely wrapped around his waist. He began to feel himself becoming aroused.

"Sir, sir, here's your credit card," the desk clerk interrupted as she handed him his Visa.

"Thanks," he replied, grabbing his card before heading to Natalya.

She rose to her feet and began to walk to the door as he followed.

"Is everything okay, babe?" he asked. "You look like you have a lot on your mind."

"Yeah, I'm fine, sweetie. I just need to get home," Natalya replied casually.

He knew getting her to tell him what she was thinking about wouldn't happen. In her mind it wasn't any of his business.

"Are you sure you don't want to grab a bite to eat?" Lamar asked as Natalya sat back glaring out of the tinted window of his black 2019 Audi S5.

Natalya turned and stared Lamar coldly in the eyes without replying. After staring at him for two minutes straight, she turned her focus back to the window.

"I'm sorry, baby," Lamar replied timidly. "I know you

need to get home. Forget I asked." He focused straight ahead. He couldn't help but think that suddenly Natalya seemed annoyed. Her silence confirmed his thoughts. She obviously assumed that since they had spent the previous night together and today was Saturday, a new day; it was time for her to go home and time for him to do whatever it is twenty-two-year-olds do.

Her phone began to ring. She looked at the caller ID. "Carl," she said, sucking her teeth.

Lamar looked at Natalya, and before she could press the TALK button, he reached over and turned on the radio. He knew it would make her upset, but he didn't care. He wanted her to get upset and yell at him so that maybe she would miss the call. It wasn't that he was jealous. He just didn't understand how a man could be so passive, so weak, and so soft.

If she was my wife, there's no way in the world she'd be disappearing without calling. I would have kicked her ass the first time she tried that shit. It wasn't that Lamar disliked Carl Adler. He just didn't respect him as a man, but he played the game at work because Carl was his boss.

"Good morning, Mr. Adler. How are you today? Can I get you some coffee? Would that be all, sir?" But inside he was laughing. *Do you know I'm fucking your wife, you fat bastard?* Lamar smiled at his inner thoughts.

He didn't understand how a man with so much going for himself settled for a woman who couldn't care less if he dropped dead today. Lamar didn't have a problem with giving credit where credit was due, and he respected Carl's professionalism, but that was as far as it went. People in the office called him a "kiss up," but he wasn't concerned. He was, "getting paid and getting laid."

Natalya reached over and slowly turned the radio down interrupting his thoughts. "Don't be a smart ass!" she said, rolling her eyes.

"Hello?" she answered in a warm, inviting tone. She slowly ran her tongue across her top lip. She used that same tone to introduce herself to Lamar at Carl's annual Christmas party almost a year ago.

* * *

Carl paced back and forth in the kitchen. It was 12:45 p.m., and he still hadn't heard from Natalya. He had been trying to get in contact with her all night. She wasn't at her mother's; she couldn't have been out shopping for twenty-four hours, and she wasn't at Abby's. Carl picked up the cordless phone and called for the eighteenth time. He got her voicemail and decided to leave another message.

"Babe, it's me. Carl." His voice trembled. "Please call me as soon as you get this message. Natalya, I'm worried. I love you. Goodbye."

Once he returned the telephone to the receiver, he headed to the living room and grabbed the remote control near the television and flopped down on the couch. He glanced at his watch and couldn't take his mind off of Natalya. He was used to her pulling disappearing acts, but she'd usually call after seeing his number at least ten times. He glanced over at the telephone on the kitchen counter.

"Maybe I didn't hang it up all the way." He walked over to the kitchen counter and dialed her number once more. "Natalya? Natalya!" Carl shouted angrily and out of breath on the other end. "Where in the hell are you?"

"Hi, baby. I'm terribly sorry. I'm on my way home. I'm going to stop at Mega Mart grocery store. Do you want me

31

to pick you up anything special? I miss you so much!" she replied in a cunning and sexual tone.

Carl's eyes and mouth were frozen wide open. "Why are you going to Mega Mart? We never shop there. That's an hour away from the house!"

"I know, baby, but I wanted to pick up something special for you."

He didn't expect that reply. He was waiting for a different response, a response with a few insults and expletives, maybe even an elaborate excuse with expletives and insults; anything but that response. He was at a loss for words. Natalya hadn't spoken to him like that in months. It had probably been a year since she called him "baby," and it had been a year since they had had sex. Carl melted like butter. Where Natalya had been, who she had been with, and why she hadn't called was the last thing on his mind. Carl refused to press the issue; he just wanted her home.

"I miss you too, baby. I was so worried about you, Talya. Are you okay?" he asked sincerely.

"Yes, daddy. I'm fine. I had such a rough day yesterday, cleaning, running errands, and just feeling overwhelmed with life, and I really needed some time alone!"

"I'm sorry for yelling at you, Talya. I didn't know. Please forgive me, baby. How long will you be?"

"I'm pulling into the parking lot of the grocery store right now. I'll be home shortly. Oh, and Carl, baby?" she moaned. "Get some bath water ready. I'll pick up the whip cream." Natalya quickly ended the call.

Carl sat with his mouth open, with the phone pressed to his ear. He was in a state of shock. He couldn't believe what he had heard. He kept replaying the conversation back in his mind just to make sure he heard her correctly. "Did she say whip cream?" Carl didn't know whether to drop to his knees and thank God, or run around the house naked. All he knew was that within the next few hours he was going to be making love to the woman he loved, instead of jerking off to his collection of old *Hustler* magazines he kept hidden in a toolbox in the garage. He was unsure if he still knew how to make love. He began to panic as he questioned his stamina. Carl stood to his feet and looked down at the front of his pants. He heaved a sigh at the huge bulge that protruded to the front.

"Tonight's the night!" he shouted excitedly. He began to do the running man around the entire house.

* * *

"That was easy!" she said, dusting her hands off and turning to Lamar with a smile.

Lamar crinkled his nose, curled his lip and turned away. Natalya quickly reached out and placed both hands on his shoulder and swung him around.

"Lamar, you know how I feel about you. I was only telling him those things so that he wouldn't be suspicious of my whereabouts. You do understand, don't you?" She looked at him and waited for a response. "Come here," she said, gently stroking the right side of his face with the back of her hand. "I care for you, Lamar, and I would never hurt you." She placed her hand over her heart and kissed him on the cheek. She loved Lamar to death, but she just couldn't take any chances on ruining her marriage. Where else was she going to find an overweight white man with a great job and low self-esteem to take care of her? She felt bad for talking in front of Lamar, but sometimes she needed to remind him that he was only the side dish and not the main course. He had to learn how to respect her personal life because he was starting to get out of hand, and it was her duty to keep him in check. Lamar pulled into the parking lot of the grocery store where she had left her car.

"You could have at least pulled up to my car," she complained, before getting out.

She walked across the parking lot to her car and placed her purse inside before walking over to the driver's side of Lamar's black 2019 Benz Coupe. Natalya stuck her head through the open window.

"Well, I guess this is it. Are you still upset with me, sweetheart?" she asked in a baby voice with his chin in her hand. "I love you, and you know that, Lamar. I just don't want things to get out of hand. I thought you understood."

"Yeah, I understand," Lamar replied, looking down.

"You better," she joked, as she leaned through the window and softly kissed his lips.

Lamar grabbed the back of her head with his right hand and slowly eased his tongue in her mouth. Natalya pulled away. "Boy, are you hard at hearing? Didn't you just hear me tell that fat fuck I was on my way home?"

"Really, Natalya?"

She crossed her arms, aware of the power she had over him. "What? Do you have a problem, Lamar? Do you have something you want to say?" She irritably tapped her foot on the ground and waited for a response. Intimidated by her demeanor, he lowered his head and looked at the ground.

She walked toward him. "Hello, earth to Lamar!"

"Uh, umm … no I don't have a problem, babe," he said after he regained control of his voice.

"That's what I thought!" she replied, hopping into her car with a smirk.

* * *

Natalya raced across town, her heart pounding, knowing what she was about to face. She pulled into the driveway of her three-level home. She wiped the smudged lipstick from her mouth as she stared at her reflection through the rearview mirror.

"Back to the bullshit!" she said "And that fat bitch better not even think about touching me!" She shivered with the creeps, feeling herself sinking into depression at the thought of Carl touching her with his long, fat white Vienna sausage fingers. She placed her hand over her mouth, but quickly regained her composure. The thought of him made her heart drop to her stomach as she rang the doorbell.

Chapter 6

The scent of cinnamon air freshener and bowel movement nauseated her the moment she stepped into the crowded restroom. Sdia hated when maintenance tried to mask funk with fragrance. She looked down at the wet floor as she made her way to an empty stall. She lifted her dress, squatted and relieved herself. After using the restroom, she walked to the sink to wash her hands. She looked around; the restroom had gotten crowded. Sdia stepped out. *Do I want to buy a cinnamon bun?* Her stomach began to growl, reminding her that she hadn't eaten since breakfast and waiting until she reached DC to eat wouldn't be the best decision. As she walked over to the stand, she heard someone calling her name.

"Sdia!" the male voice called from behind.

She turned and to her surprise, it was the guy from the parking lot. "Yes?" she asked, warily.

"I don't want you to think that I am stalking you, but I just wanted to know if I could talk to you for a second," he said as he flashed a smile, revealing a set of perfect teeth.

"You're talking now!" she said sarcastically as she scoped him up and down.

"Yes, I am, aren't I?" He chuckled. "So you like cinnamon buns, huh?"

"Yup. I love 'em," She turned her back to him and reached into her purse for her money.

"Here, let me get that." He reached into his pocket and handed the young lady behind the register a crisp hundred dollar bill.

"Thank you. Have a good one," the cashier replied at the sight of the ten dollar bill he dropped in the tip cup.

"Thank you," Sdia replied politely, exposing her deep dimples.

"You're welcome." He smiled.

The two walked side by side as they made their way to the exit. He was way taller than she was. He stood six-foot-two and he smelled of Issey Miyake. Sdia loved the scent of men's cologne. It could have been anyone wearing it. A man wearing cologne really turned her on. As they walked, he introduced himself. Mel was twenty-eight years old and lived in Jersey City about twenty minutes away from her. He owned a barbershop, didn't have any children, and was on his way to Washington, DC to visit his sister.

By the sound of things, he seemed as if he had himself together, but then again she thought, *Sean showed his best side in the beginning.* Sdia didn't give a lot of information about herself when he inquired. She told him that she was twenty-four years old, on her way to Virginia, and worked full-time as an editor for a small company. She believed that he had all of the information he needed. It was bad enough he had found her credit card and knew her full name. Mel asked if she was in a relationship and she kindly dismissed the topic.

Being mysterious always keeps a man excited, her mother once said. Sdia didn't want to give him too much too soon; she had made that mistake in the past, and it ended up being a recipe for disaster.

A man needs to be kept on his toes at all times, and never let a man feel as though he has won you over completely, because if he does, he becomes comfortable.

When he gets comfortable, he gets lazy. When he gets lazy, he slacks, and slacking eventually leads to him taking you for granted' Sharon had cautioned.

'Ma, you always have the answers!' Sdia replied.

Sharon had taught her daughter to be independent and to never depend on a man.

Remember, Dia, always make sure they like you more than you like them. Men like a challenge, and remember you're the prize!

Numerous times Sdia had fallen short of many of the guidelines Sharon had given her when she had been in a relationship with Sean. One of the main ones was showing him how much she cared. Everyday Sean had an excuse as to why he didn't return her calls, why his cell phone was off, why he didn't show up for their dates, and why he would disappear for days at a time. He would constantly use the excuse of school and working late, but eventually those excuses got old. Sdia had to learn the hard way, and the next time around, she promised herself she'd be prepared.

I don't know what's wrong with you, Dia. Why don't you have confidence in yourself? Sharon asked with every ending conversation.

"Well, it was nice meeting you," Sdia said as they approached her car.

"I enjoyed chatting with you. I was wondering if we could exchange numbers," he asked with a slight smirk.

"Sure." Sdia laughed. She knew that question was coming. "Do you have a cellphone?"

"Of course I have a cellphone." He pulled his iPhone from his pocket.

"I see you're a fan of the iPhone too."

"Yeah, isn't everyone these days?"

After exchanging numbers, Sdia got into her car and within minutes, she was on the road. She had another hour and a half before she reached Maryland. As she drove, she couldn't help but think of Mel. *He seemed like a really nice guy.* She was surprised she had given him her number; she had been turning down every guy that approached her, but there was something about him that intrigued her. Sdia had to stay on her toes, and as far as she was concerned, every man was like Sean. She had already made up her mind that she wasn't going to call him first; that wasn't even an option. The last thing she wanted to do was seem desperate. She thought of their conversation from beginning to end. It was easy for her to remember what she had said because she hadn't said much. Mel had dominated the conversation.

Even if you lack self-confidence and your self-esteem isn't where you want it to be, you must put it into action and eventually you will start to believe it, she recalled a passage from her book.

Sdia smiled. "I can do that!" She replayed the conversation with Mel once more and nodded with satisfaction. "I didn't say too little, and I didn't say too much. I said just enough to have him curious, and that's exactly what I want!"

Chapter 7

"You should have been at least an hour away!" Jasmine yelled into the phone.

"Damn, Jaz, you sound just like Mommy." Mel laughed.

"Seriously, Mel, you promised you would be here," Jasmine continued, her voice beginning to crack as she tried her best to hold back the tears. "If you miss my graduation, I swear I'll never speak to your ass again. And I hope you aren't late because you decided to spend time with one of your air head bitches!"

Mel laughed. "Fuck no. Do you really think I'd put a bitch before you?"

Jasmine sighed. "Who the fuck knows with your crazy ass. You need to get married and stop messing around with all of these women."

"Here we go again," Mel sang.

"I'm not going to lecture you. Just get here!" she replied

Jasmine was five years younger than Mel. Their parents were murdered ten years prior during a robbery that took place at the mini market they owned in Jersey. Mel and Jasmine were left with their maternal grandmother, and she passed away two years ago. Their grandmother left them her house, which was worth over a half million dollars and the money from their parent's will. Mel purchased a condo and opened a barbershop while Jasmine moved to Washington, DC to attend Howard University, where she was studying to receive her Master's in Political Science.

"Jaz, you know I wouldn't miss your graduation for the world," he replied.

"Please don't, you know how much this means to me," she whined.

"Yes, Jaz, I know. Believe me. I'm on my way. I'll call you once I get closer, okay?"

"By the way, what did you get me?" she asked.

"You'll see when I get there. I have to go now. I need to pay attention to the road."

"Okay, see you soon."

God is good! I'm twenty-eight years old, single, no kids, handsome, got my own business, and I'm cruising down 395 in my brand new 6 series on my way to DC to see my little sister.

"Shit!" he cursed, frustrated as his cellphone softly vibrated on his hip. He looked at the caller ID. It was Niki, his girlfriend of six months.

"Hey, babe. Where are you?" she asked in her thick New York accent.

"I'm on my way. What's up?"

"Nothing, just sitting here wondering when you were going to call."

"Let me call you back," he replied, annoyed.

"Why? What's wrong?" she asked, high-pitched.

"First of all, what the fuck did I tell you about questioning me?"

There was a long pause.

"Bitch, do you hear me talking to you?" he yelled, holding the phone like a walkie-talkie as spit flew from his mouth. "I swear to my mother, if you don't open your mouth, I'm gonna smack the shit outta you when I see you!"

Niki swallowed. "I'm sorry, Mel. I didn't mean to yell. I just was worried."

Mel smiled as he recalled the last time he had seen Niki and how she had guzzled his baby batter. He had never met a girl who gave head like that. The last time he got head was three days ago, but it was nothing like Niki's. Mel couldn't wait to get to DC.

"Stupid ass bitch!" He sighed, hanging up on her.

* * *

Carl had been watching Natalya from their bedroom window. Before going down to answer the door, he took one last glance in the mirror. He unbuttoned the first three buttons on his flannel short-sleeved shirt—one of the three gifts Natalya had bought him for his birthday the previous year. The gold cross that hung on a gold chain lay buried between his coarse black, thick chest hairs. Carl removed his toothbrush from his dresser drawer and began to brush his thin chestnut colored imaginary hairline in a downward motion. Carl's father, brothers, and uncles also had receding hairlines. They all started losing their hair in their mid-twenties. He headed downstairs to let Natalya in, who had begun to bang on the door. Excitedly, Carl swung the door open with a friendly grin.

"It took you long enough," Natalya shouted as she brushed past him in a hurry and stomped up the stairs to their bedroom.

Carl stood there with his hand resting on the doorknob. He hadn't gathered what just happened. His grin slowly transformed into a frown. He cleared his throat and shut the door. Disappointed, Carl looked down at the floor and slowly headed up the stairs to his bedroom. There he peeked through the half-opened door and watched Natalya's reflection in the mirror as she undressed. She wore a black lace thong with a matching bra. He stared at her crotch as he tried to detect the pubic hair from the lace. She had a Brazilian wax; just the way he liked it. Carl licked his lips as her round, plump behind jiggled from the motion of her jerking a pair of panties that were stuck between the dresser drawers.

"What the hell are you looking at?" Natalya shouted, after she noticed Carl staring at her in the mirror. She rushed over to the door and jerked it open. "You are so fucking weird, I swear," she said, pointing her index finger at his forehead. "You know, you really turn me off!"

He stood dumbfounded, searching for words. His eyes frantically searched the room; from the walls, to the floor, to the ceiling and under the bed as if his words would magically appear.

"Uh, do want me to try to get your panties out?" he muffled, rushing past her with his head down.

Natalya stepped to the side with her hands on her hips and looked on in disgust.

"Why me?" she asked, raising her head toward the ceiling.

Carl squatted down with his crack exposed. That was his signature style. Whenever he wore any type of bottoms, whether it was jeans or shorts, the crack of his behind was revealed. Natalya took a deep breath as if she were about to make a life-changing decision and walked over to Carl. She stroked his head as he continued to work on the stuck garment.

"I'm sorry, baby," she said seductively. "Did you wear

that shirt for me? You look great. So, what's on the schedule tonight?"

That was music to Carl's ears. He jumped to his feet, immediately leaving the dresser drawer halfway open. "Whatever you want to do." His heart pounded as he looked Natalya in the eyes. He wanted to throw her across the bed right then and there and hump the life out of her. He wiped the sweat from his forehead with the back of his hand and smiled.

"Do you have any suggestions?" he asked.

"I'll think of something while I'm in the shower. I'm feeling a little sticky down there," she replied.

Carl grinned. "The stickier, the better," he said as he wiggled his plaque-covered tongue like a lizard.

"Not with your white-ass tongue. You need to go and brush that shit!" she replied as she went into the bathroom slamming the door behind her.

* * *

Natalya walked over to her purse and removed her cell. She discreetly slid it under her towel. She walked over to the sink and removed her earrings, bracelets, and chain. "Oh, shit!" she whispered, holding her naked ring finger. "What the fuck!" She bit her bottom lip and mentally backtracked her actions. "Lamar!" She removed her cellphone from underneath the towel and dialed his number. "Have you seen my wedding ring?"

"No. You don't have it?" he asked, amused.

"Evidently I don't, if I'm asking. Do me a favor and check in your car. Call me back when you're done."

She put her phone on vibrate and waited for his call. After waiting ten minutes, she turned on the water in the bathtub and sinks to mask her voice. *This could get ugly.* Natalya dialed Lamar for the second time.

* * *

Carl sat down on their California king-sized bed and waited for Natalya to finish. He unbuttoned his shirt, revealing a chest full of lamb's wool. Carl hated shaving his chest and thought it was for sissies. Eager to finally get an opportunity to touch his wife, he removed his jeans and slithered under the satin comforter. He then flipped through the channels, rocking his leg back and forth impatiently. After watching a few minutes of football, he looked at the time on the cable box.

"Natalya went in the bathroom at 1:50, and its 1:57. She should be done by now. Seven minutes is long enough," he blurted. "Shit, I ain't had none in a year. She better hurry her ass up."

Carl got up from the bed and walked over to the bathroom door. He could hear Natalya speaking low. He glanced over at the dresser to see if the cordless phone was on the hook.

"She must be on her cellphone with Abby. Damn, I didn't even see when she took her phone into the bathroom." He put his ear to the door and listened. He could barely hear what she was saying. The running water veiled her voice. Carl pressed his ear harder against the bathroom door.

* * *

"Didn't I tell you to call me back? When were you going to call?"

"I was about to call you back in a few minutes," Lamar replied.

"Did you check?" Natalya whispered.

"Yeah, it's not in my car."

"What do you mean it's not in your car?" Natalya replied, gritting her teeth.

"I told you, it's not there. I searched the whole damn car."

"Are you getting smart with me?" she asked.

"I'm telling you that I checked. Maybe you left it in the hotel room."

"No, I didn't leave it in the … Fuck!" She gasped. "I took it off before I got in the shower."

"Damn, Natalya," Lamar whined. "I guess you want me to go back and get it, right?"

"Hell yeah. You need to go back and get it. What the fuck do you think?"

"Yeah, okay," Lamar responded resentfully, before hanging up.

She cut the water off from the sink and proceeded to get into the shower when she noticed how it had gotten mysteriously quiet in the bedroom. She remembered hearing the TV earlier. Natalya dropped down to her knees and looked under the bathroom door.

"Oh, hell no, this motherfucker didn't!" She could see Carl's feet under the crack. She snatched the door open as hard as she could, causing him to stumble forward.

"What the fuck are you doing?" she shouted.

"Uh, just, nothing. I was …"

"You were listening to my conversation!" She walked toward him until they were back into the bedroom. He fell backward onto the bed.

"You nosy bastard!" She jumped on top of him in a riding position. "You want to be nosy, huh?" she asked seductively, as she began to stroke his neck and ears with her tongue.

Carl's eyes rolled back in his head as his penis stiffened. Natalya could feel his heart pounding against her breasts. She pressed her body as hard as she could against him. She stroked his chest with her right hand while slowly moving down to his navel and into his boxers, where she removed his penis. She gently yanked it using her thumb and index finger. Carl wasn't worth fucking. Natalya continued to yank his long Vienna sausage in hopes of him ejaculating soon. Carl grunted and moaned. He thought he was dreaming. He gently bit her nipples while gazing up at her to see her facial expression.

"Does this feel good? Do you like it?" He wanted confirmation, but instead, her eyes remained closed as she tilted her head back toward the ceiling. Carl refused to let this night go to waste. In one quick motion, he jumped up and turned Natalya on her back and roughly opened her legs, positioning his penis for insertion.

"Wait, wait, wait, Carl!" she shouted, pushing her foot in his chest. "Do you have condoms?"

"What?" he asked, confused and recovering from a missionary position. "A condom? What do you mean a condom?" His natural high was blown. He stood back and looked down at his wife with pain in his eyes. "What are you trying to say, Talya?"

She stared at him with revulsion. "Who the fuck do you think you're talking to?" She scooted to the edge of the bed and stood to her feet.

"What are you trying to say, Talya?" she mocked. "I'm

trying to tell your fat ass I don't want to get pregnant. What part don't you understand, Ronald McDonald?" she asked, staring at his hair. She placed her left hand on her hip, being careful not to reveal her bare ring finger. "Answer me, goddammit!" she said.

"I understand. I ... I ... I didn't know. It's been so long since we made love. I just thought that ..."

"Thought what? That I wouldn't make you wear a condom? I don't know where your dick has been!"

"Baby, you know I would never cheat on you. How can you say something like that?"

"You might as well cheat as much as you jerk that jalapeño off to all of those fucking magazines in your toolbox!"

Carl's jaw dropped in humiliation. At that moment, whatever ounce of pride he had, had been snatched from his body. He lowered his head and walked out of the bedroom. Natalya took a deep breath, threw herself backwards onto the bed, and smiled.

"Mission accomplished!"

Chapter 8

"Dia, Dia, you there?" a recognizable voice on the other end called out.

"Charmaine?" Sdia shouted. She pulled the phone away from her ear and looked down at the screen.

"Where you at?" Charmaine demanded.

"I was trying to dial my hairstylist, Danice. How in the hell did you get on the phone?"

Charmaine laughed. "No, seriously, Dia. What's your location?"

"I'm driving up Georgetown. I should be pulling up to my parents in about five minutes. Where are you?"

"Oh, okay. I'll be there in about a half-hour. Your annoying ass mother asked me to pick up some ice. Shit, I see she don't let nothing past her." Charmaine tried to sound serious.

"You betta watch your mouth." Sdia laughed. "But seriously, I'll see you when I get there. You know I can't talk on the phone in D.C. They got that stupid ass cellphone law because of the people who can't drive, such as yourself."

"No, sweetie. It's called a Bluetooth. Upgrade your shit wit cha broke ass!" Charmaine laughed and quickly hung up. She wanted the last word because she knew Sdia's comeback jokes were lethal.

Sdia pulled up in front of her parent's home on 8th Street in North West DC. She could smell the charcoal from the grill and she heard the bass from the speakers playing, "Bustin Loose," by the late Chuck Brown.

"Oh, my God! Daddy must be the DJ."

She knew she might as well prepare herself for a night of old school music so she decided to grab her case full of old CDs; her new playlist on *Apple Music* was not an option. Her father, Thomas used to DJ when he was younger for local house parties and family affairs. He continued to DJ part-time for older crowds at special events and worked full-time as an Engineer in Northern Virginia.

"Looks like Daddy ended up getting that Harley Davidson," she said, glancing over in the driveway.

"There's my baby girl!" Thomas yelled as Sdia walked into the backyard where he was standing behind his turntable that Sharon had bought him for his forty-fifth birthday. Thomas grinned from ear to ear and extended his arms for a hug.

"Hey, Daddy!"

"How's my baby girl?"

"I'm good. I see you're going to be the DJ for the night. Pahleeeease don't be playing all that 70s stuff!" she said, looking up in the air.

"Whatever. Don't hate. You know I got skizillz!" he replied, doing the b-boy stance.

Sdia smiled. "I'm just kidding. You know you're the best DJ in Chocolate City. Where's Mommy?"

"She's in the house. Hey, how long you here for?"

"I'm leaving tomorrow."

"Good!" he shouted back, with his hands in a praying position.

"Whatever," she replied, waving him off as she walked toward the back door.

"Dia?" he called after her.

"Yes, Daddy?" She turned.

"Did you see the Harley or what?"

"You the man!" she replied, giving him a thumbs up.

Thomas threw up the black power fist.

Sdia smiled and thought, *He is too old school.* She made her way inside.

"Boo!" she shouted, sneaking up behind her mother who was chopping onions.

"Dia, don't scare me like that!" Sharon replied, jumping. She dropped the knife and hugged her daughter.

"You look so pretty. Your hair looks good. Did you do it yourself?" she asked, as she stood back looking her daughter up and down.

"Yeah, I did the best I could," Sdia replied, pulling her fingers through her hair.

"It looks good."

"Thanks, so does yours!"

"Chile, please. I ain't even dressed yet."

"I'm so glad you're here, baby. Now you can take over. Cut these onions. I have to go upstairs and get ready." Sharon removed her apron and shoved it in Sdia's hand with a smirk.

"Ma!" Sdia whined. "I don't want to smell like onions!"

"That's nothing new," Sharon replied, sticking out her tongue. She had jokes, too.

"No, I'm only kidding, sweetie. Let me go upstairs and get ready. We can leave the onions for Charmaine or Loretta to cut." She winked.

Sdia smiled. "I'm coming upstairs. Hold on." She

dropped the apron on the table and followed her mother.

Once upstairs, Sdia removed her shoes as she sat on her parent's chrome and black framed king-size bed. She looked around at the chrome and black decorated room. There were matching nightstands on each side of the bed. A chrome and black lamp resided in the corner, followed by Sharon's black vanity set.

On the wall hung two chrome framed paintings. "Picasso paintings?" she thought. "Shit, I am definitely hitting Daddy up for some money before I leave."

"Hey, when did y'all get that plasma?" she called out to Sharon who was in the bathroom undressing.

"About three weeks ago. It's nice, isn't it?"

"Yeah, that's the same TV I was looking at last weekend."

"Don't you already have two TVs?"

"Yeah, but I was going to give the one in my living room away."

"Girl, you ain't rich. You're always trying to play Ms. Rich Bitch. You betta be saving your damn money. You're twenty-four years old. Me and your father aren't going to be here forever, you know!"

"I know, I know. I just get bored easily. I've had that TV for a year."

"Well, since you're so damn bored, you can iron my outfit in that chair by my nightstand."

"Damn!" Sdia whispered. "Okay, Ma," she politely replied. She grabbed the black sundress that sat in the chair by the nightstand.

"Hey, Ma, who's coming?"

"Huh?" Sharon called out, trying to talk over the

running water.

"I said who's coming?" Sdia shouted.

"Oh, let me see . . . Loretta, a couple of your father's co-workers, Charmaine, and I think Simone is coming.

"Who's coming from Daddy's job, those little rascals?"

Sdia remembered how upset Sharon was the last time her father's co-worker brought his kids over.

"Hell no, he better not bring those little fuckers!"

"Ma, you're crazy." She laughed.

"Shit, I'm serious, Dia. Those little fuckers pissed me off!" she replied, walking out of the bathroom in a black towel, shaking her hair dry.

"Do you know how much I had to clean up? Every time I think about that shit, I get pissed, and to top it all off, his daughter was your damn size if not bigger. Have you seen your room? Your father bought a daybed."

"No. Is this okay?" she asked, holding up the ironed dress.

"Yeah, that's fine, baby. Thanks." She leaned over and kissed Sdia's forehead. Sharon tugged on the bottom of the dress and smiled. "You know what this reminds me of?"

"Nooo, Ma. What does it remind you of?" Sdia's eyes rolled skyward. Sharon always had long drawn out stories.

"It reminds me of the times I'd sit in my parent's bedroom with my mother while she ironed her uniform for work. She'd talk about how her mother and her younger brother, Uncle George would drive her grandparents crazy and this was in their adult years." Sharon paused and glared down at the floor. "That Uncle George was a trip, I tell ya! Damn ... I miss that crazy old man. I still can't believe he's gone," she said, her eyes raked with disdain.

"I don't," Sdia blurted out.

"Don't what?" Sharon asked with a quizzical expression.

"I mean . . . I'm not happy he's dead. I'm just saying that I don't miss seeing him in pain."

"I don't miss seeing him in pain either, but damn. You said that like you're glad the man is gone."

"I am," Sdia mumbled. "I'm going to check on Dad. Do you need anything else?"

"No, I'm good. I'll be down in a minute."

Sdia walked down the hall to her old bedroom and opened the door. "Fuck!" *I should've just told her. I had the perfect opportunity and my dumb ass blew it!* "Uncle George touched me. Uncle George *fucking* touched me!" she said as she approached her bedroom door.

"Uncle George what?" her father asked, rather perplexed.

Sdia turned around, stunned. "Oh . . . hey Dad. I said, may he rest in peace. Mommy and I were just talking about him."

"Yeah he was a great guy."

Chapter 9

"No kiss?" Lamar asked, pouting as he stood at the door of his apartment.

"Of course," Will replied, leaning forward and gently kissing him. Lamar cuffed Will's behind with both hands.

"I gotta go," Will said, pulling away. "I'ma be late for work. I'll call you later." He turned and headed toward the elevator.

"You know you're wrong, right?" Lamar called out.

"Shut up." Will laughed as he got onto the elevator.

This was Will's third time spending the night. They had met three weeks ago at a local gay club. Lamar had never met a guy like Will. All the men he had previously messed around with in the past were flamboyant and drama queens. Will was more masculine and into manly things. However, Lamar didn't consider himself gay. He just enjoyed crossing over from time to time, and he didn't see anything wrong with that. *Natalya knows I'm a man*, he thought. *I've only been with three men. I've had more women than men.*

"Shit, I know I ain't gay!"

It was 7:45 in the morning.

"Good, I still have time to sleep; service doesn't start until nine."

The air conditioner softly hummed. The room was nice and cool—just the way he liked it. He climbed into bed and pulled the soft comforter to his chin. "At least I go to church and repent for my sins!" He closed his eyes with a slight grin and dozed off.

* * *

Will sat frustrated at the traffic light, surprised at the amount of traffic on a Sunday; not many people worked on Sundays. He turned on the radio and popped in a CD. The bass from the speakers caused his windows to vibrate. Will pulled the visor down on the driver's side and looked at himself in the mirror. He licked his index finger and gently ran it across his eyebrows.

"Oooh, I need my eyebrows done."

The rays from the sun reflected off of the mirror, turning his hazel eyes green. Will opened his mouth to examine his teeth, tongue, and gums. He scraped the white residue that coated his tongue and jaws with his long pinky nail.

"What the fuck?" he said angrily. "I just brushed my teeth!" He slammed the visor closed. Will was twenty-eight years old and worked as a personal trainer at a local gym. He had recently moved from North Carolina where he was born and raised. He hated working on the weekends, especially when the weather was nice. He'd rather be out stunting, something he enjoyed doing. It brought him great pleasure the way women looked in awe at his lean and muscular physique. However, the most satisfaction he got was when he'd catch straight men looking at him. Once they realized they were caught, they'd quickly try to cover their embarrassment by asking questions like, "Is there a gentlemen's club around here?" As if they were trying to convince him they weren't curious. It wasn't easy maintaining such a physique, which was that of a model. Although that wasn't the look he was trying to accomplish, he had no complaints with the results, so he also stuck to a strict diet. The traffic began to move.

"Thank God," he said, pulling his Chapstick from his glove compartment and greasing his lips. "He tryna 69 like Tekashi call him Papi, work that ASAP keep me Rocky," he rapped along as Tekashi 69 and Nick *Minaj's* song "Fefe" banged from the speakers. "Yaaaas, Nicki bitch! This is my shit!" he shouted, turning up the volume. It made him think back on his earlier years when he was young, sexier, and promiscuous. The music kept his mind off the fact he was at a standstill with what seemed to be hundreds of other cars. After listening to a few more songs, he turned the radio off and directed his attention to the road.

"Damn!" he shouted, banging on the steering wheel. "This shit is ridiculous!" He turned from side to side to scan the crowded road until he saw a small opening that led to the exit. "Bingo!" his reveled both rows of teeth from the true nature of this thoughts. *I need to kill time with a big fat juicy dick!* He was only feet away from exit that led to Stelo's neighborhood. "I'm about to pop up on his ass. I need some dick. Yup... that's exactly what I'm going to do. And that motherfucker better not have another nigga at his house!"

Chapter 10

Oh my God! My back! Carl's feet touched the cold wooden floor as he stood up and stretched. He hated sleeping on the couch; it really did a number on his back. The smell of hickory smoked bacon filled the air. He walked into the kitchen where Natalya was preparing breakfast. She stood at the stove wearing a black silk robe with a pink apron around her waist. Her back faced him as she stood like a stalk removing the bacon from the hot pan.

"Good morning, babes," she cheerfully called out, turning to him.

Carl was amazed. *Did she just call me babes? Am I dreaming?* He rubbed his eyes to make sure it wasn't an illusion. He quickly replied, "Uh, hey, Talya." He didn't want to waste another minute. Whatever she was feeling he didn't want to spoil it.

Natalya removed the apron and tossed it on the counter. "How are you this morning?" she asked, approaching him with her arms open for a hug.

Carl looked from left to right and then behind him, as if she could have been talking to someone else.

"Yeah you, silly," she smiled, grabbing him and wrapping her arms around his big neck.

Carl held her by the waist and embraced her. He closed his eyes and placed his head on her shoulder. He wanted that moment to last forever. He breathed heavily as she stroked the back of his head.

"Are you hungry?" she asked, gently pulling away to look him in the eyes.

"Uh, yeah, of course," he replied, still on cloud nine.

Natalya smiled. "Well, go upstairs and freshen up. By the time you're done, breakfast will be ready."

She poured the waffle batter into the waffle maker and slowly closed it. Carl rushed to the powder room down the hall.

"Hey, baby cakes."

Natalya jumped, startled. "Hey, Carl." She smiled. "Are you ready to eat?"

"Hell yeah, I'm starving," he said, rushing over to the glass top black and chrome dining room table. He jerked the black leather stool from under the table and sat down.

Natalya slid the magazine in her robe, being careful not to lose the page. "Espresso?" she asked.

"Yes, please," he replied, dousing his waffles in syrup.

She walked to the cupboard and removed a clear glass Espresso cup. "Foam, babe?" she called out as she placed the cup under the dispenser of the all-chrome Espresso machine. Carl nodded yes. She licked her lips as she poured the hot contents into the cup.

"Carl?" She swallowed. "I want to show you something."

"Yeah?" he asked, with a mouthful of waffles as he sucked his syrup soaked stubby fingers.

Natalya walked over and placed the coffee cup next to him. She pulled a chair from the table and sat down.

He looked at her and smiled. "Is there something wrong?"

"No, no. I'm fine," she replied, pulling her long, black hair behind her ear. She reached into her robe and pulled out the Tiffany's catalog. Carl continued to eat, occasionally slurping his coffee here and there.

"I was wondering if maybe ..." She handed him the catalog.

Carl wiped his hands on his green plaid pajama pants before taking the magazine from her hand. He raised his eyebrows.

"Sixteen thousand dollars for a bracelet? That's ridiculous!" He looked up at Natalya. It was a Victoria line platinum bracelet with diamonds.

"Yes, Carl, $16,000 for a bracelet. Are you saying that I'm not worth it?" she asked, staring coldly.

"No. Oh, God, no. Are you serious?" he replied, changing his tone; he didn't want to make her angry.

"Just imagine how it's going to look with nothing on." She winked, slowly running her tongue across her top lip.

Carl swallowed. He looked at her with such admiration as he imagined that view. She leaned over and softy kissed his lips. He could feel the breath from her nostrils on his beard. Natalya slowly pulled away and waited for his response. Carl's eyes remained closed with his lips protruding. Natalya cleared her throat.

"Oh," he said, and opened his eyes. He shook his head as if he were recovering from a trance. "Well, I guess it would be okay."

Natalya jumped from the table and smiled. "Thanks, baby." She took his face in her hands and kissed his forehead. "You're the best!" She tossed the magazine on top of the black marble countertop. "I'm so happy!" she sang as she made her way out of the kitchen, her bare feet softly padding on the black heated marble floor.

Carl smiled as he studied her plump behind jiggling

under the robe. "Hey, Talya. Why aren't you wearing your ring?" he called out.

"Damn!" she grunted low and quickly turned. "Um, I—" She fished for words and smiled, nervously trying her best to look calm.

"Phoung from the spa has it. I took it off when I was getting a manicure yesterday. I am going to pick it up this afternoon."

Carl nodded. "Oh, okay, just asking." He slurped his coffee as he watched her exit the kitchen. Suddenly she dropped the catalog and slowly bent down to retrieve it, revealing her bare behind. Carl's jaw dropped.

"Where's your credit card, dear?" she asked.

* * *

"Dia, Charmaine!" Sharon called from the bottom of the stairs. "Y'all, breakfast is going to get cold! Get y'all asses down here!"

Sdia rolled over on her left side to face Charmaine, who was smiling. "Eww! You are definitely not a morning person," Sdia teased. "Thank God for make-up, bitch. You look like a totally different person without it!"

"Shut up." Charmaine grabbed the pillow from under Sdia and hit her. "Your ass wears make-up too, bitch."

"Barely. And if I do, I still look the same in the morning. Oh . . . I almost forgot. Can you grab my purse from that chair?" Sdia asked, pointing to the pink recliner that sat in the corner.

"Yeah." Charmaine rose from the bed while adjusting her black boy shorts.

"That's a really cute bag, Dia."

"Thanks. It's Chloè." Sdia opened her purse and

removed her cellphone.

"What time is it?" Charmaine asked as she sat at the pink vanity set, pulling her curly, honey-blonde hair in a bun.

"Almost ten."

"You know, Dia. I was thinking about cutting my hair. I want to do something different."

"You have the face for it. If you do cut your hair, you should let Danice do it." Sdia grabbed her robe from her suitcase and stood to her feet. "I'm starving. I think my mother made pancakes."

"Oh, my gosh! I love her pancakes. They're better than IHOP!" Charmaine replied, excitedly. "Hey, you gotta pair of sweats I can throw on?"

"Yeah, I think so. Let me use the bathroom first," Sdia replied.

Sdia entered her bathroom. Everything was the way she'd left it, from the pink and yellow shower curtains to the yellow rug that lay by the tub. She grabbed her wash rag from the back of the door and ran it under the running faucet. "I need to start eating healthier," she said aloud at the sight of two small bumps on her cheek.

She brushed her teeth and exited the bathroom. Charmaine was on the phone when she entered her room.

"Who did you call on my phone?" Sdia asked as she plopped down on the bed next to her.

"Shhhh!" Charmaine demanded, putting her finger over her mouth. "I didn't call anyone. It's for you," she said, nodding toward Sdia.

"For me?" Sdia asked, pushing her index finger in her chest. "Well, who is it?" Sdia tried to think of who could have been calling her on a Sunday morning.

"So what's up?" Charmaine asked in a sexy tone.

Quickly, Sdia snatched the phone from her and looked at the caller ID. "Area code 609 is Jersey," she said, confused. "Hello?" She put on her professional tone. She wanted to be on the safe side just in case it was a business call.

"Hello," a smooth voice replied.

"Who is this?" she asked.

"This is Mel. Can I please speak to Sdia?"

Sdia smiled. "This is she." She nudged Charmaine. "I didn't catch your voice. Is this your home number?"

He chuckled. "No, this is the number to the barbershop. Did I catch you at a bad time, sweetheart?" he asked.

As much as she wanted to stay on the phone to hear his sexy voice, she knew it would be best to hang up. She didn't want to be available—at least not in the beginning.

"Well, actually, I was on my way out."

"Oh, okay. My bad, sweetheart."

Sdia laughed seductively. "I'll tell you what … how about I give you a call a little later on?" she asked, as if she were offering him the deal of a lifetime.

"No problem. Enjoy the rest of the day."

"You, too." Sdia ended the call and tossed her phone onto the bed. "Oh, my God!" she shouted, with her hand over her mouth. "Charmaine, he is so fucking fine! Did I play it off or what?" She placed her hands on her hips.

Charmaine looked up at Sdia, perplexed. "Who the hell was that?"

"A cutie I met on the turnpike." Sdia closed her eyes as

she tried to picture his face.

"So what's his situation? I mean, where's he from? Does he work? Does he have any money, a car, any kids and most of all, does he have a girlfriend?"

"Damn! Slow down. I just met him yesterday. He's twenty-eight years old; he's from Jersey City; he owns a barbershop, owns a condo, no kids, and I don't know if he has a girlfriend. We didn't get into all of that," Sdia replied.

"Well, that's one of the main questions," Charmaine replied in a "you know better" tone.

"Look, I just met the man. It's my first time talking to him since yesterday. And besides, you know men lie about being in relationships," she said sarcastically, rolling her neck.

"Yeah, that's true, but as a woman, you still need to ask those types of questions." Charmaine folded her arms.

"Yeah, I know, but we didn't get to that part."

"How about the part where you take a break? You and I both know that you're not over Sean."

"Oh boy, Charmaine. Here we go again!" Sdia whined.

"Seriously, Sdia. You should think about taking a little break. Get some me time."

"Girl, I have enough me time at home, and look who's talking, Ms. I'm-Going-to-Be-Your-Roommate," Sdia teased.

"Okay, okay, you got me with that one," Charmaine said, fanning her hand, . "But at least think about what I said!"

"That's why I love you, girl. You are always looking out," Sdia replied, hugging her.

Suddenly, Sharon pushed the door open as she stood there with her hands on her hips. She pushed her tongue in her jaw before speaking. "See, I wake up after throwing a huge barbeque yesterday just to make y'all hungry asses something to eat, then I cut my finger cutting cantaloupe, and then I stand at the bottom of the stairs calling y'all for almost ten goddamn minutes. Your plates have been on the table for almost half an hour!" she shouted. "Sdia," she continued, "I don't want to hear shit about Ma, you never cook when I come here. Mommy this, Mommy that, and all that other bullshit you be talking. Now get y'all asses downstairs!" she said, pointing to the staircase. The two brushed past Sharon, snickering with their hands over their mouths.

After breakfast, Sdia and Charmaine showed their gratitude to Sharon by cleaning the kitchen while she and Thomas cuddled on the couch watching the classic, *Willie Dynamite*, one of Thomas's favorite films.

"Hey, Dia, can you pass me a beer?" he called from the living room.

"Yeah, Daddy, just a sec," she replied as she swept the floor.

Charmaine hand-dried the last plate and said, "I got it, girl." She retrieved a Corona from the fridge and handed it to Thomas. She watched the movie as it played from the large plasma TV that hung over the fireplace.

"Charmaine, whatchu know about Willie D?" Thomas teased.

"Oh, please, Mr. Mitchell. You are just too old school," she replied, finding a comfortable spot on the brown and gold Persian rug.

Thomas filled her in on the movie plot as the three

continued to watch the movie.

"Not this movie again." Sdia smiled, joining in on the film.

"Hush," Charmaine replied, "I can't hear."

"Are you serious? You can't be serious?" Sdia replied, taken aback.

"Look, if you're gonna come in here talking, you can just leave," Sharon teased, winking at Thomas and Charmaine. "Because no one wants to hear that shit."

Sdia laughed. "Anyway, I'm about to go to Georgetown. I want to pick up a few things."

"Dia, I don't want you leaving too late," Thomas said.

"It's not even twelve o'clock," she replied.

"Yeah, but if you plan to do any shopping, make sure you do it early because I don't want you traveling back home at ten, or eleven o'clock at night. Do you understand?"

Sdia nodded. "Yes sir!" She playfully saluted him like a soldier.

"Good," Thomas replied.

Sdia stood there without saying another word, waiting for an opportunity to ask him for a few dollars.

"You're still standing here, so I know you have something to ask. Or better yet, let me ask, how much do you need?" He pulled out his wallet.

Sdia looked at Sharon, who was sitting beside him and silently assisting Sdia with a bid. She concentrated on her mother's lips as her father repeated the question with his head down, looking into his wallet.

"Uh, five hundred—no, six hundred," she replied, never

taking her eyes off Sharon, who was fanning her hand in an upward motion, signaling for Sdia to ask for more. "Eight hundred," she called, as if she were at an auction.

Thomas looked up at her blankly. "What the hell is wrong witchu? You must not need any money because you can't make up your mind!" he replied, aggravated.

"No, I do. I was just trying to calculate some of my expenses in my head," she reassured.

"How's fifteen?" he asked, looking at Sharon for support.

Sharon shrugged. When Thomas turned to Sdia, Sharon began to fan her hand in an upward motion. "Five thousand," her lips read as if she were speaking to a mute.

"Five," Sdia called out.

"Five what?" he replied, looking at her as if she had lost her mind.

"Daddy, I have so many bills, and I would like to buy a couple of things for my apartment." She pouted.

Thomas turned to Sharon, who was looking at her nails. "Babe, what chu' think?"

Sharon looked up, startled. "I'm sorry, were you talking to me?" she asked, confused.

"I'm giving Dia $5,000. Do you think that's too much with Christmas around the corner?" he added.

"No baby, that's fine." Sharon smiled.

Thomas pulled his credit card from his wallet. "You're going to have to go to the ATM and withdraw some. And I'll have to put the remainder on a check," he said, straight-faced.

"Thanks, Dad." *Being an only child definitely has its advantages.*

67

She kissed both parents on the cheek and headed to her bedroom to get dressed.

Sure she had some shopping to do, but unbeknownst to them and Charmaine she was going to spend half of that on Mel!

Chapter 11

Lamar grabbed a pair of navy blue slacks and a white collar shirt from his closet. He ransacked through the white laundry basket in his room for a pair of trouser socks. His search ended with a mismatched pair—one blue and one black. He reached under his bed, removed his black Kenneth Cole shoes, and rammed them on his feet. He took his Jean Paul cologne from the top of the television and sprayed his neck and wrist before leaving.

"Come on, come on!" Lamar shouted at the bus in front of him as it collected a small line of kindergartners who waited on the corner. *Why did I have to pull behind this stupid ass bus?*

He nervously peeked at the clock on the dashboard and sucked his breath. "Let me tell these fools I'm running late!"

"Micro Media, can I help you?" a whiny voice answered.

"Hey, Marina. It's me. Lamar. Can you let Mr. Adler know that I'll be a few minutes late?"

"Okay, Lamar. See you soon."

His other line beeped. Lamar looked at the caller ID and shook his head, displeased. "Okay. Thanks, Marina. Bye." He clicked over.

"Why haven't I heard from you all week?" Natalya shouted.

"Well, good morning to you, too," Lamar replied.

"I'm waiting."

"I'm sorry, Natalya. I had a lot to do. I got sidetracked."

"Well, next time, call. I thought something may have happened to you."

"Listen Will, I'm fine!"

"What? Will?" Natalya replied.

"Huh?" Lamar replied in a shaky voice.

"You said Will. Who is will?" Natalya demanded.

Lamar let out a quick bark of laughter. "I meant . . . will you give me a break please? I said I got sidetracked!"

She replied, "Oh. Okay."

"Babe, I'm fine," Lamar reassured her.

So are we still on for lunch?" Natalya asked.

"Yeah."

"Great. So what time do you think you'll get here?"

"Around twelve."

"Great. See you when you get here."

"Okay."

"Don't be late."

Lamar ended the call without a response. "Damn that was close!" Lamar stated as his heartbeat finally returned to normal.

* * *

Carl stepped onto the crowded elevator.

"Good morning, Mr. Adler," the elevator operator said in a cheerful tone.

"Good morning," he replied, politely smiling. Carl placed his black leather briefcase on the floor and adjusted his tie.

"Fourth floor, sir," the operator informed.

"Thank you," Carl replied, before stepping off.

"Good morning, Mr. Adler," voices called out as he walked to his office.

Carl nodded from left to right, being sure to reciprocate the greeting. He entered his office and set his briefcase on his cherry wood desk before walking to his window and opening the blinds. The sun peered through the pale blue blinds and onto his desk. Carl looked at the busy street below; everyone seemed to be in a rush. Cars zoomed by one another, people passed one another, sometimes bumping shoulders as they walked on the crowded sidewalk. Even the birds in the sky seemed busy. Everyone and every living creature seemed to have a purpose. Everyone had a reason to wake up in the morning, a reason to be in such a hurry; and a reason to keep them going. He couldn't figure out his reason and took a deep sigh, feeling himself getting choked up.

"What's wrong with me?" he said barely above a whisper.

Just then, there was a knock on the door. Carl wiped his eyes with the back of his sleeve.

"Come in," he called.

"Hello, Mr. Adler," Marina said, sticking her head in the door. "Lamar is on his way. He's running late." She smiled.

"Thanks, Marina," he replied.

Marina had been working for Carl for six months. She was originally from Boston but had moved to DC after her mother died. She was only twenty-two years old and was already making close to $60,000. Carl found her quite attractive and often wondered why such a beautiful girl was single. He thought for sure that one of the younger guys in his department would have snatched her up. Then again, most of the young men in his department had girlfriends, except Lamar. *Lamar and Marina would make a nice couple*, he thought. *They're both good-looking kids with good heads on their shoulders.*

Carl sat at his desk and picked up the chrome framed picture of Natalya. He remembered the times she would tell him she loved him, and how good she used to make him feel, but that was a long time ago. Throughout the years, her personality had changed, and the more he gave, the more distant she became. The last time she promised him sex was three months ago when he paid an arm and leg for a diamond bracelet she had her heart set on. Then when it came time for her to pay her debt, she complained about having a nasty yeast infection.

"It's been eleven months since we made love," he complained, before settling for a three-minute hand job.

Carl felt the tears emerging from his eyes the more he thought about the condition of his marriage. "I hate myself. I am such a failure!"

His phone rang and he pushed the red flashing button. "Yes, Marina," he answered, half-dead.

"Your wife's on line one. Do you want me to put her through?"

"Sure," he replied, regenerated.

"Hi, Carl," Natalya said dryly.

"Hey, Talya. Is everything okay?"

"I'm fine. I was calling to tell you that I'm having problems with my cell, and I won't be home."

"So how will I contact you throughout the day?"

"I'm taking it to get serviced. I'll call you when I'm done!"

"Okay, that's fine. See you when I get home. I love you." She quickly hung up.

Carl stared at the telephone before placing it on the receiver. Suddenly there was a knock on the door. He cleared his throat. "Come in."

Lamar opened the door and stepped in flashing a Colgate smile. "Good morning,

Mr. Adler."

"Hello, Lamariel," Carl replied, taking notice of the way Lamariel flexed his jaw after the greeting.

"Hey now … you know a young stud like me prefers to be called, Lamar. I really dislike when people address me by my birth name." He winked at Carl.

"Yeah sure … Lamar."

He handed him a thick folder containing customer contracts, the company's budget, and a goal plan for the month. Carl was sure it would keep Lamar busy for the day. He smiled as Lamar took the folder.

"Did you see the game this weekend, Mr. Adler?" he asked.

Carl clasped both hands together. "No, Unfortunately I didn't have time. How was it?" he asked.

"We beat the Giants by fourteen. It was a really close game."

Perhaps Lamar didn't realize it, but his never-ending smile made Carl take notice. *Was it genuine?* he mused. Lamar had smiled so long Carl wondered if his cheeks were cramping. "I told you the Redskins would make a comeback." Carl smiled.

"Yes, you did. Oh, I'd better get to work," Lamar quickly replied, slightly holding up the folder and easing back toward his desk.

Carl smiled, and thought to himself, *What a nice kid.*

Lamar headed for the door. "Oh, Mr. Adler?" He turned back. "I was wondering if I could take my lunch a little early, say around twelve? I need to meet with the Youth Ministry to go over a couple of notes."

"Most definitely. Take as much time as you need."

"Thanks, Mr. Adler."

Carl nodded. "Hey, Lamariel, maybe we can catch a game one weekend. A friend of mine works at the Nationals Football Arena."

"Okay," he replied.

"Yeah, it's been a while since I've taken my wife Natalya to a game. Maybe we can double date," Carl hinted. It was his way of seeing if Lamar was dating anyone.

"Oh. Um, double date?" Lamar asked.

"Yeah." Carl chuckled. "I'm sure a great-looking kid like you can't keep the ladies away. I know you have options." Lamar shrugged.

"Sounds like a plan?" Carl reiterated.

Lamar peered down at the floor.

"Okay, soo . . ." Carl sang, motioning for Lamar to give a response.

"Yeah, sounds good, Mr. Adler." Lamar quickly rushed toward the door.

"So, do you shoot hoops?" Carl asked.

"All the time." Lamar turned and smiled.

"Good. Maybe we can hit the gym on 7th Ave. I know a few personal trainers over there. They gotta nice size basketball court too."

"Um ... sounds like a plan," Lamar said, slightly raising the thick folder in his hand.

Carl chuckled. "Right. My bad. You have a lot of work to do. Carry on, good man. Carry on."

Lamar snatched the door open and quickly exited the office.

Carl shook his head and smiled. *Wow, interesting kid! That Lamariel . . .*

Chapter 12

"What the fuck is wrong with you?" Natalya snapped, removing Lamar's penis from her mouth. She stood to her feet and placed her hands on her naked hips. "What's your problem?"

Lamar raised his head toward the ceiling and closed his eyes. *Get hard, get hard . . . Fuck! Why isn't my dick getting hard? Damn!* "Nothing, baby. I got a lot on my mind, that's all," he replied, sitting up on the bed and grabbing her by the waist. He gently pulled her closer and kissed the palm of her hand.

"A lot like what?" she shouted.

"I don't know . . . things."

"You know, you've been acting funny lately," she continued. "You know you can easily be replaced!"

He looked up, confused. "Why would you say something like that?"

"Because y'all young boys start to get shit twisted!" She snatched her hands from his grip and walked away.

"Natalya, please don't say that," he begged, pulling up his boxers and gently grabbing her from behind. Her soft ass pressed against his bare stomach and immediately he thought of Will. *Damn I miss Will's tight, wet, muscular ass*; his penis quickly stiffened. *I wish he was here right now so I could fuck the shit out of him.*

Natalya smiled devilishly as she felt his arousal. She turned and pouted. "Maybe we should just end this." She began to pull away.

"No, Natalya, please!" Lamar whined, tugging at her

hand like a child.

"I ... I just don't know, Lamar." She placed the back of her hand on top of her forehead, as if she were about to faint.

"Please, baby," he begged, dropping down to his knees.

Natalya continued with her award-winning performance. "Yes, Lamar. We have to end it. It's for the best." She began to sniffle.

He remained on his knees, holding her waist. He looked up at her with tears in his eyes. "Please, Natalya. I love you," he said, placing soft wet kisses on her stomach.

Natalya closed her eyes as he slowly circled her navel with his tongue. He caressed her butt cheeks before gently parting her nature with his tongue. She grabbed the back of his head and pressed his face into her as she moaned loudly, slightly lifting her leg. Lamar grabbed her right thigh and placed it over his shoulder as he feathered her clit with his tongue. Natalya slowly orbited on his face until she could feel the love juices ooze from her vagina. Lamar closed his eyes as he imagined being Will's wet asshole. "Mmmm" he moaned. Natalya unapologetically pushed as much vaginal secretions from her vagina as she could until his entire beard was saturated. *Damn Will. Fuck! You taste so good*, Lamar slurped and sucked every drop; his dick was now harder than ever!

* * *

My first date since Sean! I almost can't believe this! Sdia reached down and turned the volume up on her stereo as Drake's latest hit blasted from the speakers. It felt great to finally be settled in her own place. She rushed to the linen closet and grabbed the iron. "Shit, I'm gonna be fucking late!" she screamed, after looking at the clock.

She had a half hour to get ready for her date with Mel, and hadn't yet showered. Her stomach flipped at the thought of seeing Mel's face again. She had been speaking to him every day since they met two weeks ago, and tonight she had finally agreed to go out with him after declining several times. Sdia wasn't one to hang out during the week, but since she wasn't due for work until noon the following afternoon, she figured she would go out. She turned her jeans inside out before ironing them and huffed.

"I should have worn my light jeans. Why didn't I get them out of the cleaners?" She quickly ironed her jeans and placed them over the arm of the couch.

"Where the hell is my sweater?" she yelled as she ran into her room and peeled through the shirts that hung on the closet rack. "I know I put it in here."

The house phone rang loudly, interrupting her search. "Damn it!" she said, tossing the sweater onto her bed and running into the living room to answer the phone.

"Hello?" she answered, frustrated.

"Hey, girl. What's up?" Charmaine asked.

"Hey, Maine. Can I call you back?"

"Oh okay. Yeah," Charmaine replied, confused.

"As a matter of fact, I'ma put you on speaker phone," Sdia replied, remorseful.

"No, Dia. You can call me back. It's okay," Charmaine insisted.

"Girl, quit. I wanna talk to you. What's up?"

"Ain't shit, just sittin' here watchin' videos, bored outta my mind." Charmaine laughed.

"I'm in here tryin' to get ready for this date," Sdia stated as she turned the shower on.

"A date? A date with who?" Charmaine asked, excitedly.

"Mel."

"Mel, Mel . . ." Charmaine tried to recall the familiar name.

"The dude I met on the turnpike. Don't you remember I told you about him?" Sdia quickly undressed and got into the shower.

"Oh, okay. Is that the nut who called the next day at seven in the mornin'?" Charmaine teased. "I ain't know you be talkin' to him."

"Whateva, you know damn well he ain't call at no seven in the mornin'." Sdia ignored that last remark.

"Where y'all goin'?"

"I don't know. I feel like some seafood, and I definitely need a drink."

"Damn, too bad y'all not out here, 'cause I could recommend some good spots."

"I know, but I'm sure we're gonna go somewhere nice. He seems like a cool dude."

"Well, make sure you get all that nigga's info. Does Sharon know you going on a date?"

"I could have sworn I was talking to her," Sdia joked.

"Whatever. Well, my lips are sealed."

"Good, cuz' I don't feel like hearing her mouth. Anyway, let me call you back after I'm done getting dressed."

"Okay, have fun and call me when you get home."

"A'ight, girl. Talk to you later." Sdia ran into the living room and placed the phone on the charger. She glanced at the clock.

"Shit!" she sang, running into her bedroom to get dressed.

Within minutes she was dressed in tight jeans and a cute sweater. She adorned her wrists and neck with jewelry and perfume, then rushed down to the lobby to meet Mel.

As Sdia walked out, she spotted Mel rolling the window down on the passenger's side.

He quickly got out of his truck to greet her. Sdia's stomach did flips as she approached the tall, dark handsome man.

Wow, he looks even better than I remembered, she thought as she extended her hand for a handshake.

"Hello, I'm sorry I took so long," Mel explained as he softly took her hand into his. "I lost track of time."

"You're fine. Don't worry about it," Sdia replied.

Mel quickly turned to his truck and opened the passenger's side door. "Allow me."

Sdia walked past him and smiled. "Thanks, Mel," she said, slowly getting in.

He closed the door and walked around to the driver's side. Sdia leaned over and opened the door for him.

"You must be the one!" Mel teased.

"*A Bronx Tale*, right?" Sdia asked.

"Yeah, that's one of my favorite movies, too!" He reached toward the rearview mirror, turned on the light and looked at her.

"I want to look at you. You're so pretty!" he said, tilting his head from side to side as he studied her face.

"Thank you," Sdia replied, shyly turning toward the

window. *Oh, shit, he's fine!*

Mel turned and reached into the backseat. "I got you something," he said, retrieving a beautiful bouquet of red roses.

"They're beautiful. Thank you," she replied, taking the roses from his hand.

"You're welcome, beautiful." Mel started the ignition.

Sdia smelled the roses. "I can put these in the vase on my kitchen table."

Mel glanced over at her and smiled. "I can't believe you're sitting next to me. I thought you were gonna turn me down again. You're just too beautiful."

Sdia giggled. "No, it wasn't even like that. That's not even my style."

After about fifteen minutes of shooting the breeze on how one another's day went, the upcoming weather forecast and more compliments on her beauty, Sdia was grateful to see they had arrived at the restaurant. She was running out of things to talk about.

Sdia looked up at the name silently pronounced it. A tall white male came to the driver's side of the window and greeted them.

"Good evening. Will you be valet parking this evening?" he said, revealing a set of perfect white teeth.

"Yes, thank you," Mel replied, putting the car in park and stepping out. He walked around to the passenger's side and opened the door for Sdia.

"Here, let me help you out, babe," he said, taking her by the hand and helping her over the curb.

Wow. Did he just call me babe? Damn that sounds so sexy! Sdia shivered. "Fish Bowl? I've never been here before." She glanced up at the blue cement bowl-shaped building.

"A friend of mine told me about this place. He said the food was delicious and that they have excellent service. I believe it's two levels." Mel placed his hand around Sdia's small waist and led her through the restaurant's double doors.

"It's beautiful in here," she sang as she slowly glanced around at the aquatic themed restaurant. Embedded in the walls were fish tanks filled with some of the most exotic fresh water fish she'd ever seen. The light aqua blue water elevated throughout the dimly lit restaurant causing everything to glow. The scent of Old Bay seasoning and seafood filled the air. "This is amazing," she said as the soft, fluffy, baby blue sand rested below her feet.

"I like your boots. What are they?" he asked, looking down at the black leather knee boots she wore.

"Thank you. They're Marc Jacobs," she replied, proudly.

I see he's observant, Sdia thought. She liked a man with a sense of style and couldn't wait for Mel to be at least six feet away from her so that she could check out his gear. She didn't want to be obvious and look him up and down, but the suspense was killing her. Sharon always told her that a person's shoes said a lot about them.

"Wow, it's pretty crowded in here," Sdia said. She wasn't quite sure how to handle Mel. Although they had been talking on the phone for some time, being face to face was always different.

Mel shook his head and said, "Yeah, the food must be good." Sdia put her hands in her pockets as she pressed her back against the wall.

"Are your hands cold, baby?" he asked, taking her right hand from out of her pocket and cuffing it between his.

"Yes," she replied, goo-goo eyed.

There were so many questions she wanted to ask him, like: Why didn't he have a girlfriend? Where were his parents? What were his aspirations and goals, etc.? Most people would have asked those questions during the second phone conversation, but they were questions she felt she should only ask in person because she believed, "The eyes never lie," and his reaction to each question would make or break their friendship. Sdia could feel her hand becoming sweaty as he continued to warm it with his. He opened both his hands releasing hers.

The hostess informed them that the wait would be another fifteen minutes after taking Mel's name.

"You're welcome to go to the hostelry while you await your name to be called," she said in an English accent. She held out her hand and bowed kindly, signaling them to walk ahead.

"Let me get that for you." Mel said, pulling out the baby blue and white suede stool.

"Thanks," Sdia replied as she stood on her tiptoes and slid backward onto the stool.

He took a seat next to her, and looked her up and down until their eyes met. "Do you wear make-up?" he asked.

"No, not really." Sdia laughed. "I'm good with my Mac lip gloss and a little bit of Rihanna's Fenty mascara."

He was sitting a reasonable distance for her to scope out his outfit. "Nice sneakers. Gucci?" she asked, flaunting her knowledge of fashion.

Mel raised his eyebrow. "You already know. You must

have bought your man a pair," he mocked.

"I don't have a man," she replied, sarcastically.

Mel pulled his seat in closer. "So you mean to tell me that a beautiful woman such as yourself is really single?" He smirked. "I find that shit hard to believe."

"Well, it's the truth." Sdia shrugged. "I could say the same about you. Why don't you have a girlfriend?"

"Hello, can I get you all something to drink?" the bartender interrupted.

Mel looked at Sdia. "You drinking?"

Sdia scanned the beverages that sat on the shelf behind the counter. "Sure. Can I have a lemon drop?"

"And for you, sir?"

"Lemme get a double shot of Hennessy."

"Hennessy? God, I hate that drink!" Sdia replied, scrunching up her nose.

"You have the cutest nose," Mel replied with admiration.

"So back to the question," she said, removing her coat.

"I'm single, sweetheart. I've been single for a while."

"I'm sure you're messing around with someone."

"Messing around? *No.* Friends? Yes!"

"Uh-huh."

"Uh-huh, what does that mean?"

"Nothing. Just uh-huh." She turned to take her drink from the bartender.

"You wanna take our shots at the same time?" he asked, switching the topic.

"Sure," she replied, removing the sugar-coated lemon

from the rim of the glass. She innocently sucked the sugar off, catching Mel studying her lips.

Sdia twisted her face from the bitter taste. "Wooo! That's the part I hate!" she said, raising her glass. "You ready?"

Mel smiled. "I'll give you a head start."

"I don't need a head start."

"No, no, ladies first," he insisted.

"One, two, three," she said, quickly turning up the small fish bowl glass to her mouth.

Mel waited until she was halfway done and proceeded with his. He slammed the empty glass down on the table. "Now that's what you call a shot." He motioned for the bartender to bring another round.

"Would you like another one?" he asked.

"No, I'm good," Sdia replied.

I know his ass is not tryna get me drunk. I don't fucking think so! She could already feel the drink starting to take effect.

"You sure?" he asked, before sending the bartender off.

"No, thank you," she replied politely. *I hope I don't have an alcoholic on my hands!*

"Okay, just a double shot for me." He fanned the bartender off.

"So do your parents live close by?" Sdia asked.

Mel looked down before replying. "Nah, my parents died when I was younger."

Way to fucking go! she thought. "I am so sorry." She placed her hand on top of his.

Mel looked up and laughed. "It's cool."

"I am truly sorry to hear that." She turned away, slightly embarrassed.

"Yeah, thanks. They were killed when I was younger, but hey, that's life, right?"

Sdia looked down. *Damn! That's fucked up. I can't imagine losing my parents.*

"How about your parents? Are they still together?" he asked.

"Yes, they are. My parents live in DC."

"Are they married?"

"Of course." She laughed.

"Really?" he asked, surprised. "Not many people I know have parents who are still together, let alone married."

"So you don't have any kids or a girlfriend? That's crazy!" she said.

"If I got paid every time I heard that, then I would be rich."

"No, seriously. I mean, it's very rare to find a man without any kids nowadays— particularly, a brotha."

"You don't think that's a little cliché?"

"Cliché? No. Reality? Yes."

Mel nodded. "I guess you do have a point, but it doesn't necessarily mean it's a bad thing either."

Why is he trying to make this a debate? Sdia smiled. "What do you mean?"

"I mean, just because a nigga got kids, doesn't mean he's a bad dude."

"I didn't say that." Sdia laughed. "But I'm going to say that I would prefer a man without kids."

"Really, and why is that?"

"It's just my personal preference. I don't have time for the baby mama drama, and I need to come first at all times." She smiled. "Would you date a woman with kids?"

"Of course I would. Why not?"

"It just seems like a lot of responsibility on your end, you know?"

"If you care for someone, then it doesn't matter. You accept those things."

Sdia shrugged. "If that's what you like."

"So I guess I should consider myself lucky then, right?" he asked, smiling.

"Why would you say that?"

"Because, if I had a kid, then you wouldn't have given me a chance."

"Who said you had a chance?" She softly hit him on the shoulder.

"Oh, shit!"

"Simmons, your table is ready," a voice on the loud speaker called out.

Mel got up from his seat and pulled the stool out for Sdia.

"Thank you." she said as she cautiously got up.

They were seated and placed their orders right away.

"So, the barbershop is doing well," Mel said, stuffing a fork full of salad into his mouth.

"That's so nice to hear that you're doing what you love. Not many people can say they're doing something they actually like, you know?" Sdia replied, picking up a breadstick.

"Yeah. A nigga is blessed though. I can't complain even if I wanted to."

"Have you ever been incarcerated?" she asked.

Mel drank from his water and began choking violently, pounding on his chest and turning red. He slammed the glass down and banged his fist against his chest.

"Hey, you okay?" she asked, as he kept trying to clear his throat.

"I think so," he said, still coughing and getting the attention of other patrons in the restaurant.

Sdia stood and rushed over and gave him a couple of hard wacks on the back. He coughed twice more and seemed to stop suddenly. Satisfied that he was okay, she took her seat and stared at him.

"You've obviously been arrested," Sdia surmised.

Chapter 13

Mel cleared his throat and laughed. "Who hasn't?" he said, answering her question about being incarcerated. *I'll be damned. If I tell her I was in prison a year ago for attempted murder, she'll think I'm a fucking psycho, and I'd probably never see her again.*

"I know," she said, finally looking up at the ceiling.

"But it was for a bullshit gun charge . . . nothing too serious," he lied.

"Well, thank God you're home, right? " *RED FLAG! A gun charge? What the fuck?*

"Hell yeah!" He smiled. "So tell me about your line of work," he mimicked a professional tone.

"You're silly. Well, I write for a magazine called, *Reach*. It's a small magazine that focuses on culture, issues in the community, and current events."

"Oh, I know what magazine you're talking about. That's that shit with the lady reaching up towards the sun, right?" he said proudly.

Sdia bucked her eyes, surprised. "Yeah, you read that?" she asked, astounded.

"What? You don't think a street dude can be concerned with worldly issues?"

"No. It's just that I wouldn't expect many men to read that!"

"Yeah. I mean, you gotta be aware of what's going on around you, you know?"

"Wow! A lil hood and educated. Umph!" She stared at

him as he spoke.

"I mean, you have to be able to socialize, you know. How can I call myself a businessman and not be able to have a discussion with someone about politics or the perils of the world."

"I understand," she replied. "You know what? I think I will have another drink."

"Yeah, I think I'ma have me another shot, too," he said, waving for the waiter to come over.

"Will you be all right to drive?" she asked.

"What? Will I be all right to drive? This is what I do!"

"All right now," she said, raising her eyebrows.

"How was your salmon?" Mel asked, looking over at her half-eaten plate.

"It was really good. Would you like a piece?" she asked, forgetting her manners.

"Nah, I'm good. I'm not too big on seafood. Would you like a piece of steak?" he asked, breaking off a piece with his fork.

"No, thank you."

Mel laughed. "I know you hungry. I don't know why women do that."

"Do what?"

"Too shy to eat, knowing y'all asses be hungry."

"I'm not that hungry."

"Yeah, okay!" Mel twisted his lips to the side.

"Is everything all right over here?" the waiter came over and asked.

"Can we have another round of drinks? As a matter of fact, let me have a bottle of Moet," he ordered. "Go ahead and order some dessert, babe," he said, handing Sdia the dessert menu.

"May I suggest the Valrhona Chocolate Sphere at the price of $48?" the waiter stated.

"Did he just say $48 for some goddamn dessert?" Sdia muttered.

"What exactly is that?" Mel asked the waiter, holding in his laughter.

"Well, it's one of Dubai's signature deserts, however, every month we feature a different dessert that's inspired by one of the world's most beautiful countries. It's basically chocolate poured over a chocolate shell with raspberries and chocolate cake inside. It goes excellent with champagne!" he said, looking up at the ceiling, overjoyed.

"Do you like chocolate cake?"

"Yes, I do."

"Can you bring out a few strawberries, too?" Mel asked.

"Certainly, sir," the waiter replied, scooping the menus from the table. "I'll be back with your champagne and dessert."

"Expensive dessert, chocolate, strawberries and champagne, huh? What are you over there trying to do?"

"Get a second date," Mel responded.

"Really?"

"Absolutely. So . . ." he said. His cellphone began ringing. He looked at the screen and rolled his eyes. "Excuse me," he said, holding up one finger. Sdia nodded.

The female's voice on the other end and by her tone she didn't seem too happy.

"I have been trying to reach you for the past thirty minutes. My period is late!"

"So what the fuck do you want me to-?" He paused mid-sentence and waited.

Sdia looked at him as if he had sprouted an extra head. Her expression said: *What the fuck?*

"Pardon me," Mel said, quickly standing to his feet and dismissing himself from the table. He stepped outside of the restaurant before continuing his conversation.

"Who the fuck do you think you talking to bitch?"

"My period is late. I think I may be pregnant!" Niki sobbed.

"Well instead of calling me your stupid ass she be on the phone making an appointment for an abortion!"

"Are you serious?"

"Look. You either get an abortion or I'll beat the little bastard out of your stupid ass. The choice is yours!"

There was a long pause.

"Bitch do you hear me talking to you?'

"Yes daddy."

"Cool. I'll call you when I'm done handling some business." He shoved the phone into his pocket before heading back over to the table where Sdia sat scrolling through her text messages.

This bitch better not be texting no nigga on my time! Mel slowly crept up behind her. "Boo!" he shouted, causing her to jump.

"Oh my God. You scared the shit out of me," She spun around stunned.

"I'm sorry sweetheart."

"Is everything okay?" Sdia inquired.

"Yeah. Just some barbershop shit. The new receptionist calls me for everything. I mean...she could lose the top to a pen and call me asking me what I think she should do," He replied rubbing the back of his neck.

Bull shit! "Well it's getting late and I have a few articles that are due in the morning." Sdia fidgeted with the collar of her shirt, "So..."

"Oh...sure. I- I'm actually tired myself." Mel looked down and turned away. He fumbled with the set of key in his pocket.

Sdia smirked. *Sure you were!*

"Well shall we?" Mel asked taking her by the nd leading her to the entrance of the restaurant.

* * *

Sdia stepped out of the truck and waited for Mel to close the door behind her.

"Thanks for a wonderful evening," she said as he stepped in front of her.

Mel looked at her and smiled. "No. Thank you for allowing me to take you out!"

"You're welcome." She looked down.

Mel held his hand out. "Here, let me walk you to your apartment."

"Okay." She stuck her key inside the front door.

"Hello," she said, passing the clerk at the front desk.

"Good evening. How are you?" the older white woman asked.

"Fine, thank you," Sdia replied as she and Mel walked to the elevator.

"Will I be all right double parked?" he asked, turning in the direction of his truck.

"Yeah, you'll be fine," she said as she stepped onto the elevator first.

Mel followed.

"I hope I didn't keep you out too late," he said, looking at his watch.

"No, I'm okay. I usually don't go to bed until about twelve so I have an hour." She tried to appear as normal as possible, but he knew the call he'd received only an hour earlier still lingered in her mind.

"Are you okay?" Mel asked.

"Huh?" Sdia tilted her head to make certain she had heard him correctly.

"You look like you're struggling with something. Are you okay?"

"Oh. I'm sorry. I was thinking about something I had to do."

"So when can I see you again?"

"I'm just gonna say it. I wouldn't be surprised if you have a girlfriend! Only a scorned lover would call yelling like that. "

"I know. I could see why someone would think that!" Mel laughed.

"Why is that?" Sdia asked narrow eyes.

"She's younger and I guess she thought she had a chance, but I had to let her know that I don't mix business with pleasure!" He had trouble making eye contact.

This nigga must think I was born yesterday! "Well—I"

The elevator disrupted her sentence as it stopped on the

eighth floor. She stepped out and led the way to her apartment door.

"This is really nice!" Mel said as he glanced around at the cultivated hallway. Everything was spotless, even the walls. He was thankful for the interruption.

"Thanks," she replied, indecisively. *Why is he complimenting me on the damn hallway, like I'm the one who cleans the building? Do I look like a damn custodian?* She stopped in front of her door where a green and yellow flowered welcome mat rested. "Well, this is it," she said, turning to face him.

"Thanks again for a wonderful night." Mel took her by the hand and kissed it.

"You're welcome and thank you."

He stood back and skimmed her body from head to toe. "I definitely can't let you slip away from me!" He placed his hands in his pockets and shook his head. "Damn, let me go. I know you gotta wake up for work in the morning."

Sdia laughed. "Yeah, I do."

Mel stepped in closer, and asked, "Can I have a hug good night?"

"Of course." She placed her arms around his neck, being ultra-careful their pelvises didn't touch.

Mel smirked and thought, *Fake ass hug.*

Sdia pulled away. "Call me," she said, turning her back to him and entering her apartment.

Mel nodded. "All right now. I'll call you tomorrow." He waited for her to enter her apartment before heading back to the elevator. As he walked onto the elevator, he pulled out his cell phone and smiled.

"This should be interesting."

TAHANEE

Chapter 14

Impatiently, Natalya looked at her watch. "If she isn't here in five minutes, I'm leaving." She took a sip of her vanilla latte and looked out the café window. She regretted inviting her mother out for brunch. "God, please let her be on her best behavior!" From afar she could see people snickering and covering their mouths.

"Oh, shut the hell up and show me where my bitch of a daughter is!" Phyllis said.

Natalya heard her mother's sober voice and put her head in her hands. "Oh, my God."

Phyllis walked toward her, following the waitress. "Hey, Talya!" she yelled, waving her hand from side to side.

Customers watched as Phyllis passed by, bumping into some and knocking others upside the head with the huge ragged plastic purse she held. Natalya watched in repulsion.

"Hey, boo!" Phyllis shouted as she approached the table.

"Hey, Ma," Natalya replied dispassionately, glimpsing her black patent leather jacket marred with white scratches.

The waitress stepped aside as Phyllis removed her coat.

"Ooh, it's cold out there. I started to wear my sheepskin, but I ain't wanna be overdressed." She looked at Natalya, disgusted. "You look like you put on a few pounds."

Natalya forced a smile on her face. *She's more worried about my weight than that hideous, tight purple sweater and acid washed jeans she's wearing.*

"Really? I don't think I have."

Phyllis rolled her eyes as she grabbed the menu from the table. "I'm starving. What y'all got to eat here?" she said, looking at the waitress.

The waitress leaned over and looked at Phyllis's menu. "Well, let's see, we have the—"

Phyllis jerked her menu to the opposite side. "I don't like that. Just get me a glass of vodka!" she ordered.

The waitress blinked. "Uh . . ." she said, looking at Natalya for assistance.

"Ma, they don't have a bar," Natalya said.

"How y'all not gonna have a bar?" Phyllis raised her tone. "That's some bullshit. I need to see the manager!"

Natalya placed her hand on top of Phyllis's and said, "Ma, please … I'll buy you a bottle when we leave here." She picked up the menu and showed Phyllis the different entrees. Phyllis sucked her teeth.

"Let me see that," she said, snatching the menu from Natalya's hand.

Natalya looked at the waitress and signaled her to come back in a few minutes.

"Get me some water!" Phyllis called out.

Natalya shook her head. "So how are things on your side of town?" she asked as she inspected her mother's white patent-leather, knee-high boots that slightly flipped up at the toe and on her head she wore a black leather tam. *Did this bitch get dressed in the dark? What the fuck is she wearing?*

Phyllis reached in her purse and removed a cigarette. "I tell you one thing, it ain't as good as it is on your side," she replied, looking at Natalya's wedding ring.

Natalaya looked down at her finger. "Ma, you've seen this ring a thousand times. I actually thought I lost it." She chuckled.

"Hmm. I'm sure if you did, that cracker husband of yours would have gotten you another one."

Frustration rising, Natalya looked out the window. *Hold ya head, Natalya. This woman is your mother.* She wanted to take the glass of water and toss it in her mother's face. "How are your finances?" she asked.

Phyllis removed a small box of matches. "Not good. I could use a few hundred if you don't mind. I know you and that rich ass husband of yours won't miss it!" She proceeded to light the cigarette.

"Excuse me, madam, but we don't allow smoking in here," the waitress said nervously, as she returned with the glass of water.

"Who the hell you calling Madam?" Phyllis said in a phony British accent. "Do I look like I'm from Britain?"

The waitress stepped back. "Oh, I'm terribly sorry. I was just—"

Natalya cut in. "Ma, they can fine you for smoking in restaurants. It's against the law. And for the record it's British."

"Britain, British, American, who gives a shit!" Phyllis roared.

"Ma, it's against the law. You remember what happened the last time you tried to light a cigarette in the post office."

Phyllis' hand trembled as she placed the cigarette back into the carton.

The waitress looked at Natalya and smiled.

Natalya knew the chances of her mother being friendly without a drink was a million to one.

* * *

"Bitch, get ya lazy ass up. I'm out of Wild Irish!" her mother yelled from the living room as she sat on the couch with rollers in her hair sifting through the ashtray for cigarette butts.

Sixteen-year-old Natalya sat up, wiping the cold from her eyes. Her head pounded as she staggered out of bed trying to find a pair of shorts, just in case one of her mother's boyfriends was visiting—the very reason she and Natalya's father divorced over a year ago. Phyllis loved men. Natalya looked at the clock and sucked her teeth. It was eight o'clock in the morning, and she had just gotten in from work only an hour ago. She had just turned sixteen two months ago and was already working seven days a week at the gas station just to make ends meet. Her mother, Phyllis, was on the verge of losing her job as a delivery woman at the local Chinese restaurant.

"Bitch!" Phyllis called out from the living room again. "I know you ain't in there trying to get all dressed up. Get your ass out here!"

When Phyllis was out of booze, she was another person and her patience was very low. Natalya scanned the room frantically in her bra and panties looking through mountains of dirty clothes for a pair of shorts. The door burst open as Phyllis stood there with her hands on her hips.

"Didn't I tell you to get your motherfucking ass up and go to the store?" she shouted, charging toward her. "Get up!" she said, snatching Natalya by her hair and dragging her across the room.

Natalya's legs and buttocks burned as her mother towed her across the rough carpet. Her underwear fell off her hips, slightly revealing her buttocks.

"Get in the living room!" she demanded as she pulled her up by the arm.

Tears ran down Natalya's face as she rose to her feet.

"Leave them damn panties the way they are!" Phyllis ordered.

Natalya complied and slowly walked into the living room where Darren, her mother's boyfriend, had been sitting on the couch with an empty bottle of whiskey in his hand.

Darren shook his head in disbelief. "You sure are growing up. You even got pubic hair and everything." He smiled as he inspected her body, distinctively focusing on her crotch. Natalya held her hands over the front of her underwear and looked down at the floor.

"Here, dumb ass!" Phyllis said as she entered the living room, tossing a pair of dirty pants onto Natalya's head. "Tell Leon I owe him, and pick up a box of Newports while you're at it. You just got paid, right?"

***

Revenge has finally come! Happiness radiated through Natalya. "Come on, Ma. I'm going to take you to this nice restaurant where they make the best martinis."

Phyllis's face lit up like a Christmas tree. "Thank you!" she replied, gleefully. "Come to think of it, Talya, you don't look fat, now that I'm looking at you."

Natalya put her coat on her arm and walked ahead as Phyllis followed, babbling on and on about weight gain and how women over the age of thirty should eat healthy. At one point, Natalya could have sworn she heard her talking about Barbie dolls.

"Go ahead and wait for me in the car," she told Phyllis as she held the automatic key toward her car, unlocking the door.

Phyllis passed the waitress as she walked outside and said, "Y'all need to get some liquor in here!"

Natalya handed the waitress a twenty dollar bill and told her to keep the change. She looked at her watch before stepping outside into the cold and shook her head. *After all these years I'm finally the shot-caller. Who would've thought?*

"It's eleven o'clock in the morning, and I'm about to give my mother liquor. God forgive me! "

Chapter 15

"Damn!" Sdia stared at the flashing cursor on her laptop. *I have a review due in a week, and I'm not even past the first sentence.* She wanted to smack herself for staying up late on the phone with Mel for the past two weeks. If she were using that time to work on her report like she intended, she wouldn't be in this position. She placed her head in her hands. "Shit!" she shouted.

She walked to the living room window and gazed at the pale blue sky. The rain softly drummed on her window sill, worsening her mood. The last thing she needed was another cold, rainy day. She stood there with her pen hanging from her mouth. *Time flies,* she thought. Only three months ago it was July, and Thanksgiving was right around the corner. She could definitely use a drink.

Ring, ring, ring.

Quickly she turned, looking toward her apartment door. "I hope that isn't Ms. Wallace. I don't feel like socializing." Sdia decided to ignore the doorbell. Luckily she had turned off her kitchen lights and parked her car in the garage to keep it from the rain. So whoever was at the door would realize she wasn't home, eventually. She smiled as she turned back to the window.

Bang, bang, bang.

Her apartment door shook furiously, causing the small sheep figurine to fall from her armoire.

"Now I know that isn't Ms. Wallace knocking like that," she said, storming towards the door.

She stood on her tiptoes and looked through the

peephole. Sdia stood back, perplexed. "What the fuck?" It was Mel.

"Just a second," she called out, running to the bathroom to remove the silk scarf from her head.

Grabbing the comb from on top of the sink, she combed her hair, then ran to her bedroom and flung her closet door open in hopes of finding a pair of sweatpants. She didn't want Mel to see her in boxers, at least not now. "What the hell is he doing here? I'm not even dressed! Fuck!" she shouted as a stack of folded shirts fell from the top shelf onto the floor.

Using her foot, she shoved them to the back of the closet. All of her sweatpants were dirty, so she decided to answer the door in her boxers and wife beater. Mel smiled from ear to ear as she opened the door.

"Hey, sweetheart." He leaned forward and kissed her on the cheek.

"Hi, Mel." She blushed. "How'd you know I was home?" she asked, confused.

Mel stepped inside wearing a platinum diamond-faced dog tag, a black, long- sleeve thermal, a pair of dark jeans, and black suede Tims. He removed his black leather jacket.

"I called you on your cellphone like three times and you didn't answer, so I got worried and decided to drop by. Did I disturb you?" he asked.

"It's okay. I was just working on this report for work. It's due in a week. Have a seat." She pointed to the tan suede couch in the living room.

"Ladies first." he replied, stepping to the side.

Sdia smiled sarcastically as she quickly walked past

him. *He thinks he is so slick. Trying to get a good view of my legs.*

"Damn!" he murmured, stealing a peek at her thick thighs and strong calves.

Mel licked his lips as her round, plump behind made waves under the silk pink boxers. He removed his black New York Yankees cap and placed it in front of his jeans before walking over to the couch to join her.

I can't believe he's here, she thought. *I'm not even dressed. What the hell was he thinking?* Sdia scooted over, putting distance between them. Her panties grew moist from the sight of his face.

"How did you know I was home?" she repeated.

"I saw your car in the garage." He winked.

I hope he isn't some kind of stalker, she thought.

They had seen each other several times after their first date, but she had never invited him into her apartment—not because she didn't want to, but because she never got a chance to. He was always inviting her out or over to his place. Sdia was impressed with his exquisite taste. His condo looked like as if it should have had a page in *Better Homes* magazine. He had all types of antique furniture and expensive paintings. When she asked who helped him with his décor, he said he hired someone. But she had her suspicions. Sdia felt guilty that he had never visited her place, but she figured she would invite him over once she redecorated, especially after seeing his.

Charmaine had said, "You might as well invite him over. It's not like you haven't been to his place, which is crazy to me 'cause he could've raped you!"

"That is not why I haven't invited him over, Miss Know

It All! Besides, he wouldn't have raped me. He is too fine to be raping somebody!" Sdia replied.

She promised herself she would stop sharing certain things with Charmaine because she always looked for the negative in people, and that was something Sdia tried to break away from. Besides, she liked the way Mel carried himself. He wasn't like any other man she had ever dated; his personality was magnificent. Not only was he charming, he was caring, wise, funny, and just plain ole' perfect! It's like he was God sent. Ever since they'd been dating, he had showered her with flowers, candy, and teddy bears. They'd gone to Atlantic City twice, and he'd taken her to the most exquisite restaurants New Jersey had to offer. A few weeks ago when her car was being serviced he offered his Range Rover, but she declined. She didn't want to be held responsible if anything happened. Sdia knew he had a hidden agenda like most men, so she fed him with a long spoon. At times, toward the end of their dates, she wanted to kiss him, but she knew she couldn't. She had to keep him off balance, and she knew that sleeping with him in the short timeframe in which they'd known each other would be the biggest mistake she could possibly make.

She knew all about giving in too soon without making a man work. It led her to a dead end time after time, and this time she wanted to do things differently.

"Close your eyes, baby. I have something for you," Mel said.

"You have something for me?" she asked, batting her eyes.

"You are so beautiful!" He stared her in the eyes before reaching into his pocket and pulling out a gold rectangular box.

Sdia smiled as he opened the box and removed a platinum charm bracelet that held five huge charms—a heart, butterfly, elephant, dancer, and a horse. Each charm held a diamond centerpiece. He grabbed her hand and gently placed the bracelet on her wrist.

"It's beautiful," she replied, leaning forward and kissing him on the cheek.

Softly, Mel grabbed the back of her head until their lips touched. Slyly he eased his tongue in her mouth and moaned softly as he pulled her closer, running his fingers through her soft hair. Mel eased his left hand up and down her thigh. He could taste mint on her breath.

Quickly, Sdia pulled away. "Are you thirsty?" she asked, standing to her feet.

Mel looked up, wiped his lips with the back of his hand, and nodded. "Yeah," he replied, almost laughing.

As she walked into the kitchen, Sdia felt the moistness between her legs. She opened the refrigerator, pulled out a two-liter bottle of Sprite, and grabbed two glasses from the cabinet. *Oh my God!* she thought. *I can't believe I kissed him!*

She returned with two glasses of soda, a bag of chips, and onion dip. She placed the refreshments on the coffee table.

"I'll be right back." She smiled.

"If you like him, I suggest you keep your legs closed," Sharon's words popped in her head every time she fantasized about being intimate with him.

She went into her bedroom and grabbed a pair of panties along with some jeans. Sdia placed the panties inside of the jeans to conceal them and went into the bathroom to freshen up. *Glad I threw on some clothes. I definitely don't want to get myself into some trouble I can't get out of. Sean was enough. Maybe I should rush Mel up out of here. I don't trust my own self.*

* * *

Niki: *I miss you.*

Mel read the text message on his cellphone when Sdia first left the room. That was the third message Niki had sent him within twenty minutes. He turned his phone on silent and placed it in his pocket. Not even a minute had gone by before he felt the need to check his phone. *I better see if anyone else called. Could be my lil sis.* Mel opened his phone. There were five missed calls from Niki. "What the fuck does this bitch want?" he said, dialing her number.

"Hello?" Niki answered.

"Why are you blowing up my phone? What did I tell you about that shit?"

"I haven't heard from you all day. I sent you several text messages and you didn't reply."

"If I don't reply, that means I'm busy. Shit!" Mel shook his head in annoyance. Sdia's house phone began to ring.

"Where are you?" Niki asked.

Sdia suddenly came running from the bathroom to answer.

"I'm at home. Let me call you back!" He quickly hung up before Sdia reached the living room.

"I was just about to answer that," he teased, winking his eye.

"Really?" Sdia asked, picking up the phone. "Hello? . . .

Hey, Ma!" she said excitedly. "Nothing, just sitting here talking to Mel." Sdia turned to him and smiled.

Mel waved and whispered, "Tell her I said hello."

"He said hello," Sdia answered.

Mel knew her mother must have been grilling her about him because all Sdia said was yes or no. He glanced at his watch as she continued her conversation. Then someone else must've got on the phone and asked if she had company because Sdia said, "He's sitting right here . . . Hold on. I'm going to put you on speaker phone," she said, placing the phone down. "It's my aunt. She wants to say hi." Sdia said and bit her lip nervously. "This is my aunt Loretta."

"Hello?" Mel answered.

"Who is this? Mel?" Loretta asked.

"Yes. How are you?"

"You tryna fuck my niece?"

Mel's eyes widened in shock. "What!"

"You heard what I said. I heard you were a sexy motherfucker—buying her all kinds of shit!"

"Yeah, I bought a few things, but I don't expect anything in return." He laughed and looked at Sdia, pointing to the phone. "She's a trip!" he mouthed.

"And so you don't want no ass, huh?" she asked, astonished.

"Not at all. I like your niece, and that's far from my mind!"

"Oh, okay, so you must have a girlfriend. Well, you tell that tack head bitch don't start no shit, 'cause Auntie will come up there and fuck her up," she replied, laughing, and then began coughing uncontrollably.

"Nah, I don't have a girlfriend. Your niece is in good hands. Trust me," he reassured her, before handing the phone to Sdia, who gave him a light shrug.

"Okay, Aunt Loretta. Can I speak to my mother?"

"Damn, is this twenty-one questions?" Sdia murmured to Mel.

After a few more minutes of talking, she finally brought the call to an end and placed the phone on the receiver. Then she walked over to the couch to join Mel, who had become intrigued with his phone once again.

"Sorry about my aunt. Sometimes she gets out of hand."

"It's nothing," he replied, closing his phone.

Sdia laughed. She took a sip of her soda. "What are you doing for Thanksgiving?"

"I'm not sure. I was thinking about sending for my sister, since it's just us, or maybe go with my man to see his family."

"Yeah, I know." Sdia looked down. She felt guilty about asking, after remembering his parents and grandmother were dead.

"That would be nice. Where does your best friend live?"

"About twenty minutes from me." He grabbed a potato chip from the bag and placed it in his mouth. At the same time, he was thinking, *I wonder what the lips below her navel taste like. Once I lick that, I know this bitch is gonna be hooked.*

"Those are my plans if you don't invite me to spend Thanksgiving with you," he added.

So far, Mel had invested almost $10,000 in her, all within a matter of two months. He wasn't about to blow his chances, let alone make any hasty moves. He wanted to take things slow. He wanted to master her. He was going to play by her rules until she felt it was safe to drop her guard. Then, as soon as she dropped her guard, he would go for the kill. Mel wanted to see the source of her strength, and see if he had what it took to break her down. *This bitch needs to come off of that high horse.* Mel smiled and gently stroked the side of her face with his fingertips.

Chapter 16

"Uh, uh, ah, ah!" Lamar groaned as he bit the pillow in agony. Will continued to plunge his penis deeper into Lamar's rectum.

"Oh, shit, uh, uh."

Lamar could feel his asshole stretching with each thrust. This was his first time being on the bottom and as far as he was concerned, it was the last. Will removed his feces-covered penis before ejaculating on Lamar's back.

"Oh, shit!" Will said, out of breath. He threw himself down on the pillow next to Lamar. "Are you all right?" he asked.

"Hell no! That shit hurt!" Lamar yelled, standing to his feet. He rubbed his asshole with his index finger. He could still feel the wet lubricant that rested on his rectum along with the semen that had drizzled down his back. His asshole continued to throb as he walked to the bathroom to wash.

"Can you grab me a washcloth while you're in there?" Will called from the bedroom.

"Hold on," Lamar replied. He grabbed a washcloth from the shelf and ran it under the cold water. "Aaaah!" He sighed as he gently dabbed his rectum with the cloth. He looked at himself in the mirror. "Never again," he said as he looked at his bloodshot eyes. Lamar looked down at the washcloth and gasped. "Will!" he called.

Will ran into the bathroom naked in a pair of white ankle socks. He grabbed the door frame to keep from sliding. "What?"

"I'm bleeding!" Lamar replied, frightened.

"Pssssst," Will said, placing his hand on his forehead. "Is that all? I thought it was an emergency." He grabbed the rag from Lamar and examined it. "That's normal. You'll be okay. Turn around."

"Fuck, no!" Lamar yelled. "I ain't doing that shit no more. That's your shit."

"Man, let me see," Will ordered.

Lamar turned, placing both hands on the sink. Will separated his cheeks and examined his rectum. "I was being as gentle as possible." He ran the washcloth under the faucet and gently wiped the fluids. "Watch out," he said, patting Lamar on the waist for him to step aside. Will reached under the sink and removed a fleet. "Come here. I need to rinse you out." He grabbed Lamar by the arm and told him to squat.

"Is that vinegar in there?" Lamar asked nervously.

"No, you'll be all right," Will replied.

He inserted the nozzle into Lamar's rectum and gently squeezed. The cool liquid felt great as it soothed his rectum. It ran down the side of his leg, leaving a trail of blood and feces. Will continued to squeeze the bottle until it was empty.

"Are you okay?" he asked.

Lamar turned and kissed him. "Yes, baby."

Will smiled and then grabbed a washcloth from the shelf and cleaned his penis.

"Wanna take a bath?" Lamar asked.

"Sure!" Will replied.

He walked over and sat on the side of the tub and dropped vanilla scented bubble bath under the running water. Lamar slowly walked over and stood in front of him with his penis at attention. Will cuffed Lamar's penis with his left hand and slowly inserted himself, inch by inch into his mouth. Lamar tilted his head toward the ceiling and closed his eyes.

"Oh, shit!" Lamar sang. He gently grabbed the back of Will's head and began to guide him back and forth. His dick sucking skills were way better than Natalya's. Will was proving himself to possibly be the best lover he had ever had. "I'm 'bout to cum, I'm 'bout to cum. Ooooh shit!" Lamar's legs trembled as if the weight had lifted from his soul. "I'm never gonna let you go!" he moaned.

***

"Do you care about me?" Will asked, sitting between Lamar's legs as the steam rose from the hot bath water.

"Of course, I care about you," Lamar replied. He grabbed Will's hand and kissed it.

"You know I really care about you, Lamar."

"Yeah, I know you do, Will. What are you getting at?" he asked, suspiciously.

Will looked up at him. "Well, a few minutes ago you said you're never gonna let me go, and I want to know if you really mean it. I mean ... we've been seeing each other for the past few weeks, and I don't know . . ."

"What are you talking about?" Lamar sat up, lifting Will from his chest. "What do you mean you don't know?"

"I mean, I want to take things a step further." He stared Lamar in the eyes.

"Take it further, like how?"

"Let me ask you a question. Can you see yourself with me for the rest of your life?"

Lamar laughed. "You mean being monogamous?" The question amused him.

"Yes, monogamous," Will replied harshly.

"But we are monogamous."

"So what's the problem? If you aren't seeing anyone else, then why is it so hard for you to commit?"

"I don't think that I'm ready for all of that. That's a bit much."

"So would you say we're in a relationship?" Will pressed.

"I don't know," Lamar replied, aggravated.

Will sighed. "Well, we have to mean something to each other. There are certain things you just don't do with anyone!"

"I guess."

Lamar could see where the conversation was going, and he didn't want to go there. *I'm not going to make a commitment because I'm not gay!* he thought. He cared about Will, but he loved Natalya.

"Sit up, babe. Let me wash your back."

Lamar didn't know who he preferred sexually between the two, but one thing he knew for sure—they would never find out about each other.

* * *

Carl awoke in a cold sweat. He glanced over at Natalya, who was peacefully asleep. She hadn't even felt him jump. It was three in the morning, and he couldn't sleep. This was the second dream he had this week of being pushed from his office window. He figured the reoccurring dream had to be a result of the tremendous amount of stress he was under. He had a presentation to make the following morning that he and Lamar had been working on unrelentingly for the past month. He'd been sleeping with the notes under his pillow for the past week. That was an old trick his mother had taught him when he was younger. Whenever he had a quiz in school, she would help him study the night before and tuck him in bed, placing his notes under his pillow.

"I guarantee you will pass the test tomorrow," she'd say, before kissing his forehead and turning off the light. Hopefully his hard work would gain the interest of Ledman & Riggley, a well-known IT company he'd been trying to get the attention of for months. Carl decided to go downstairs and make himself a drink. He took his time easing out of bed and taking careful steps to the bar. Carl poured the vodka into his glass, filling it halfway and took a seat on the barstool.

"Why me, Lord?" he said aloud, looking at the ceiling. He wrapped his bare feet around the barstool legs. His face grew hot as he tried to hold back the tears, but it was no use. Tears emerged from his eyes leaving long trails on his cheek. Carl placed his head on the bar table and cried. He wanted to die. He hated himself. He hated his life, and he hated Natalya.

"Fucking bitch!" he grunted, slamming the empty glass onto the bar table and jumping from the stool before heading toward his bedroom. The more he thought about his life and Natalya, the angrier he became. Adrenaline pumped through his veins as he stomped up the stairs and burst into the bedroom. His shadow lingered on the floor of the doorway as he watched her lay with her back facing him.

"I wish your fat ass would close the door and lay down. It's almost 3:30 in the morning!" She fluffed her pillow and rolled over on her stomach.

Carl didn't move. He stood there silent, clenching his fist and biting his bottom lip, contemplating his next move. *She is so fucking disrespectful*, he thought. *I do everything for that ungrateful bitch and this is how she treats me?*

"What the fuck is your problem, you stupid motherfucker?" she shouted, turning to face him.

Carl didn't expect her reaction. He slowly unclenched his sweaty fists and wiped them on his pajama pants. Fear seeped into his body slowly, devouring his courage. Natalya quickly jumped from the bed and grabbed the pillow she lay on, along with the top sheet. She charged him, shoving it as hard as she could into his chest. Carl fell backward and slammed his back on the wall in the hallway.

"Since you can't make up your mind where you want to sleep, keep your fat ass out here!" She slammed the bedroom door and locked it. "Dumb ass! I have to wake up for a hair appointment in a few hours, and your fat ass wants to act stupid. Well, stay out there, you fucking jerk!"

Rubbing his lower back, he turned to look at the small crack he had made in the wall. He grabbed the pillow from the floor and headed to the guest room. He was too embarrassed to think about what had just happened. He was embarrassed that God had seen what his wife had just done to him. He climbed into bed and buried his head under the covers before dozing off.

When he awoke the next morning, he could hear Natalya in the next room on the phone telling someone how she had to knock him on his ass a couple of hours ago. He knew she was on the phone with Abby because she had no other friends, and she rarely spoke to her mother.

"I don't have time for his mess. Girl, you should have seen the way I pushed his fat ass. I didn't know I had that much power. I am so sick of him!"

Carl walked into the bathroom to shower. As he undressed, he noticed a small, purple bruise on his back. He felt like a bitch. Carl didn't bother looking at himself in the mirror as he brushed his teeth. Instead, he spat in the toilet. He, too, was too appalled to face himself. He wished he had the balls to hit a woman. His mother would be turning over in her grave if she knew his thoughts. Although his family wasn't too happy about him marrying a black woman, he did know for sure that they would not approve of him putting his hands on any female, no matter what her race is. A small inkling of guilty pleasure fluttered through his body. *I shouldn't even be think of such a cowardly act, but I'd sure like to slap the shit out of that nigger bitch!* He never understood how a man could hit a woman until now. By the time he got out of the shower, Natalya was gone. He had purposely spent almost an hour in the bathroom to avoid her. He ate an English muffin with jelly and drank a cup of coffee before heading to work.

He would kill himself if any of his employees found out the truth about his marriage. His office was the only place where he was appreciated, respected, and treated like a man. Sometimes, he wished he could stay at work all day. Once he entered the building, everyone scattered like roaches, breaking the small huddle they had formed in the corner.

"Good morning, Mr. Adler," Marina called from the front desk, smiling politely.

"Hello, Marina. How are you this morning?" he asked.

Marina stood up and walked over. She wore a pair of form fitting khakis, a tan and brown blouse, and a pair of Chanel loafers. Her jet black hair was pulled back in a bun and small diamond studs sparkled in her ears.

"I'm doing fine, thank you," she replied as she handed him a memorandum.

Carl nodded. "That's good," he replied, taking the note from her hand and heading into his office.

He closed the door behind him and thought, "What a nice young lady." Carl closed his eyes and smelled the note that her perfume had rubbed off on. He knew it was a Victoria's Secret fragrance, but he couldn't remember which one. Every Christmas he and Natalya threw a huge party for the office staff, and they always had a secret Santa. He figured it would be a nice way for Natalya to interact with other people since she didn't work and only had one friend. Marina ended up being Natalya's secret Santa the year before.

"What does Mrs. Adler like?" Marina had asked.

"Anything that smells good," Carl replied.

Marina went out and bought Natalya a holiday edition gift set from Victoria's Secret that had been sitting in the garage since then.

"I'm not wearing that shit," Natalya said when they arrived home from the party. "That little Puerto Rican bitch could have kept her money!"

Carl shrugged and said, "It's a nice gesture, Talya."

"Then you wear it!" she replied.

He read the memo. "Damn!" He sighed. The presentation had been moved up an hour. Carl looked at his briefcase. He needed to go over his notes. "Shit!" he cursed aloud, banging his fist on his desk.

Unfortunately, he had left the notes at home. His day had just begun and was already starting off bad. He picked up the phone and dialed Marina at the front desk.

"Can I see you for a moment?"

She rushed into the office carrying a stack of files. "Yes, Mr. Adler?"

"Can you please tell Lamar that I need to see him in my office?"

"Lamar called in sick today. I'm sorry. I forgot to tell you. Is there anything I can help you with?" she asked.

Carl gritted his teeth. He wanted to knock everything from his desk onto the floor. "Out sick? He's out sick? Of all the days he decides to get sick, he does it today?" He put his face in his hands.

"I left the presentation at home, and I would never make it back in time for the meeting." Carl walked over to the window and gazed at the busy street below.

Marina fidgeted with the folders in her hands. She looked around the room trying to think of something comforting to say in his time of distress. She twisted her lips to the side. "Bingo!" she said.

"It's going to be okay, Mr. Adler." She walked toward him, placing the folders on his desk. She reached in her pocket and pulled out a ring full of keys. "I have the key to Lamar's desk." She jingled the keys behind Carl's head. He quickly turned, astonished and smiling from ear to ear.

"You are a life saver." He patted her on the shoulder. Now all he had to do was find where Lamar kept his hard copy of the presentation. Carl took the keys and headed toward Lamar's office.

"Why not kill two birds with one stone?" she asked.

Confused, Carl turned around.

"I'm sorry." Marina smiled. "I meant while you're searching, I'll call him on his cellphone to save us some time."

"Thank you so much, Marina!" Carl said with a smile.

Marina winked. "Not a problem."

Carl fiddled with the keys. "It would have been smart to find out which key opened his desk." After trying three keys, he realized that Marina had each key labeled with the employee's first and last initial. He shook his head, looking down at each label on the remaining keys.

"Lamariel Baldwin, Lamariel Baldwin, LB—got it!" he said aloud. Carl inserted the key into the small file cabinet that sat between Lamar's desks. The drawer popped open revealing hundreds of unlabeled files.

"Fuck!" Carl shouted.

A couple of his employees poked their heads in the office before quickly removing themselves after seeing him seated at Lamar's desk. He knew that would be Friday's topic of discussion, and he didn't care.

"I tried calling Lamar on his cellphone twice and he didn't answer, so I left him a message," Marina stated as she entered the room. She searched through the files that sat on top of the bookshelf in Lamar's office while Carl continued to go through each folder in the drawer. Marina snapped her fingers. "How could I have forgotten? Mr. Adler?"

Carl looked up.

"I have a copy of the presentation in my e-mail. Lamar

asked me to do a spell check before he printed it and gave it to you." Marina felt as if she had just cracked the code to a longtime puzzle.

Carl dropped the folders from his hand. Sweat trickled down his temples. "Are you serious?" he asked, amazed.

"Yeah!" Marina nodded excitedly, revealing both rows of her teeth. She quickly walked to her desk. Carl followed and watched her wide hips sway from side to side. He wondered if Marina added extra motion in her hips because she knew he was watching. She pulled the seat from under her desk and sat down.

"Here, Mr. Adler. Have a seat," she said, pointing to the chair that sat in front of her desk.

Carl complied. He looked around at her small office space, and thought, *She could definitely use more room.*

"Who's this?" he asked, picking up a small silver-framed picture of a little girl on the beach. She wore two curly pigtails, with a pink and white striped dress. In her hand she held a bucket and shovel. She looked like she could have been two years old.

"She's a cute and chubby little thing," he teased, placing the picture back in its place.

Marina looked up and smiled. "That's my niece, Eliana. She's back home in Columbia with my sister."

Carl drummed his fingers on his knees. He looked around the small office and could tell Marina was a fan of art. "I see you have a passion for paintings, huh?" he asked, referring to a painting that hung on the wall.

Marina glanced at the picture. "Yes, I am. That's a painting by Fernando Botero. That's called, 'Still Life with Watermelon.' It's an oil painting." Her fingers gracefully tapped the keyboard as if she were playing the piano.

Carl stood. "I know this painting," he said, walking to the wall on the other side of the room. "Isn't this Francisco Goya?"

Marina looked up, astounded, and said, "Yes, he's also a famous Columbian painter."

"I guess you can say I have a liking for paintings myself." Carl chuckled.

"Got it!" she said, almost jumping from her seat.

Carl hurried over and looked at the screen. "Yup, that's it," he replied, standing behind her and reading over the presentation; her hair smelled like fruit. *Damn, this girl smells delicious!* He inhaled deeply as he continued to read the memo. Marina could feel his hot breath on her neck. Goose bumps began to form on her arm. Carl stood back.

"Can you print that out for me?" he asked, adjusting his tie.

"Sure," she replied.

He proceeded to the door, and said again, "You're a life saver, Marina." He turned and winked.

"Anytime, Mr. Adler," she replied.

Ten minutes later, Carl was sitting as his desk when Marina entered his office.

"Here you go," she said, handing him a twelve-page printout.

"Thank you," he replied, taking the documents from her hand.

"How about you go ahead and order yourself some take-out for lunch? My treat."

"No, thanks, Mr. Adler. I brought my lunch." Before

leaving the office, she turned, and said, "Besides, I'd rather have lunch with you."

Chapter 17

"Damn, ain't shit on TV!" Mel cursed as he flipped through the stations. He stood to his feet and tossed the remote on the couch.

"What the fuck does this bitch got in here to drink?" he said as he opened the refrigerator. "Bullshit, bullshit, bullshit," he called out, knocking over a jar of pickles, a carton of milk, and a carton of Chinese food.

All he wanted to do was fuck. He had things to do. The bathroom door opened and Dwana, his girlfriend of two years stepped out. Roc had introduced the two of them while he was in prison. Dwana had looked out for him while he was away. She made sure his commissary stayed full and never missed one visit. She had even snuck some work in a few times. He called her his, "Down Ass Bitch," and she loved it. She was definitely a hood chick. Mel rarely messed with hood rats, but he felt every guy needed one just in case something major went down.

"I'm back," she purred, standing in the hallway naked. The water that hadn't dried off on her body glistened on her olive skin. The chandelier that hung above gave Mel a clear view of what her body looked like, and it was a masterpiece. He bit his lip.

"Bring your sexy ass over here."

Her 36 double D's bounced as she walked toward him. Mel stared at her clean shaven vagina.

"Damn!" he said aloud, grabbing her by the hand. He slowly spun her around, examining every inch of her body. Her round ass jiggled with every step she took.

POW!

Mel smacked her left butt cheek. It flopped up and down like a bowl of Jell-O; it had a life of its own.

"Ooooh," Dwana moaned as she leaned over and placed both hands on the couch. Mel stood behind her and unzipped his jeans. He removed his penis and gently smacked her on the ass with it.

"You like when I smack ya ass?" he whispered in her ear.

He held her left cheek open with his left hand as he gently ran his index and middle finger down the crack of her ass with his right hand. Mel smelled his fingers. He had to make sure she was on point before he penetrated her. Mel didn't bother putting on a condom. He knew he was the only one Dwana was sleeping with, and if he found out different, he would break her face. Dwana screamed loudly as Mel rammed his penis inside of her. He humped vigorously.

"You like this shit, don't you? You like it when daddy fucks you like this?" He smacked her ass as hard as he could, causing her to shriek.

"Uh, baby, slow down," she managed to say, but she was talking to deaf ears.

Mel grabbed her by her hair and continued to pound her out as hard as he could. His thrusts were so fast and hard that her ass was beginning to hurt his stomach. He felt himself about to cum and quickly stopped.

"Put your face right here!" he said, pointing for her to get on her knees in front of him. Dwana did what she was told, as Mel grabbed his penis and relieved himself on her face.

After freshening up, Mel left her apartment and headed to see Roc. He decided to chirp him to make sure he was home before he drove all the way across town. Mel held the side button on his phone and began to speak loudly into the speaker.

"Yo!" he shouted.

"What up, nigga?" Roc replied, excited. "Where you at?"

"I'm about to come through. You home?" Mel asked.

"Yeah, I'm here. I'm waitin for this bitch to leave!" he replied, referring to his baby's mother.

"All right, son. I'm on my way."

Mel drove down the busy street. The burnt orange sky hovered over the tall buildings as the sun began to set. Mel looked at his watch. It was 7:07 p.m.

"I wonder if Sdia's home," he said, as he dialed her number.

Her telephone rang four times before he got her voicemail. He hung up and redialed her number only to get her voicemail once again. Mel grew frustrated. He hadn't heard from her all day, and he was beginning to have second thoughts about going to see Roc. He wondered if he should drive over to Sdia's to see if she was home. Although they had never been intimate, or made a commitment to each other, he had already decided she was his. He needed to know where she was. Mel redialed her number for the third time.

"Hello?" she answered, half asleep.

"Hi, baby," Mel replied. "Are you all right?"

"Huh, what?" she asked, confused.

"I tried calling you two times and you didn't answer. I

was a little worried."

Sdia chuckled. "I'm okay. Thanks for asking."

"How was your day?" he asked.

"Tiring and stressful. I had to turn in my report. It was due today."

"Did everything work out?"

"I don't know. I left early, but for the most part, I think so."

"Why didn't you call me when you got home?"

There was a long pause. "I fell asleep," she replied, suspiciously.

Mel laughed. "I'm only playing, beautiful."

Sdia laughed nervously. "Mel, can I call you back?"

"All right, baby."

* * *

Sdia put the phone on the receiver and walked to the window. She stared at the sky.

"Lord, please give me the ability to recognize a bad situation and the strength to walk away before it's too late!" She decided to go into her room and read a chapter from her self-esteem book.

"Never give someone the power to determine your emotional state," she said, reading a small section in the book.

She looked up at the ceiling and repeated the sentence once more. Sdia read a few more pages and decided to run water for a hot bath to ease her mind. "Take it one day at a time, Sdia," she said aloud. "I'm just going to enjoy my bath, turn the ringer off on both my phones, and have a wonderful evening alone." She sunk her body into the hot water. The smell of citrus candles filled the air as the shadows of the flame danced on the walls. *Maybe I'm being too paranoid*, she thought. *But what if I'm not?*

Chapter 18

"I don't think I'll be able to," Lamar exclaimed.

"Are you serious, Lamar? I told you about this a month ago," Will replied.

"Yeah, I know, but there was a sudden change of plans. I'm sorry."

"Okay, all right. That's cool." Will slammed the phone on the receiver. "Fucking liar!" he screamed. He had told Lamar about his mother and sister coming down from North Carolina a month ago, and Lamar agreed that he would meet them. His chin quivered as a single tear trickled down his ashen cheek. He had a fun-filled weekend set for the four of them, and now that Lamar cancelled, he was back to square one.

"Damn!" he cursed, kicking over the kitchen trashcan.

He took a seat at the table and placed his head in his hands and wondered if being angry was appropriate. It wasn't like he and Lamar were committed to each other. Every chance Lamar got, he was constantly reminding him how he wasn't ready for a relationship, and how he'd rather take things slow.

Will decided to walk outside for a breath of fresh air. The dark blue sky gaped down on him as he kicked an empty Pepsi can. His luck was nonexistent. Everything he touched turned to shit. Will knew he was about to be on the pity party, and soon he would be weeping and feeling sorry for himself. First, he would start with how his father abandoned him and his sister when he was four; second, how he had no life; and third, how every guy he ever liked seemed to reject him after they got what they wanted. He scrunched his lips as his eyes began to fill with tears. He did his best to keep from blinking but couldn't. Tears continually rolled down his cheeks. He wiped his face with the palm of his hand, trying to clear his stuffy nose of mucus. The conversation with Lamar continued to play in his mind.

"Piece of shit!" he cursed.

Will needed an outlet; a way to release his frustration. "Quick dick!" he said to himself and smiled.

He turned and quickly walked toward the direction of his car. He hopped in and headed down the street to his favorite bar.

"Fuck that shit. I'm 'bout to find me a piece of, trade!"

* * *

"I mean, I like him and he's cool, but ..." Sdia explained, balancing the silver cordless phone between her shoulder and cheek.

"I know you like him, but he seems a little off," Charmaine replied. "I didn't forget about that phone call you said he got during your first date!"

"So what should I do? We haven't even had sex or made a commitment, and he's acting all controlling and shit."

"Uh, uh, uh, that's a sign of someone obsessive and possessive. I would drop his ass now."

"Shut up, Charmaine. You're taking this too far. It's not even that serious!"

"Yeah, okay. Trust me. I know his type."

Sdia's other line beeped in. "Hold on, Charmaine. It's my other line." She looked at the caller ID before clicking over. It was Mel. *Huh? Didn't I tell him I'd call him back an hour ago? I wonder what he wants.* She felt butterflies in her stomach as she hurriedly clicked the FLASH button.

"Hello," she answered in a sexy tone.

"What's up?" Mel replied. "Whatchu' doin'?"

"I was on the other line."

"Talkin' to who?" he asked.

Once again, she was caught off guard by his aggression, but at the same time, it turned her on.

She swallowed before replying, "My friend."

"What friend?"

"Hold on." She clicked over to Charmaine. "Let me call you back."

"Must be Mel on the other line. I can't wait to meet this character."

"Whatever. I'll call you in a few," she said, quickly retrieving Mel's call.

"Yeah. So what's up?" she asked, trying to sound calm and collected.

"Nothing. So who's your friend?" he insisted.

Sdia couldn't believe how persistent he was. For a quick moment, she wondered if she should tell him it was Charmaine. She knew this was one of the many ways that men tested women. He wanted to see how far he could go. Sdia didn't want to play his game, so she flipped it on him.

"You wouldn't know them if I told you. How was your day?"

He paused before replying, "My day was cool. As a matter of fact, can I call you back?" he asked.

Sdia smiled. She could tell he was agitated by her reply,

and she knew he wasn't going to challenge her. Instead, he took the easy way out.

"Yeah, that's fine." She closed her phone and stood to her feet. "Men!" Sdia decided to go to the bar across the street for a much needed drink. Once more, she found herself brooding over uncertainties when it came to Mel, but she didn't want to write him off just yet.

Let him go, Sdia. Maybe he's not for you! the little voice in her head kept saying as she hurried across the busy street. Several drivers beeped their horns as her lovely silhouette gracefully stepped onto the sidewalk. As Sdia walked to the bar, she noticed a white Range Rover parked on the corner across the street from the bar. She squinted as she got closer to the vehicle.

"Is that—wait a minute . . . I know that isn't …" Sdia's heart dropped to her stomach, as Mel emerged from the vehicle dressed in a black Adidas sweat suit.

"What the hell?" she said aloud as he ran across the street toward her. "What are you doing here?" she asked as he approached her with a smile on his face.

"No, the question is, what are you doing?" he replied.

Sdia stood back and laughed. "Are you serious?"

Mel placed his hands in his pocket and stared at her. "Are you meeting your friend inside?"

"What friend?" she asked, trying to hide her fear.

"The nigga you were talking to on the phone."

"That was Charmaine!" she said.

Mel continued to stare at her doubtfully. "You know I was out here the whole time," he replied.

"What?" she asked, slowly backing away from him. "What do you mean you were out here the whole time?"

With his arms open, Mel began to walk toward her. Sdia stared at him blankly, not knowing what to think.

"What's wrong?" he asked, stroking her chin with the back of his hand.

The touch of his soft hand on her face caused an abrupt case of amnesia. She couldn't remember what thoughts occupied her head only seconds ago.

"What's wrong, baby?" he asked again, gently grabbing the back of her neck and softly kissing her on the lips.

She kissed him back as he pushed his pelvic area firmly against hers. She felt his penis become erect, and she quickly pulled away.

"I was about to go in for a drink. Do you want to join me?" she asked, pointing toward the bar.

Mel grabbed her arm and pulled her closer for another kiss. "You belong to me!" he whispered. His hot breath and wet lips brushed across her ear causing the hair on the back of her neck to stand up straight.

Mmmm! Her nipples grew hard and her vagina moistened.

"Get a room!" a passenger from a white Acura yelled from the window.

Their embrace came to a halt as they watched the car speed down the dark street. Sdia grabbed his hand and led him to the bar. "Come on, drinks on me!" *I belong to him, huh? I kind of like his thuggish swag. I know I should check him on that though, but I'll just let him think whatever he wants.*

Chapter 19

"Where in the hell is this boy?" Natalya asked herself as she walked over to the hostess.

"Good evening. I have a reservation for two under the last name Marks." She used her maiden name regularly when she and Lamar had dates.

The hostess slowly ran her red fingernail down the list of names before confirming, "Yes, ma'am, I see the reservation." The young hostess smiled, revealing a mouthful of braces.

"Has my date arrived?" Natalya asked rudely.

"No, ma'am, but I can—"

"Just seat me," Natalya replied, stopping her mid-sentence. She brushed past the hostess, bumping her shoulder, almost knocking the young lady to the floor.

"Please follow me, ma'am," she said, quickly walking in front of Natalya.

Natalya blew her breath, stepped to the side, and allowed the hostess to walk ahead. She switched her LV purse to her right shoulder.

"My name is Natalya."

The hostess nodded. "Certainly, Natalya. I apologize. Please follow me."

The two women walked through the crowded restaurant. Natalya looked at each couple as they dined; some chatted, some held hands across the table, and others fed one another crème brulee. She turned her nose up in disgust. *What a bunch of assholes!* she thought.

The hostess stopped at a table for two that sat by the window. "Here you are, Ma'am. I mean, Natalya," the hostess nervously said as she pulled the chair out for her.

Natalya looked her up and down. "Just get me a glass of water."

The hostess scurried to the back to fulfill the order.

"Where is this idiot?" she said as she looked down at her watch. Natalya slowly sat down and crossed her legs. Lamar was fifteen minutes late. She snatched her phone from her purse and dialed his number. His voicemail answered.

"What the hell?" she muttered, before hanging up and dialing again. "He must be trying to call me."

"Hello, you've reached the voicemail of Lamar Baldwin. Please leave a message after the beep." She gritted her teeth while holding the phone sternly. "Where the fuck are you? You stupid motherfucker. I'm sitting here in this fucking restaurant waiting for your dumb ass. You better call me back!" She closed the phone and tossed it on the table. She pulled her make-up compact from her purse and touched up her face.

The hostess returned with a glass of ice water. "Can I get you anything else while you wait for your guest?"

Natalya looked at her, revolted. She thought, *Can't this bitch see I'm busy?* The waitress took her expression as a hint and kindly walked away.

A minute later, Natalya's phone softly hummed on the table. "He'd better be on his way!" she said as she picked it up to answer. Her faced dropped when she looked at the caller ID. It was Carl.

"What!" she shouted.

"Talya, I'm, I'm, I'm working late tonight. I'm not sure what time I'm going to be home," Carl stuttered.

"Whatever," Natalya replied, before hanging up on him.

She took a sip of her water, glanced at her watch, and dialed Lamar once more. His phone rang one long time before his voicemail abruptly came on. Natalya's leg shook uncontrollably at the thought of him forwarding her to voicemail. She knew all about forwarding calls; that was her forte when it came to Carl. She could feel the blood from her stomach rush to her head. She rose to her feet, clenching her fist and shoved the chair under the table.

"Fuck!" she said aloud, causing the older white couple who sat behind her to turn. "Can I help you?" she asked, clutching her bag with her right hand and placed her left hand on her hips. She turned and stormed away toward the exit.

"Have a good evening," the hostess called out with a smile.

"Go to hell!" Natalya shot back, giving her the finger. Surprisingly, the waitress returned the gesture. Natalya gasped, and thought of turning back to report the waitress, but decided against it. She didn't have time for games and made her way to the valet and handed the valet her ticket. She waited for him to retrieve her car.

Once inside, she switched on the overhead light and dialed Lamar.

"Hello, you've reached Lamar."

She slammed the phone shut and tossed it in the passenger's seat. "Motherfucker!" she shouted, banging on the steering wheel. "That little piece of shit! Who does he think he is?" She rocked back and forth, biting down on her jaw, which caused it to bleed. Her plans for the evening had been crushed. She had her hopes set on getting laid before Carl came home. She and Lamar hadn't fucked in two weeks, and her body needed it.

"Stupid ass," she said as she started the ignition. "That's cool. I'll show that little fucker!"

* * *

"Who keeps on calling you?" Will asked, handing him a napkin.

Lamar quickly closed his phone. "Wrong number," he replied, wiping spaghetti sauce from the corner of his mouth. "Damn, baby, that was delicious." He leaned back in the kitchen chair and gazed at Will. "You have got to be the sexiest man I've ever seen."

Will turned away. "Stop, Lamar, you're making me blush."

Lamar smiled as he stood and picked up his plate from the table. "I'm really sorry about Thanksgiving, man."

Will quickly interrupted. "Don't sweat it. I understand." He walked over and kissed him on the cheek.

"As long as you're here now, that's all that matters." He grabbed the broom and began to sweep the floor.

"Do you want to watch a movie after we're done?"

Lamar looked at him while grabbing his crotch, and said, "I'd rather make one."

Suddenly Will dropped the broom and ran to the bathroom. "Damn!" he shouted.

"What's wrong?" Lamar asked, running behind him.

Will dropped his pants and sat on the toilet. The water in the commode splashed as a foul stench filled the air. Lamar held his nose.

"Damn, baby!" Gurgling sounds came from Will's rectum. "What the hell did you eat?" Lamar asked, handing him a can of Glade air freshener.

"I ate the same thing you ate," Will strained. "I've had diarrhea for three weeks. I've been meaning to make an appointment with my doctor, but I've been procrastinating."

Lamar walked into the living room and opened the window. "Well, you need to get on the ball with that. You shouldn't play with your health." He wiped his hands off on his jeans. "So I guess this means I don't get any tonight, huh?"

Will stuck his head through the bathroom door. "Most definitely not. You know I'm going to take care of you before the night is over," he said, signaling oral sex.

"I'm going to run to the store. Do you need me to pick up a Gatorade?" Lamar reached for his phone.

Will poked his head out from the bathroom. "Yes, baby, please."

Lamar grabbed his jacket and stepped outside. Once he was halfway down the hall, he dialed Natalya. His heart raced as he thought of a lie to tell her. He let out a sigh of relief at the sound of her voicemail.

"Natalya, its Lamar. Call me back when you get a chance. I'm in the hospital." *Damn, why did I say that?* He knew that once he spoke to Natalya, she would do a full investigation and ask for a doctor's note. *I'll tell her a friend of mine was in a car accident, and I rushed to the hospital to see them and the nurses told me to turn my phone off.* With that thought, he smiled. He had the perfect lie.

The cool November air was brisk and the stars above

glistened in the pitch-black sky. *I wonder what she decided to do for the rest of the night. She probably went home to pick a fight with Carl.* He shrugged in response to his internal conversation. He hadn't seen her in a couple of weeks, and he knew she was depending on him to break her off, but tonight he just didn't feel like being with Natalya. He needed something bare, tighter, and wetter. He knew just where to find it—in Will's pants.

Chapter 20

"Hey, Ma!" Sdia cheered on the other end.

"Hi, pumpkin head. How are you?"

"Fine, where are you? I just called the house."

"Just finished grocery shopping."

"Oh, I see. Hey, Ma, I wanted to ask you a question."

"Sure. What is it?"

"Well, it's about Mel."

"Okay," Sharon replied.

"Well, I was wondering if he could join us for Thanksgiving."

Sharon took a deep breath. "And where is he supposed to stay?"

"He has a sister that lives out there," Sdia replied.

"Did he say he would be staying with his sister?" Sharon asked.

"Actually, he didn't say, but I'm sure he's gonna stay with her."

Sharon sighed. "Don't be surprised if he asks you to spend the night with him."

"I doubt it."

"Like I said, don't be surprised because you know he definitely thinks it's only a matter of time before he gets what's in your pants."

"I doubt he's thinking that. He can't possibly think that," Sdia replied, trying to convince herself as well.

"You aren't stupid, Dia. You are twenty-four years old,

and you know how men think. Wasn't Sean a prime example?"

"I know, Ma. I know."

"Just keep your eyes open, Sdia. That's all."

"Damn it. I am so pissed I have to go back to the nail shop after I empty these groceries. I broke my nail." A loud honking sound followed.

"Ouch!" Sdia shouted. "You could have warned me before you did that. Why don't you just call me back?"

"I'm sorry, pumpkin. Your father needs to come out and help me with these bags."

"Thomas," she shouted. "Dia, let me call you back. Love you."

Sdia tossed her phone on the couch. She turned on the television and propped herself on the couch. "What the hell?" she said aloud as she flipped through a station showing a man barking like a dog. She felt the urge to call Mel, but she didn't want to seem desperate. It was already 3:00 p.m. on a Saturday, and she hadn't heard from him since 11:30 the night before. The last time they spoke, he was on his way home, and he promised to call her when he got in the house.

"Get it together, Sdia, and stop acting so damn desperate!" she coached herself. Her stomach twisted in knots as she questioned his whereabouts. Sdia decided to do some housework to clear her mind. Normally, she would clean her house during the week, but for the past couple of weeks she had been spending most of her time with Mel—putting a lot of her priorities aside.

She entered her bedroom and removed her cellphone from under her pillow to see if she had any missed calls from him. She knew she was falling for him from that simple act in itself. Self-consciously, she had placed her phone under her pillow so that she could come back to see who had called her, and to keep herself from answering when he called. She didn't want him to think she was sitting by the phone anxiously anticipating his call. She didn't want him to ever know the truth about her actions. She couldn't believe how much she was obsessing over a telephone call. *I don't want to even imagine how I'd feel if I had been intimate with him. Thank God for that!*

Sdia entered her kitchen and grabbed a pair of rubber gloves and cleaning products from the cabinet. Then she proceeded to clean the oven. It was almost 4:30 p.m. when she was finished, and she still hadn't heard from Mel. She stood and removed the gloves from her hands, and angrily threw them in the sink. She walked to her bedroom and checked her cellphone.

"One missed call," she said aloud, smiling as she pressed the "view" button on her phone. Her smile immediately turned into a frown after seeing the name, "Charmaine," on the caller ID.

"What the hell does she want?" She was definitely not in the mood to talk, especially to Charmaine. She removed her sweatpants and crawled into bed. She glanced at the pink clock that hung on the wall and said, "It's 4:40, and this nigga still hasn't called. I swear to God I better not find out he's seeing someone else!"

* * *

"Where the hell did I put it?" he said aloud, looking at himself in the mirror, before shamefully turning away. Carl frantically searched his drawers for his brown cashmere sweater. He walked into the bathroom, removed

143

his toothbrush and ran it under the lukewarm water.

"Where the hell are you going?" Natalya called from behind him. She stood there with her arms crossed waiting for a response.

"I have a meeting," he said turning in her direction as little drops of toothpaste flew from his mouth.

"A meeting on a Sunday at 4:00 in the afternoon?"

Carl turned to the sink and rinsed his mouth. "Yes, it's the only day I could meet with Mr. Wells." He brushed past Natalya and grabbed his beige slacks from the bed.

"You sure look casual," she replied, following him.

"Well, you know, it's Sunday and I don't want to look too professional," he replied, pulling his pants to his waist and zipping them.

"So what time will you be home?" Natalya continued to stare at him.

Carl looked up in surprise and said, "What?" He couldn't believe what he was hearing. *She's actually concerned about what time I'll be home?* He cleared his throat and said, "I'm not sure. I'll call to let you know." He walked over to his closet and grabbed his black wool sweater and his black Gucci shoes. He completed his outfit with his Rolex.

Natalya sat on the edge of the bed watching his every move. She raised her eyebrows. Carl grabbed his car keys from the dresser and headed for the door.

"Aren't you forgetting something?" Natalya called out. He returned to the bedroom where she remained sitting on the edge of the bed. Carl leaned over and gave her a kiss on the cheek.

"No, not a kiss, fat ass. What kind of meeting are you

having without your briefcase?" she said, pointing to the briefcase that sat in the corner of the room. Natalya roughly wiped her cheek and stood.

"Thanks, Talya. I would have been in trouble without this," he said, and grabbed the briefcase while glancing at his watch. "I have to go. Love you."

"Whatever." Natalya rolled her eyes as she shooed him away with her right hand.

Relieved, Carl just about raced out of the house and into his car where he placed his briefcase on the passenger seat. His hands shook uncontrollably as he put the key in the ignition. When he got to the end of the block, he put his car in park and removed his cellphone from his briefcase.

"Hello?" a soft voice on the other end answered.

"Uh . . . hello, Marina?" he replied nervously.

"Hi, Mr. Adler," she said excitedly.

"I'm on my way. I should be there in about twenty minutes."

"Okay, Mr. Adler. I'll let the waiter know. See you soon!"

"What the hell are you doing?" he asked himself as he looked in the rearview mirror. His palms grew sweaty as he put the car in drive and continued to ride down the dark streets. He popped in his Blue Magic CD as he reminisced about the days when he was younger and much happier with himself. He sang the tunes, "What's Come Over Me," as it softly vibrated through the speakers. It had taken Carl ten minutes before he was pulling into the parking lot of Orcniccis. He stepped out of his car and handed his keys to the valet. Nervously Carl looked around, hoping no one had noticed him. Even though he had taken the back streets once he left the neighborhood and picked a restaurant forty-five minutes away from his home, he was still a bit jittery.

It's only dinner with my employee. It's not like I'm cheating. For heaven's sake, she's a child! he thought. The aroma of entrees filled the air as he walked through the double doors of the restaurant.

He was greeted by the friendly server and then led to a table. Carl looked down at the empty table that was covered with a white tablecloth. On the table laid two menus, a lipstick-stained champagne glass half-filled with water, and a long white candle sat in the centerpiece. His heart dropped to his feet. *Oh, no! She left!* Carl stood there in shock.

"Hey, Mr. Adler," a familiar voice called from behind.

Carl quickly turned. His eyes widened at the slender vision of Marina standing there dressed in all black.

"Hi," he replied in a cracked voice, glimpsing her form-fitted short black skirt that revealed her vanilla toned Beyoncè thighs. She wore a black turtleneck and a black blazer that hugged her waist and a pair of black pumps. He extended his hand for a handshake, but instead she moved in for a hug while pushing her pelvis firmly against his. Carl quickly pulled away and gently held her off by holding her shoulder.

"You look wonderful!" he said in a professional tone. "Wow!" he said, referring to her hair.

"Thanks, I decided to get a wash and set," she replied flirtatiously, running her fingers through her hair. "You're looking good yourself!" she replied, with a love tap on his arm.

"Shall we?" Carl asked, pulling out her chair.

Marina gracefully walked over and sat in the chair. He took the seat across from her and opened the menu. "So, what are you going to have?" he politely asked.

"I see something that I want, but it isn't on the menu," she replied.

Carl gasped. His eyes widened in shock. *I can't believe she just said that!* he thought.

Marina saw the nervousness in his face as he smiled and opened the menu. "Oh, do I make you nervous? I can see it all over your face."

"No, no … I'm fine." He wiped his sweaty palms on this pants.

"Well, I think I'm going to have the crab cakes as an appetizer and a glass of wine." She placed the menu on the table and stared at Carl.

"Hello, how are you all this evening? My name is Denise, and I'll be your server for the evening," a tall, dark-skinned woman said as she stood with perfect posture over the two.

Carl looked up, relieved. *I'm so glad she came over and saved me.* "Hello, Denise, may we have a glass of water?" He smiled and glanced at Marina's half-filled glass.

"Sure. Can I start you two off with an appetizer, or an alcoholic beverage?" She cuffed both hands together.

"Yes, please. May I have the crab cakes and an apple margarita?" Marina replied.

Denise nodded and turned to Carl. "I'll have the same and a glass of Merlot," he replied. The waitress left the table. Carl unfolded a napkin and gently placed it in his lap.

"Is that your favorite drink?" he asked, trying to make

conversation.

Marina pulled her hair behind her ear before responding. "Well, I usually would have a glass of Hennessy, but tonight I want to take it easy. I'm hanging with the boss." She winked.

Carl chuckled. "I would really like to thank you for all of the help around the office, Marina. You're wonderful."

She reached over the table and placed her hand on top of his. "You're welcome, Mr. Adler. You're the greatest boss a girl could have."

Denise returned with the drinks, crab cakes, and hot rolls with butter. "Are you ready to order?"

Carl looked at Marina and waited for her reply. "Can you please give me a few minutes?"

"Definitely. I'll be back in a few."

The two sat at the table for several minutes conversing before turning their attention to the menu and ordering. Carl was surprised to find out how comfortable Marina was with sharing her personal business. She told him that her father abandoned her, her mother, and seven sisters and brothers when she was five years old, and that he was currently in the Bronx struggling with a heroin addiction. She also shared that she was trying to save up to visit Columbia with her older sister, and that no one would really miss her because she and her family weren't close. Carl asked general questions and answered quite a few. From what he concluded, Marina was definitely a young lady who was comfortable with herself and not afraid to express how she felt. She asked how long he'd been married, if he wanted children, and what he enjoyed doing in his spare time. She volunteered that she didn't have a boyfriend, and she wasn't interested in having children or getting married. She'd been living on her own ever since she was eighteen years old and she used to have a roommate, but they parted ways after an argument over the rent.

After the fourth round of drinks, Carl asked for the check. "Wow, I didn't know it was this late!" he said, looking at his watch.

It was nine on the dot. Marina looked around. "Yeah, there's only one, two, three …" she said, trying to count the remaining couples seated. Her head wobbled from side to side as she tried to pull her phone from her purse.

Carl chuckled. "I don't think you should be driving."

Marina looked up at him sarcastically and said, "I can't. I didn't drive," she replied, as if she had cracked the DaVinci code. "I was trying to call my brother to tell him that I already have a ride. He's the one who dropped me off."

"Yes, you have to be very careful nowadays. People are crazy." He walked over and pulled out her chair. She stumbled to her feet, pulling her skirt down on her thighs.

"I need to use the restroom," she slurred.

After she turned the corner, Carl called Natalya three times before she answered the phone.

"Hello?" she answered, out of breath.

"Are you okay? Did I wake you?" he asked, concerned.

"Yeah," she replied, breathing heavily.

"Are you sure you're okay?"

"Yeah," Natalya replied.

"I was calling to tell you that I'll be home shortly. I have to stop by the office."

"Yeah, okay. I have to go." The dial tone rang in his ears.

Carl returned his phone to his pocket. "Why do I even bother?" he said aloud as he dropped a forty dollar tip on the table and walked toward the women's restroom.

By the time he reached the restroom, Marina was coming out. She looked as if she had sobered up and was inching up her skirt to fix her stockings. Carl could partially see the brick wall behind her through the gap between her legs. Quickly, he turned away. He didn't want her to think he was a pervert. She approached the bench and stood in front of him with one hand on her hip.

"I'm ready."

Carl held his hand out for her to lead the way. They walked out the front door and waited for the valet.

"So what are you doing for the holidays?" he asked, breaking the silence. Marina pulled a pair of black leather gloves from her purse and placed them on her hands.

"I'm not sure. I was thinking about going to a friend's house. How about you?"

Carl looked up at the star-filled sky. "Well, last year my wife and I spent Thanksgiving at my brother's in Ireland, but this year I think we're going to stay home."

"Wow, Ireland? That's interesting."

The valet returned with his car and opened the passenger's side for Marina. Carl handed him a twenty and hopped in the driver's side.

"Are you okay?" he asked as he turned on the heat.

"Yes, I'm fine. Do you mind if I put the seat back?" she asked, already pushing the button. Slowly, she laid her head back on the headrest, licked her lips, and closed her eyes.

Carl looked over at her and asked, "Where did you say you lived again?"

Marina opened her eyes and smiled. "I live off of Pennsylvania Avenue." She unbuttoned her coat and removed it.

"Is it too hot for you? I can cut the heat off." Carl reached for the switch to turn it off.

She slowly grabbed his hand and pulled it toward her chest. "I feel sick. Tell me if my head is hot." She gently placed his hand on her forehead and waited for a reply.

"No, uh, you don't feel hot," he said nervously and tried to pull away.

"Well, feel my neck!" She held his hand firmly with her right hand and unbuttoned her shirt halfway with her left.

Carl gulped. Her pink nipples were visible through her black sheer bra.

She placed his hands on her warm chest and moaned, "I don't feel hot to you?" She looked over at him.

Carl quickly patted her chest and pulled his hand away. "No, you don't have a temperature. Do I turn here?"

Marina sat up and looked out the window. "No, make a right on the next block." She returned to her previous position and took his hand once more.

"Can you hand me a piece of tissue?" he asked. Sweat fell from his temples as he rubbed his lips together and nervously reached for the glove compartment.

Marina grabbed his hand and placed it over her left breast. "Do I have a temperature here?" Carl's hand grew limp and fell onto her lap. She quickly grabbed his hand and placed it between her legs. His palm was greeted by the soft pubic hairs that stuck out from her stockings. Carl's neck made a cracking sound as he immediately turned to verify where his hand was.

"Touch it, touch it!" she whispered, slowly moving her hips in a circular motion.

Carl focused his attention back on the road, and his left hand remained on the wheel. His heart pounded as he tried to make sense of what was happening. *Is that what I think it is?* he thought. It had been months since he had touched a woman. He began to tickle her softly with the tip of his fingers. Marina reached over and grabbed the bulge that sat in the front of his slacks. Carl excitedly pressed the accelerator, which caused his tires to skid on the wet pavement. He was on the prowl for the first parking spot. Their bodies jumped up and down as he drove recklessly, ignoring the speed bumps in the parking lot. Carl pulled into the next available spot in sight—a handicapped parking space. He breathed heavily as he unfastened his seat belt and removed her hand from between his legs and roughly kissed it.

"Marina, you are so beautiful!" He grabbed the back of her neck and pulled her forward for a kiss.

"Let's go!" she demanded, pulling away and reaching for the door.

Carl leaned forward with his lips protruding and tried his best to land kisses on her neck. Marina broke free. She stepped out of the car, grabbed her shoes and coat, and began to walk toward her building. Carl watched anxiously. "Marina, Marina?" he called out as he fumbled with the door. He snatched his keys from the ignition and followed her.

She continued to walk barefoot to her building without

turning around once. A Korean man stood outside smoking a cigarette. He turned as Marina walked past and raised his eyebrows at the sight of her right butt cheek that her twisted skirt revealed.

Carl ran into the building, through the empty lobby, and onto the elevator with Marina. They rode silently on the elevator until they reached the third floor.

"This is us," she said as she stepped off the elevator and peeked around the corner. "I really have some nosy neighbors. I don't want everyone in my business." She walked to apartment 301 and removed her key from her purse. Carl kissed the back of her neck tenderly. He closed his eyes and inhaled the sweet scent of perfume. Marina led him into her small apartment.

"Make yourself at home," she said, walking into the back room.

Carl took a seat on the small crème loveseat that sat in the corner by a window. He looked around the small apartment. Everything was brown and crème, even the portraits that hung on the wall. Brown and crème plates lay displayed on the small breakfast bar in the kitchen; crème placemats lay on the round wooden kitchen table accompanied by brown plastic roses that sat in a brown and crème striped vase. Tall crème candles sat on each coffee table in the living room. Carl wondered what her bathroom looked like.

"I'm going to hop in the shower. I'll be out in a second. Go ahead and make yourself a drink," she called from the back room.

Carl glanced at the small bar next to the fireplace. "Not too safe," he said as he stood. He walked over to see if she had any beverages of his choice. "Remy Martin, Hennessy,

Paul Mason, Bacardi 151, Captain Morgan—young people stuff," he said and smiled. He reached for a shot glass and poured himself some Hennessy. Carl walked around the small living room and picked up a small portrait of an older woman with long gray hair. She looked as if she could have been attractive in her younger days. He placed the portrait back on top of the fireplace.

"That's my *abuela*," Marina called from behind. "That means grandmother in Spanish."

Carl turned, startled. Marina stood there in a sheer, light-pink nylon body suit, which revealed her perky breasts and neatly groomed bikini area. "Victoria's Secret." She winked as she spun around.

"You look beautiful." Carl grinned and tilted his head back and emptied his glass. Marina walked over to the lamp in the living room and dimmed it before lying on her side in front of the fireplace. "I wish I could take a picture," Carl added as he looked down at her perfect posture.

"Why don't you join me?" Marina smiled and raised her hand for him to take.

Kneeling on each knee, Carl sat in front of her. "I'm really speechless at this point," he replied. "What happened in the car . . ."

Marina placed her hands over his lips, and whispered, "Don't, Mr. Adler, please." She leaned forward and kissed him. Carl closed his eyes as he softly kissed her back. She placed her hand on the side of his face and gently stroked his ear with the tip of her fingers. Carl gently caressed her arms. *What am I doing?* he asked himself, as they continued to embrace each other.

"I can't do this!" Carl shouted, pulling away. "This isn't

right, Marina. I'm your boss." He stood and looked down at her with guilt in his eyes. "Marina, we can't."

Shocked by his admission, she reached for his arm and said, "Mr. Adler, don't. Please don't leave." Her eyes filled with tears. "What's so wrong about this?" Her voice cracked. "Who said it's wrong for you to be in love with your boss?"

Carl's jaw dropped. "What?" he asked, looking confused.

Marina dropped his hand and placed her forehead in her hand. "Nothing," she replied, embarrassed, and shaking her head. "I can't believe I just said that."

Carl kneeled down. "What do you mean, Marina?"

"Mr. Adler, I care about you, and I know you feel the same! You don't think I know how you feel about me. You don't think I can't see how you stare at me, and how you look into my eyes when you ask me to do things around the office?" She waited for a response before continuing. "I know that you feel the same and you can't deny it."

Carl cuffed both of his hands together and stared at her. "Marina, I'm a married man," he replied.

"Yes, Mr. Adler." Marina laughed. "You are a married man, but are you happy?" she asked sarcastically, rolling her neck with her arms folded.

"I—" Carl slowly raised his head.

Marina cut him off. "If you're happy, then leave. We can pretend like none of this ever happened. We can go back to work on Monday and pretend like this night never occurred and these words were never spoken!" she said, staring at him with sincerity in her eyes.

He couldn't believe what was happening. *How did she*

know I wasn't happy? What am I doing here? No one in that office knows my personal business! I love Natalya! He argued back and forth with himself. Carl stood abruptly and walked to the door. He detached the chain and left. He fought with his conscience as he strolled the hallway toward the elevator. There he stood unmoving, thinking if his marriage was worth saving. For precisely ten minutes, he tried quieting his mind but had no real success. Finally he decided to act on the first thought that came afterward.

Carl rushed back to Marina's door and knocked desperately. "Marina?" he called out. "Please open the door," he begged, but she didn't reply. "Marina, please open the door!" his voice grew louder.

Slowly the door opened and she stepped aside to let him in.

"I had to move my car. I was parked in a handicapped spot." He smiled.

Marina took him by the hand and led him into her dark bedroom where the two collapsed onto the bed. "So how do you feel about me, Mr. Adler?" she asked.

"For goodness sake, call me Carl when we aren't working," he replied, slightly annoyed.

"Well, okay, Carl. How do you feel about me?" she repeated, unbuttoning his shirt.

"I absolutely adore you. I haven't felt like this in a long time," he admitted. "Just being here with you makes me feel so good."

"Believe me, Carl. I feel the same way, and I know that you aren't happy!" Her voice cracked. "You deserve so much more." Marina gently played with the hairs on his chest.

Carl didn't respond. The girl was telling the truth. Marina lifted her head from her pillow and scooted up closer to the headboard. She gently pulled Carl toward her and placed his head on her bosom.

"Give me a chance. I promise I can make you happy. We don't have to rush things." *Who would've thought? Little ole me. The Spanish girl who came from nothing, laying here with a millionaire in my arms!* She smirked.

Carl closed his eyes and fell asleep to the sound of her heartbeat.

Chapter 21

It was 7:45 a.m. when Carl pulled into the driveway.

"Oh shit, oh shit, oh shit," he said as he put his car in park. He was so nervous he could feel himself about to shit his pants. *What am I going to tell her? What excuse can I use?* Carl had thought about going straight to work, but he thought it would have been best to stop at home first. He got out of his car and grabbed his briefcase from the passenger's side. He shook out his left leg in hopes of relieving some of the wrinkles. Before entering the house, he peeked inside the garage window to see if Natalya's car was there.

"Fuck!" he whispered, glancing at his watch.

Sweat poured from his forehead as he inserted the key into the keyhole with great ease. The wooden floor squeaked underneath his feet as he stepped inside. He placed his briefcase on the floor by the door and removed his shoes before going up the steps. The light from his bedroom shined through the door. *Damn!* he thought as he reached the top of the stairs. He held his shoes under his arm as he turned the doorknob. It felt like a sauna when he entered the room—hot and muggy. Carl frowned from the odor of sweat and funk that filled the air. Natalya stood there in her bra and panties placing new linen on the bed.

"Hey, Carl," she said, without looking up.

"Hi, Talya," he replied nervously. "What happened?" he asked, referring to the soiled linen that lay in the middle of the floor.

"I was doing sit-ups on the bed and sweated out the

sheets," she replied, as she unfolded a floral pillowcase and placed it over a pillow.

Carl looked at the mattress and asked, "Did you flip the mattress as well?"

Natalya placed her hands on her hips, and if looks could kill, he would have dropped dead. "What the fuck is your problem? Why are you asking me so many questions? Did you hear me questioning you and why your fat ass didn't come home last night?"

Carl took in a gulp of air as he placed his shoes on the floor. "No, I was only asking because I can see the tag."

"Well, if you know the answer, then why ask, dumb ass!" Natalya rolled her eyes. She brushed past him as she grabbed the dirty sheets from the floor and entered the bathroom. He stood in the middle of the room staring blankly at his reflection through the dresser mirror.

"She doesn't even care!"

* * *

Natalya slowly removed her panties, sliding them down her thighs, past her knees, over her ankles and onto the floor. She took a seat on the toilet and relieved herself. She strained as she tried her best to rid her vagina of Lamar's bodily fluids. Natalya stared at her semen-stained panties that lay in the middle of the bathroom floor.

"Yuck! Next time his ass is wearing a condom. That shit looks disgusting."

She had been elated when she first learned of her husband's meeting the previous day. Less lying for her. Natalya couldn't wait to get Carl out of the house so she could call Lamar and give him a piece of her mind. She hadn't spoken to him in weeks, despite his numerous phone calls, which she had ignored. Natalya had vowed to make him pay for standing her up, and she felt he had suffered long enough. Besides, she was horny as hell. But once Lamar showed up to her home, all the anger she felt subsided, and he was her lover boy once again.

She sucked her teeth and frowned. *Damn, I can't stand the thought of making my chocolate boy toy wear a condom, because the sex is so damn good! Fuck getting an STD, that's the least of my concern. Besides, Lamar loves my kitty; he'd never cheat! I just don't wanna get pregnant. What would I tell Carl? I probably wouldn't. I'd just get an abortion at his expense. She laughed. His fat ass would be paying for an abortion and wouldn't even know it. Ugh, what did I ever see in him in the first place.* She placed her head in her hand and reflected on the day she and Carl met.

"Hello, Mr. Adler. Mr. Newman will be with you shortly," Natalya said as she handed Carl a glass of water.

"Thank you, Mrs. ..." Carl replied with a smile as he watched her slim figure walk back to her desk. Her hips swayed from side to side in the black, form-fitting pencil skirt.

Natalya laughed. "It's Ms. Marks. I'm not married," she replied, taking a seat back at her desk.

"So how long have you been working here?" Carl asked, taking a sip of water.

"For about two months." Natalya smiled. "I used to work for Wynn & Brinks, but the office space was too small," she replied, seductively licking her licks.

Little did Carl know she had already gotten first dibs on him and his high position in the district by going through Mr. Newman's files. She wasn't expecting Carl to be so heavyset, but she figured something might be wrong with an unmarried man making over three-hundred thousand a year. Natalya wasn't particularly into dating white men, but she knew that if she wanted an early retirement and better life, that was the best way to go.

Carl loosened his tie and cleared his throat. "I see. I noticed things look a bit different since the last time I was here. I don't ever remember Mr. Newman's old secretary, Victoria having such wonderful taste in interior décor." He was referring to the antique-designed office.

Natalya looked up in the air with her eyes wide and a slight smirk. "Well, what can I say? I don't want to toot my own horn." She rocked her head from side to side.

Carl chuckled. "No, I'm doing all of that for you."

That was her queue. She reached inside of her dark brown wood office desk and removed a business card with her number on it. "Here you go, Mr. Alder," she said, slowly sliding the card across the shiny desk top.

Carl abruptly stood and picked the card up. "Thank you, Ms. Natalya Marks," he said, looking down and reading the name on the card. "Expect a call from me." He winked.

"Back to reality!" *If I could turn back the hands of time, I would have just stayed at the law firm and fucked Mr. Newman. At least I could bear looking at him.* She flushed the toilet, grabbed her panties from the floor, and hand-washed them. She smiled as she tried to imagine what was going on in Carl's head. She knew he had either stayed in a hotel, or possibly slept in his car the night before. *He's just testing me. He wants to see how roused up he could get me if he didn't come home, but I ain't even about to give his fat ass the satisfaction.* Not mentioning the situation would hurt Carl the most, and that's exactly what she wanted. She continued to analyze the whole set up. *Like really—since when does Carl get all dressed up for a meeting? And who has business meetings on a Sunday?*

After washing her panties, she dried her hands on a face towel and hopped in the shower. She laughed.

"Thanks, Carl."

Chapter 22

"Sdia, it's Mel. Call me when you get this message."

Mel pressed a button on his phone and got the dial tone before calling again. The phone continued to ring before he got her voicemail once more.

"Baby, call me when you get this message. I left my phone in my man's car. That's why I couldn't call you," he said.

Mel slammed the phone on the receiver so hard that he cracked the mouthpiece. "Shit!" he shouted. He contemplated whether he should drive to her house. He hadn't spoken to her since Thursday, and it was now Monday and 5:30 in the morning. He walked into the bedroom and crawled into bed.

"Move ova!" he yelled, shoving Dwana's naked body aside.

* * *

"I don't answer private calls," Sdia yawned as she tossed the cordless phone under her bed.

She had an hour and a half to sleep before she had to awaken for work. She hadn't done anything all weekend, and she still was dreadfully tired. Mel had promised they'd go to Atlantic City for the weekend, but he failed to show up. They hadn't spoken in three days. She tried to call him several times and left three messages on his voicemail. After calling him a third time, amazingly, his phone stopped ringing and went straight to voicemail. Sdia went against the grain and called him, knowing she shouldn't have, but coaxed herself into thinking that maybe he was hurt or in jail.

"Something must have happened to him. I was calling to see if he was okay!" she told Charmaine over the phone the night before last. Now she was feeling like an idiot after hearing his voicemail.

"He left his phone in his man's car?" she repeated aloud. "Yeah, okay!" She turned over and fell asleep.

* * *

"Good morning, Ms. Wallace!" Sdia called out as she unlocked the car door. Ms. Wallace stood on her balcony with a coffee mug in her left hand.

"Hello, honey. How are you on this wonderful morning that the Lord has blessed us with?"

Sdia looked up and smiled. "I'm doing pretty good and yourself?"

"I am blessed!" Ms. Wallace placed her right hand over her heart.

Sdia waved goodbye before getting into her car. "It's freezing in here!" she said aloud as she put the keys in the ignition. Her cellphone vibrated in her purse. She retrieved the phone and blew her breath.

"What the fuck does he want?" she asked, referring to Mel.

I refuse to be taken on an emotional roller coaster by another man, especially after dealing with Sean, Sdia thought. "Sean," she said, "I haven't mentioned that name in a while." She laughed. "I wonder how he's doing." She placed the phone between her legs as she slowly backed out of the parking lot and proceeded to drive down the deserted street. It was a drag having to arrive at work an hour early, but she had mounds of work to do. She was starting to feel cranky, and she hadn't even arrived there yet.

"I need a cup of coffee," she said as she made a U-turn after accidentally passing the Bagel Shop. Her phone beeped loudly. Someone was alerting her on her walkie-talkie. Sdia snatched her phone from her purse, aggravated.

"Shit!" she yelled. "Yes?" she answered, pressing firmly on the side button and quickly releasing it.

"What's up with ya phone?" Mel asked.

"Hey, how are you?" she asked nonchalantly.

"I been trying to call you all morning!"

"I know."

"So if you know, then why didn't you answer?" His tone rose.

Sdia rolled her eyes. *I know he didn't just go there!*

"Helloooo?" Mel sang.

"Mel, I have to call you back. I'm driving!"

"Oh, yeah. Well, let me hang up and call you. You can put the phone on speaker."

Before she could reply, her phone began to vibrate. Sdia picked up the phone and decided to ignore the call. She didn't feel like talking.

"He's definitely got the game twisted. Poor thing."

Sdia knew if she didn't put Mel in his place that things were going to get worse. He was already starting to raise his tone and question her. In her eyes, they weren't even a couple. At this point, she wasn't even sure if she wanted to be with him, let alone take him to meet her parents for the holidays. Her stomach began to cramp at the thought of spending another holiday alone.

* * *

Seated comfortably at her office desk Sdia flipped through a hard copy of the interview she had done with a director at a women's shelter.

"Damn!" she whispered harshly.

"Something wrong, Ms. Mitchell?" her boss, John, called from behind. He was a short, chubby white man with a receding hairline. He smiled as he approached her desk. "How's everything going?" he asked.

Sdia spun in her chair and smiled politely, turning on her professional charm. "Couldn't be better, John. How are you?"

He held his coffee with this right hand, while his left hand remained in his pants pocket jingling his keys.

"Well," he replied.

Oh, Lord, no; please don't let this man go into how he spent his weekend ice fishing and how his cat did the funniest thing! She was not in the mood to play phony, nor was she in the mood to pretend as if she were interested in what went on in his boring life. She tried to mentally prepare herself for the long ordeal. *Please forgive me. I am so sorry!* She asked her cheeks for forgiveness for she knew the strain they were about to endure. Around 9:00 a.m. every Monday, rest assured, John would be at her desk, boring her with a list of events that took place over the weekend. Sdia slowly crossed her legs and wiggled her left foot rapidly. From time to time, she'd placed her hand over her mouth while saying, "Are you serious?" or "No way!" as if the topic of discussion intrigued her. If ever there were any conversations and John was around, they were always one-sided; he was always dominating them and that was because no one was interested in what he had to say. John was definitely one of the downfalls of working for Reach.

"Nora loved the article, however, she feels like you could've delved deeper into the lives of the women you interviewed.

Wrinkles of surprise appeared on Sdia's forehead. "Oh ... really?"

John took a deep breath and sighed. He looked down at his beige Clark's dress shoes and nodded. "Yes. I'm afraid so."

Sdia reclined in her seat and looked up at the ceiling. "What does she want me to do? The article has already been printed."

John looked up. "I'm going to have to do a recall before the next order goes out. Elaine has already taken it down from the website."

"This is ridiculous, John." Sdia's voice trembled.

"Don't go getting yourself all upset."

"So what am I supposed to do? Go back to the shelter and interview the same people all over again?"

"Yes. If that's what it takes. You're one of our best writers, Sdia. I know you can do it!" He leaned forward and nudged her on the shoulder.

It was 9:45 a.m. by the time John left her desk. Sdia sighed as she opened her e-mail.

"Fuck Nora ... with her big ass face. Pale plate-face bitch!" she said under her breath as she deleted junk e-mail. Sdia's head began to pound. She gently rubbed her eyes with her index finger and yawned. There were mounds of files on her desk that needed to be sorted and shredded. Sdia knew she'd be working late if she didn't get those piles down, and that was something she hated doing. Her stomach growled as she softly tapped on the keyboard trying her best to go over her article on women who lived in shelters . She had worked so hard to have that article featured in the magazine this month, and now this. She thought about the hopelessness in some of the homeless people's eyes when she visited the shelter just weeks ago. It was definitely an experience she would never forget, and one didn't want to revisit. Years of drug and alcohol abuse had devoured the souls of many. They walked around emotionless, wearing tattered clothes and carrying their lively possessions, which consisted of bags of all sorts of things—from garbage to groceries, even shopping carts. If you owned a shopping cart, you were one of the "blessed ones." Sdia could recall wiping the tears from her eyes several times while trying to answer the question that plagued her mind: "How does someone get to this point?"

Damn. Back to square one, she thought. But she had to play by John's rules, and John had to play by Nora Miller's rules, who was the founder of *Reach* magazine. Sdia placed her hand on her head.

"It could always be worse!" Her co-worker Iptahaj called out as she walked over and took a seat on the corner of Sdia's desk.

"I don't see how."

"You could be assigned to shadow Norma for a whole full week." Iptahaj frowned.

"Wow. Are you kidding me?" Sdia placed her hands over her mouth.

"I wish I were." Iptahaj bowed her head.

She was quite a beautiful woman. She stood about five feet-four inches tall. Her long ginger curly hair could be seen through the shear pink and white hijab she wore. The shiny curls rested on her shoulders. "Wanna trade?" she brought her head up and smiled.

Sdia brought her head back and chuckled. "No girl. I'm good!" She slapped her thigh.

"I figured you'd see the bright side of things." Iptahaj winked before standing to her feet.

Chapter 23

"I'm sorry, Mr. Edwards, but we don't have any appointments until after the holiday," the young lady said on the other end of the phone.

Will sighed. "So if I come in after the holiday, will I be able to get a full physical?" he asked.

"You sure can," she replied, relieved.

They had spent a total of fifteen minutes on the phone trying to make an appointment for Will. He had finally taken Lamar's advice and called his doctor. His diarrhea had lasted for a total of four weeks.

"Something isn't right, baby. You may be dehydrated," Lamar said, only days before.

Will would have called the same day, but Lamar insisted he drink plenty of fluids and eat hot cereal, potatoes, and plenty of bread before calling. Will smiled at the thought of Lamar. He held the phone in his hand as he looked up at the ceiling, imagining Lamar's hypnotizing eyes.

"Wheew!" he said, shaking his head.

"Give me just a second, sir. The system is slow," the nurse replied, assuming he was getting impatient.

"No problem," he replied as he walked into the kitchen and grabbed his cellphone from the counter.

He decided to send Lamar an "I love you" text. He knew Lamar was at work and he didn't want to bother him. Lamar had complained about how strict his boss was when it came to using his cellphone during work hours, and how he never allowed Lamar to take lunch breaks.

"Okay, Mr. Edwards, we have you scheduled for Monday, November 27, at 10:30 a.m."

Will grabbed a paper towel from off the roll and jotted down the information.

"Okay, thank you," he replied, placing a magnet over the paper towel and hanging it on the refrigerator.

"Have a wonderful Thanksgiving, Mr. Edwards. See you on the twenty-seventh."

* * *

Will stared at the chicken and broccoli as he dissected it with his fork. He just didn't have an appetite. *I wish I knew exactly where Lamar worked. It would've been nice to take him some lunch. Like what boyfriends do when they are in a relationship. Hopefully we'll be making it official soon!*

"What's wrong with you, man?" his co-worker, Dre asked.

"Do you want the rest of this?" Will asked, shoving the carton of Chinese food across the table.

"Hell yeah!" the young man replied, reaching over and grabbing it. "You need to be eating, though. Looks like you've lost some weight," he said as brown sauce dripped down his chin.

"I know, but I figured I could lose about ten pounds. You should be happy I lost a few pounds. I was getting tired of being the sexiest trainer!" he teased, standing up and flexing his muscles.

A couple of their other co-workers in the break room chuckled. Will was known for being a jokester. Even in high school, he was considered the class clown.

"Damn, man. I think I lifted too many yesterday," he said as he rubbed under his arm. "I think I may have pulled

171

a muscle."

Dre stood on his feet and wiped his mouth with a paper towel. "Look at you, sounding like a little bitch." He grinned. "I told you, you can't be like me!" He slapped Will on the arm and proceeded to the door.

"Whateva, man." Will continued to rub under his arm.

He sat down and removed his phone from his pocket to call Lamar. "It won't hurt if I call him just this once at work." He had just spoken to him about an hour ago, but he wanted to hear his voice. Plus, he could pretend as if he was calling to ask about the soreness under his arm.

"Hey, what's up?" Lamar answered.

"Nothing, just called to say what's up and to ask you a question," he replied.

"What kind of question?"

Will laughed. "Calm down, it has nothing to do with relationships."

Lamar sighed. "Oh, okay, so what's going on?"

"I wanted to ask you if you've ever had a lump under your arm?"

"What? What kind of question is that?" Lamar joked.

"Nah, seriously, Lamar. I got this lump. Well, I mean it's kind of swollen under my arms, and I was wondering if you've ever experienced that after lifting weights."

"I don't recall. I mean, I never lift more than I can handle. But you know, it may be your deodorant. I remember when I was younger I would get a small bump under my arm when I would switch deodorants. Besides, you're the trainer. If anything, I should be asking you these questions."

"Hey, I don't know everything. But yeah, you may be

right. It could be my deodorant. I did just switch to *Dove*."

Lamar laughed. "That's what you get for using female deodorant."

"Whatever. You still love me though." Will chuckled.

There was a moment of silence.

"*Herrrhem*," Lamar cleared his throat. "So um … did you make an appointment with the doctor?" he asked in a serious tone.

"Yeah, my appointment is next week Monday."

"Cool. So what's for dinner?"

"Me … your favorite dish," Will replied, licking his lips.

"Well, I hope you made enough for seconds," Lamar teased.

"So I guess I will see you after work then?"

"I wouldn't miss that meal for the world."

Will returned to the gym and prepared for his next client. He felt sick to his stomach thinking about the six hours he had left before he'd be off. All he wanted to do was get home, get naked, and wait for Lamar. He wanted to spend as much time with him as possible. Lamar was leaving for Connecticut on Wednesday, and he wanted to be on the road by at least noon. Traffic was going to be crazy if he decided to leave on Thanksgiving. Besides, this year he told his mother he'd bake the sweet potato pie. Will's stomach began to bubble.

"Oh shit! Not again," he said and bent down to pick up a set of dumbbells.

The last thing he wanted to do was take a crap at work, and then train someone. "I'll be damned if my clients will be talking about how I smelled like shit today while I'm spotting them." He tried his best to hold out, but he couldn't, so he quickly returned the dumbbells to the rack and ran to the bathroom to relieve himself. This was the fifth time today he had diarrhea. *What the hell is wrong with my stomach?*

Chapter 24

"That bitch is acting up. If she know like I know, she betta call me back!" Mel shouted as he slammed the phone down.

"Chill out, man. You gonna break my damn phone," Roc replied, handing him a fresh rolled blunt.

"Nah, I'm good," Mel replied.

"This bitch really got you in ya feelings." Roc laughed.

He shook his head, disappointed. "Yeah, all right, you know how I get down, nigga. A bitch could never have me stressed!" Mel smiled. He removed his vibrating cell from his pocket, and pressed the IGNORE button.

"See? That's exactly what I mean. That bitch Dwana is on a nigga!" Mel lit a cigarette and stepped on the balcony. "You got a nice view out here," he yelled to Roc who was sitting in the living room smoking.

"Yeah, I know," he called back.

Mel stared twelve stories down at the city below. The cold winter breeze brushed his face causing his eyes to water.

"Damn, nigga, do you mind closing the door? It's freezing."

Mel plucked his cigarette from the balcony and walked through the sliding doors, closing them behind him. He sat across from Roc.

"How much you pay for your Rolex?" Roc asked, admiring the diamond face.

"Twenty, why?" Mel asked.

Roc stood to his feet and tossed a wad of money onto the coffee table. "I know this Arab who could've hooked you up for ten."

Mel smiled. "Nah nigga, I'm good. I'm sticking to my jeweler."

Roc laughed. "Question."

"What?" Mel asked as he looked up with a confused expression.

Roc walked over to the balcony door and gazed outside. "Do you think you could pick something up for me while you out of town?" He turned and looked at Mel.

"No doubt, I got you," he replied, retrieving his phone from his pocket to call Sdia once more. He stood and motioned with his hand for Roc to give him a second as he stepped outside into the hallway.

"Where you been?" he snapped, as soon as she picked up.

"What?" she asked, stunned. "Why are you coming at me like that?"

"I've been calling you all day, Sdia. Why you ain't call me back?"

Sdia laughed. "Because I was busy."

Mel grinded his teeth. "Yeah, all right."

"So how are you?" she asked, trying to change the topic.

"Good!" he quickly replied. "You still going home for the holidays?"

"Of course I'm going home. You already know that."

"So what time we leaving?" Mel asked.

"We ... we aren't going anywhere!"

"What? So you telling me I'm not invited anymore?" he asked.

"Look, Mel. I don't have time for games."

"What you talking about? Who's playing games?"

"I have to go," Sdia said, and hung up.

Mel stormed back into the apartment.

"I'll be back." He grabbed his chinchilla from the couch and headed for the door.

"Later," Roc replied, his eyes halfway open, resembling an Asian.

"I need to ask you a question," he called out to Mel.

"What?" Mel asked, frustrated.

"When you go to DC—"

Mel interrupted, "You already asked me that. Stick to drinking, man!" he shouted as he closed the door behind him.

Within forty-five minutes, Mel was entering Sdia's apartment building.

"She better be home!" he muttered as he stepped onto the elevator and stood next to an older Hispanic woman. "Excuse me," he said as he reached over her head to press the button for the eighth floor.

She stood about four feet eleven with straight gray hair that fell to her back. Her wrinkled, olive complexioned hand rested on an old metal shopping cart filled with grocery bags. Her gray wool coat stopped at her knees. There were three missing buttons on the front, and several pieces of what looked like cat hair covered the back. She turned and looked up at the tall dark figure standing over her. Mel looked her up and down until his eyes met with her glacial blue eyes. He was always up for the challenge of staring someone down; he loved to see if they'd turn away first. The woman returned the stare. Within two minutes, her eyes were watering. Mel studied the crow's feet in the corner of each eye. The elevator bell rang as it stopped on the eighth floor. She placed both hands on the shopping cart's handle, placed her foot on the bottom of the cart, and tilted it back on both wheels, heading for the exit. Mel quickly stepped in front of the woman and nearly knocked her into the elevator buttons.

She quickly grabbed the side of the wall to catch her balance and yelled in a thick Spanish accent, "Wat cha way you go!" She breathed heavily as she tried to lift herself up.

"Shut the fuck up!" Mel shouted as he walked down the hall. He reached Sdia's door and began to turn the doorknob.

"Sdia?" he yelled. "Open the door!" He banged on the door.

* * *

Sdia flung the door open. "Why are you banging on my door like that?" She turned her back and walked toward the kitchen table where she continued to check her e-mail.

"Silent treatment?" Mel asked as he walked into the kitchen and stood behind her.

She continued on her laptop, reading the content of the e-mail aloud: "For women only—what the hell is this?" She pretended to be intrigued with what was on her screen.

Mel reached over and closed the screen. "That's real disrespectful!" he shouted.

Sdia jumped to her feet and hollered, "You must be out of your goddamn mind raising your voice in my house!"

She stared him coldly in the eyes.

"I think it's time for you to leave!" She couldn't believe what was happening.

Mel smiled. "Come here." He placed his hands on her hips and began to kiss her neck. Sdia pulled away.

"Mel, we need to talk. I don't like how things are going between us."

He placed both hands in his pockets and looked down at the floor. "What you mean—don't like what?"

Sdia walked over to the couch as she sat down on one knee. "Here, come sit." She patted the seat next to her. Mel complied.

Questions filled her head as she sat with her elbow in her knee and her chin in her hand. She wanted to tell him how she felt. How he scared her, how confused she was about their relationship, how territorial he had become even though they hadn't even been intimate and how he disappeared for days at a time.

"I'm listening. What's on ya mind, baby?" he asked as he reached over and ran his thumb across her eyebrow, fixing a hair that was out of place.

Sdia looked down, bit the inside of her jaw, and quickly spat out, "I don't appreciate the way you question me at times, and I don't like how you just pop up over here. That shit scares the hell out of me!"

Mel nodded. "Oh, okay, so basically what you're telling me is not to be concerned about my girl?" He brought his face down to hers and looked at her, dumbfounded. "Is that what you telling me?" he asked, widening his eyes.

Sdia scrunched up her nose. "Ya girl?" she replied.

"Yeah, my girl!" he repeated, demandingly.

"Are you asking me or telling me?" She tried to sound objective to the idea as she stared at him. "You just can't tell a woman that she belongs to you without her consent!" She was stern and her face remained serious.

Mel shook his head in disbelief. "If you don't feel the same way, then why you taking me to meet ya parents? Do you take all ya male friends to meet ya parents?"

"Whatever," she replied. She was already hip to the game. This was his way of seeing how she felt about him.

She wasn't going to deny that she wanted him to meet her family, nor was she going to admit how much she liked him. She had so many questions she wanted to ask him, but she just didn't have the guts.

"Why is your phone always off? Why don't I hear from you for two and three days at a time? Are you seeing otha people?"

"So what time are we heading to DC?" Mel asked as he reached over and grabbed the remote control from the coffee table. He put his feet on the coffee table.

"I don't know," she replied, shrugging.

"Well, I've got a surprise for you!" he said, turning to look at her.

"What kind of surprise?" Sdia continued to look down at him.

"When can you take a vacation?" Mel's phone began to ring loudly. He looked at the caller ID and lowered the volume.

Sdia walked away as if she weren't interested. "Not sure. I need to check and see how much leave I have."

He nodded. "Do you know how to swim?"

His cell began to vibrate. He slyly grabbed it from his

hip and looked at it.

"Uh huh," she replied, with her back still turned.

"What's the deepest body of water you've swam in?" he asked.

"Where are we going?" she asked, turning to face him.

He walked over, took her hand, and kissed it. "I can't tell you, but I promise you won't be upset. Come on, let's go out and grab a bite to eat."

Mel wrapped his hands around her waist and softly kissed her lips.

For some reason, she wasn't feeling right. Something about him made her feel uncomfortable, but she couldn't put her finger on it.

"Let me get changed." She slowly pulled away and walked toward her bedroom.

"A'ight, babe. I'll wait for you in the truck." She turned to look back at him, pressing buttons on his cellphone and stealing glimpses of Sdia as he did so.

"Sneaky ass," she said under her breath as she continued to her room.

Chapter 25

Just then, the elevator button rang and Carl raced into his office. He tossed his briefcase on the desk and removed his jacket.

"Good morning, Mr. Adler." Marina pulled her blouse down to reveal more cleavage. Carl hadn't noticed her standing there. He cursed under his breath as he fumbled through the file cabinets in his office. Marina tapped on the open door.

"Good morning!" he replied, without looking up.

"Everyone is in the conference room waiting for you. Would like me to inform them that you will be there momentarily?" she said.

"Yes, would you please? Tell them that—" He looked up and smiled. "Hi, Marina. How are you?"

Marina sighed. "I'm doing well and you?"

"Much better now," Carl replied.

She blushed. "Okay, see you in a few." She walked away, putting extra sway in her hips.

Carl's adrenaline rushed. He sniffed the air like a dog. The sweet scent of her perfume put him on cloud nine. He gathered the rest of his belongings and entered the conference room as he wiped his forehead with the back of his sleeve.

"I know that we were scheduled for a meeting this morning, and I apologize for the delay. Therefore, I will reschedule the meeting for next week Monday and allow you all to leave early today!"

Voices mumbled in shock. Some employees thanked him aloud while others nodded in agreement while talking to one another.

Carl watched Marina from the corner of his eye. She sat with her legs crossed rocking her foot up and down while biting on her pen. Carl didn't want to bring any attention to him or her, so he continued to talk to the right side of the room. "You are welcome to stay later to finish up your work, but as of twelve o'clock, you are free to leave."

"I have a lot to catch up on, Mr. Adler!" Marina blurted out.

Carl turned toward her, astonished. He tried his best to look normal, but couldn't help but notice that her raised skirt revealed her thigh.

"That's fine, Marina," he replied, looking past her. He didn't want to give off any vibes, so he stared at the wall overlooking her beautiful face.

"Do you still need those contracts done by today?" Lamar called out, shoving the rest of his half-finished bagel into his mouth.

Carl spun to the left. "Good morning, Mr. Baldwin. I didn't see you sitting over there. I need to review those reports I gave you last week, so please bring them into my office before you leave."

"Most definitely, Mr. Adler," Lamar replied nervously.

"If I don't see any of you before you leave, I would like to say, Enjoy your holiday!" Carl smiled as he left the room, catching Marina frowning. She rolled her eyes, clearly annoyed with him.

* * *

Lamar contemplated whether he wanted to get some from Natalya or Will before he left town. He didn't want to risk Carl arriving home, so he decided to give her a call and ask her to meet him in a discreet location. Then he would stop by Will's afterward.

"Dammit!" Lamar cursed under his breath. "It's going to take me forever to organize those files." He stuffed the remainder of his bagel in a paper towel, balling it up in his fist.

"I had a lot of errands I wanted to run before leaving town." He continued to talk to himself aloud. He watched Marina from the corner of his eye to see if she was listening. Marina looked at him and smiled.

"I'll tell you what—why don't you just give them to me, and I will take care of them for you?"

Lamar's face lit up. "Really, Marina?" Damn, I owe you, girl." He reached over and hugged her. Marina pulled away and laughed.

"It's okay, Lamar. I know how it is preparing for a road trip." She nudged him on the shoulder and walked away.

Delighted, he looked at his watch as he headed to Carl's office. He placed his phone on silent as he approached the open door. "Hey, Mr. Adler," Lamar said, entering the office with an imitation smile.

Carl placed his phone on the receiver and looked up. "How's it going, Lamariel? I didn't expect those records so ..." He stopped after noticing Lamar's hands were empty of any paperwork.

"That's what I was coming in to tell you. Marina volunteered to take care of them for me. I'm going to see my folks for the holiday, and I still have a lot of running around to do," he replied, nervously fiddling with his fingers.

Carl nodded in agreement with Lamar's decision. "So,

you're going back home for the holidays?" he asked as he directed Lamar to take a seat in the chair in front of his desk.

Slowly, Lamar walked over, unsure of whether he should have come into his office. He loathed sitting face to face with Carl. "Yes, I am, Mr. Adler. I'm driving up north to see my parents. This year I'm in charge of the sweet potato pie," he joked.

Carl chuckled. "Not only are you a college graduate, but you're also a baker?" he replied.

"Yeah, I guess so." Lamar laughed.

Something seemed different about Lamar today. Carl studied him closely. There was an eerie feeling that took over the room. The two men sat in silence before Carl broke the ice.

"I don't know what the misses and I are doing for the holidays. We haven't really discussed anything."

Lamar looked away and focused on the plaques that hung on Carl's wall. "There are several restaurants open if Mrs. Adler doesn't want to cook," he stated, trying his best to seem helpful.

Carl snickered as he pushed himself back in his recliner. "Now that's an idea. I'm pretty much up for anything."

Although Lamar could see Carl's lips moving, he didn't hear a word he had said. All he could think about was getting out of the office. His hands became clammy and a knot formed in the pit of his stomach. Guilt about sleeping with Natalya slowly began to consume him. He silently prayed, *Why doesn't the phone ring? Marina walk into the office, fire alarm go off—anything. Anything, God, please just get me out of this office!*

"You know, Lamar—"

Lamar snapped back to reality at the sound of his name.

"I wanted to congratulate you on the work that you do around the office. I really didn't get a chance to tell you how proud I am of you as a young man, a young black man," he corrected himself. "You would definitely be an asset in the finance department."

He walked over to the door and placed his hands on the doorknob, giving Lamar the queue that it was time for him to leave. Then suddenly something came over Lamar. It was as if his body was glued to Carl's seat. His mouth went dry.

"Thank you. I mean, wow! I—" *I'm a fucked up person*; his conscience finished the sentence for him. *I'm no good. Sleeping with this man's wife, fucking her in his bed. What's wrong with me?*

"It's okay, son. I know what you're trying to say." Carl laughed.

In total disbelief, Lamar struggled to his feet. Carl had told him that he was getting a promotion. The position for Finance Director was his.

"You can thank me later, Lamar," Carl replied.

Lamar's bottom lip trembled as he tried to hold back the tears. Carl looked at him and quickly turned his head, after noticing his effortless attempt to hold back his tears. He waited for Lamar to walk past him before turning to face him.

"You have a safe trip now, and Happy Thanksgiving." He patted Lamar on the back and closed his door behind him. *Such a wonderful young man! If I had a son I'd want him to be just like Lamariel.*

Carl smiled to himself at the thought of how blessed and proud he was to have the young man in his life.

Lamar opened his desk drawer and removed his small green Bible. He placed it in his back pocket and gathered the rest of his belongings before leaving the office.

Once he was inside his car, he opened it up to Psalms 51 and read it silently. Before pulling out of the driveway, he removed his cellphone from his pocket and deleted the names: "Natalya," and "Will."

* * *

It was 5:15 p.m. when Marina walked into Carl's office. He sat at his desk checking his e-mail.

"Hi, Mr. Adler," Marina said, slightly closing the door.

Surprised, Carl looked up, put on his professional demeanor and replied, "Hello, Marina. How are you?" Marina smiled as she walked toward him with one hand on her hip and the other holding a stack of folders. "I volunteered to help Lamar with these records," she replied, handing him the small stack.

Carl politely removed them from her hand and smiled. "Please have a seat." He got up from his chair and opened the office door. His gaze quickly pierced each visible cubical for employees before he returned to his seat.

Marina laughed. "Everyone is gone, Mr. Adler." She looked up at him, flattered. "You are too cute," she said.

Carl sat back in his chair. "Natalya hasn't called all day. I wonder what she's doing?"

"So?" Marina stated as she stared him in the eyes.

Carl placed his head back into the seat and looked at the ceiling. "I'm sorry for not contacting you. I just don't want

187

to rush things. I want to do things the right way, Marina. I'm still married."

With sincerity in her eyes, Marina gazed at him. "I know, and trust me, I want the same thing. Sometimes I can't believe this is happening to me." Confused, Carl looked at her. She laughed. "I mean, I prayed for this to happen. You don't understand how I feel about you!" She tried her best to convince him, and by the looks of it, it was working.

Carl leaned over his desk and softly kissed her. He glanced at his watch. It was 5:55 p.m. For a brief moment, he thought about calling home since he hadn't heard from Natalya, but as quickly as the thought came, it left after he remembered who his wife was. Carl leaned over and kissed Marina once more.

"How about a bite to eat?"

Chapter 26

Will woke up in a cold sweat. He grabbed his phone from his night stand and glanced at the screen. He had no missed calls from Lamar. It was 2:30 in the morning, and Lamar hadn't checked in with him all day. He had promised to call him when he came home from work. Will sat up as he shined the light from the phone on his sheet. It was soaked. For a moment, he thought he may have wet the bed.

"Shit!" he yelled, as he jumped to his feet and removed his saturated pajama pants. For the last few nights, he had been waking up in a cold sweat. He switched on his lamp and removed the sheet from his mattress. He entered the bathroom, grabbed a face rag from the rack, and ran it under the cold faucet. After dabbing his face with the rag, he went back into his bedroom and changed his sheets. He paused a couple of times when putting the pillowcase on the pillows because the room was spinning; or at least if felt like it. All he could think about was Lamar. "Where the hell is he?" he said aloud, strongly shaking the pillowcase.

Will had tried calling him over ten times, and each time the phone just rang. He placed the last pillow on the bed before reaching over and turning off the light switch. He placed his hand under his arm and massaged the lump, which had now grown to the size of a penny.

"Ahhhhh," he said as he gently pressed it.

He wasn't even looking forward to Thanksgiving. He wasn't in the mood. Will didn't know what was worse, the diarrhea, the white build-up on his gums, the lump under his arm, the night sweats, or not hearing from Lamar. All he knew was that he was exhausted. As much as he wanted to get angry with Lamar, he couldn't. It wasn't that he didn't want to; he just didn't have the strength.

* * *

"I'll be hitting the road at about noon tomorrow," Sdia explained to Sharon.

"Okay, sweetheart. Is that boy still coming with you?" Sharon asked.

Sdia laughed, "For the hundredth time, Ma, his name is Mel and yes, he's coming!"

"Oh yeah, so who's driving?" Sharon probed.

"I may drive the first few hours, and then he'll take ova."

"Well, make sure you get enough rest tonight, baby. You'll need it. I'm so excited you're coming, Dia," Sharon shrieked into the phone.

Sdia pulled it away from her ear and smiled, "Me, too, Ma. Where's Daddy?"

"He's downstairs cleaning the foyer. I told him to wait until tomorrow since he's off, but you know him," Sharon replied.

"He didn't have to work today?"

"Yeah, he had to work, but he came home early. He said he would need to spend the whole day tomorrow preparing his DJ equipment." She sighed.

Sdia laughed. "And I suppose he'll be playing in the garage, huh?"

"Where else is he playing? He damn sure ain't playing in here."

"Who's coming over? The same old people?" Sdia asked.

"Have you spoken to Charmaine?" Sharon replied.

"Nope, not yet, anyway. You know she usually calls once I'm on the road, or when she is fed up with her boss!"

Sharon laughed.

"That friend of yours is something else, girl."

"Yup, she sure is," Sdia replied, trying to think of something else to talk about.

"Uh-huh, I know," Sharon replied as she read the mail.

Sdia hated trying to prolong a dry phone conversation. Instead of trying to find something to talk about, she decided to end it because she knew she didn't have her mother's undivided attention.

"Hey, Dia, let me call you back. I know this phone company didn't intend to charge me twice for this month."

"All right," Sdia replied, returning her attention to work.

She read last month's issue of *Reach* magazine and read the reviews from customers. She sighed.

"They're never satisfied! Especially Nora. I can't believe that bitch. My article wasn't good enough? Tuh. Why don't you take your flat pancake ass down to the shelter and interview battered and emotionally damaged women. Let's see how you hold up!" She tossed the magazine to the side and grabbed her purse from her desk. She was in the mood for a bagel from the cafeteria. It was her last resort since she had arrived to work fifteen minutes late. She didn't have time to stop at the Bagel Shop, and thank God, John wasn't in. He decided to take off a day earlier for his trip to Arkansas. He said he was going back home to see his brothers.

Sdia walked past a couple of her co-workers who were lounging in back of the office and chatting about their plans for the holidays. *They must've finished writing their articles. No way in the world they'd be socializing like this if they weren't.* She became irritated again, thinking about how she had to re-write her article. She still had a long list of editorial changes to update, a few illustrations to go through and about twenty emails to answer. *Ugh, the perks of being a journalist!*

Most of them were older than her with the exception of one girl named Ibtihaj, who was Sudanese. Ibtihaj was a year older than her and was always bringing in food from her country for Sdia to try. They were so different, but at the same time, they had so much in common. Ibtihaj was Muslim and had only been in the U.S. for seven years. She graduated from Boston State earning her Masters in Business. She was living with her brother, his wife, and two nieces, not too far from Sdia. She was the only one out of her seven sisters and brothers who wasn't married. Like Sdia, she still believed that someday her knight in shining armor would come and sweep her off her feet.

"Good morning, Sdia," Ibtihaj called out as she held the office door open.

"Hi, Ibtihaj. How are you this morning?" Sdia asked with a wide smile.

Ibtihaj shook her head and looked down. "I'm so tired. I didn't get any sleep last night. We had company, and they didn't leave until 11:30 at night!"

"Aww, you poor thing," Sdia said and patted her on the shoulder. "How about a cup of coffee? My treat." Ibtihaj agreed and the two walked down the hall to the elevator.

Sdia pressed the button as the two waited. "I don't understand why you didn't just go to sleep. They weren't your company, right?"

"In my culture, the women are supposed to prepare a meal when we have guests."

"What do the men do?" Sdia asked as she shook her head in disagreement.

"Eat, chat, and drink tea." Ibtihaj smiled. "Besides, even if I did go to bed, I would still have to wake up to clean the dishes."

"So when you have guests, you have to prepare a meal at all times?" Sdia asked, interested.

"Well, sometimes we will offer cookies and tea, but for the most part, my family has always greeted our guests with a meal, tea, and dessert. It's just something we have always done."

They stepped onto the elevator. "I'll be glad when this day is over," Sdia complained.

"Are you going to your mother's for the holiday?" Ibtihaj asked.

"Yes, I'll be heading out tomorrow afternoon. My boyfriend and I are driving."

Ibtihaj smiled as the elevator came to a stop. "Well, well, well, your boyfriend, huh?"

"Oh, yeah. He asked me if I wanted to be with him and I accepted." Sdia blushed. She had forgotten to mention to Ibtihaj that she and Mel had become an item.

She walked into the cafeteria without waiting for a response. It was her clean getaway. On several occasions Sdia had spoken to Ibtihaj about Sean, and she knew that

Ibtihaj was a woman who strongly believed in marriage. Every time she even mentioned a friend to Ibtihaj, she would always ask if they were going to get married. She ran behind Sdia.

"So when is the wedding?"

"I haven't even thought that far! " Sdia replied and giggled at the idea afterward. *Why did I just laugh about being married?* She looked at Ibtihaj suspiciously and pretended as if that question was outrageous. *But now that she mentioned it; it would be nice to get married! I could see myself with Mel for the rest of my life. If we were married he'd feel more comfortable with our relationship and I bet he'd be less controlling!*

"You should really think about getting married this time around, Sdia. A man shouldn't be able to enjoy you unless he is your husband." Ibtihaj pointed her finger as she spoke. That was a habit she had when she was making a point or giving her opinion on a situation. "Lust now ... cry later!"

"That's the truth, girl!" Sdia said. Although Ibtihaj was a virgin, Sdia had to admit the girl knew what she was talking about when it came to men. Sometimes she wished she was still a virgin.

"I love talking to you, Sdia. You're the only one in the office who makes me feel comfortable and not out of place. Thank you so much for treating me as if we are equals."

"We are equals, girl. Thank you for your words of wisdom. You know what the hardest part is for me when I get good advice? And not just me, probably most people."

"No. What?"

"It's not only taking heed, but putting some action

behind it. It's crazy, but sometimes we can spot trouble a
mile away and run right to it."

Chapter 27

"I haven't quite thought about what I want to do just yet, Abby," Natalya said.

"Well, you know that you and Carl are more than welcome to come to my house if you'd like," Abby replied.

"I couldn't care less where his fat ass eats. Truthfully, he could skip a few meals." Natalya laughed.

"Well, the offer still stands."

"Thanks, girl. More than likely we'll stop by. Do you want me to bring anything?" Natalya asked.

"Sure. As a matter of fact, you can come by to help!" Abby replied, cheerfully.

Natalya rolled her eyes in the back of her head, and said, "Okay!"

"So, where is your little boy toy?"

Natalya's stomach dropped. "I don't know. I haven't spoken to him in the past couple of days. I hope everything's okay," she replied, as if she weren't worried.

"Looks like you won't be getting any chocolate for the holidays," Abby joked.

"Hey, that's not funny, Abby. You know I'm sensitive about my shit." Natalya laughed.

"Looks like you're gonna have to give good ol' Carl some."

"Ewwww! Please, girl. I just ate breakfast, and speaking of his fat ass, he came strolling in last night at eleven o'clock." She chuckled. "Sometimes, I wish I'd just stuck to black men!"

"Uh oh, it sounds like Carl is doing a little something on the side, or should I say someone?" Abby playfully replied.

"Oh, girl, please! Now you tell me, who in the hell would want that ton of shit for a man?"

"You never know, Natalya. You never know . . ."

"I'll tell you exactly what he's doing. He is staying out late and going to these fake ass meetings on purpose just to make me jealous. He's just upset that I didn't call him all day yesterday. Shit, I was waiting for Lamar to come over and break a sista off!" she said seductively. "But seriously, Abby, I'm kind of worried about him."

"Well, call him."

"I did, five times, and I left two messages, but he hasn't called back."

"Did you call his job?" Abby stopped as she caught herself.

"Yeah, I'm glad you realize how foolish you just sounded. Hey, why don't you call him for me?" Natalya asked.

"Me? Are you really that high sprung? You know what? Never mind. What's the number?"

Natalya happily gave Abby the number. "Please try to disguise your voice as best as you can!" she reminded her.

"I know. I've done this before," Abby said as Natalya entered the digits into her phone.

"Micro Media, this is Marina speaking. How can I help you?"

"Good afternoon, ma'am. Is Lamar Baldwin available?"

"No, he isn't. He won't be in until Monday. Can I take a message?"

"No, I'll call again on Monday. Have a good day," Abby pleasantly replied.

Natalya let out a long sigh. "That's strange. He hasn't called me all day," she complained.

"I know you aren't getting stressed out over some boy?"

"Come on, Abby. You know me better than that. A sista's just horny."

"Okay, now. I was a little worried for a second. By the way, are you two using protection?"

"Hell yeah! What do you take me for?" Natalya quickly replied.

"Wheeew! Thank you, Jesus!"

"Hey, do you want to go shopping?" Natalya asked, quickly changing the subject.

"Uh, I don't know. I have a lot to do."

"Come on. It will be fun. What else are you doing today?

"You see, that's just why Paul doesn't want me around you. You'll have me spending our mortgage!" Abby joked.

"So I'll be there around noon. I want to stop by the pharmacy to pick up some *Monistat 7* for this damn yeast infection before we go to the mall," Natalya replied, before hanging up.

* * *

Natalya pulled a pair of dark jeans and a crème turtleneck from her closet before taking a shower. After getting dressed, she went downstairs to make a fresh cup of coffee and a piece of toast. She sat at the kitchen table and waited for the toast. "I wonder if he's home?" Anticipation was killing her, so she decided to call Lamar at home. Natalya ran upstairs and grabbed her cellphone from her bed. The loud sound of the fire alarm ricocheted off the walls and the smell of burnt toast filled the air. She quickly ran into the kitchen and unplugged the toaster.

"Shit!" she cursed as she removed the rock hard bread.

She tossed the bread into the trash and headed to the living room, where she sat on the couch and slowly dialed Lamar's house number. She was greeted by his answering machine. She sucked her teeth in disgust and hung up the phone. She didn't bother leaving a third message. "If Lamar wants to talk, he has my number!" Her cellphone began to ring. She looked at the caller ID.

"Aw, fuck! Yes, Carl?" she answered irritably.

"Hello, Natalya. I just want to let you know that I will be working late tonight, so don't wait up," he quickly replied.

Natalya raised her eyebrows. *Sounds like that was rehearsed.* "Whatever!" she said. "Carl must really think I'm dumb!" She wished Lamar had answered his phone. Tonight would have been the perfect night for them to hook up. Lord knows she needed it.

It was starting to dawn on her how much her husband was a lame. *He's that desperate for my attention? He has to pretend that he's busy at work?* The thought made her angry. She didn't like the fact that he thought she was clueless.

Chapter 28

Butterflies filled her stomach every time she thought about Mel meeting her family. Sdia sat in the passenger's side and gazed out of the window. She felt awkward about the whole situation.

"Baby, can you pass me a napkin from the glove compartment?" he asked, turning for a brief moment to face her.

Sdia nodded and reached for the compartment. Inside, there was a small brown teddy bear holding a single long-stemmed rose.

"Aww, thanks, Mel," she replied, leaning over and kissing him on the cheek. Mel smiled as he stared ahead at the crowded interstate.

"What time did you tell your mother we were arriving?" he asked.

"I told her that we should be there around two or three. Why?"

Mel looked at his watch. "It's already going on 12:30. I doubt we'll make it around that time." He reached to the left of him and grabbed Sdia's hand. She pushed her seat back, placed her head in the headrest, and closed her eyes. She thought about what she would do once she got home.

"So, are we stopping by your sister's first, or my parents?" she asked, opening her eyes and looking at him.

"It doesn't matter, baby."

He was interrupted by the sound of his cellphone. He looked at the caller ID and forwarded the call to voicemail. "It's up to you, sweetheart."

Sdia didn't reply. She turned her head toward the window and peered outside at the passing cars. *I wonder who that was calling him.* Mel could feel the tension, so he decided to break the ice.

"Do you have to use the bathroom, sweetheart?"

Sdia shook her head no without looking at him. She could see the nervousness in his face out the corner of her eye. Slowly she pulled her hand away from his grip and turned on the radio.

"Here, check out The Weekends last album," he said, removing his iPhone from his pocket and plugging in the auxiliary cord. "Live For," blasted through the speakers. Sdia bobbed her head and sang along.

"Did you hear Drake's new album?" Mel asked, trying to get her attention.

Sdia looked at him and shrugged as she continued to sing.

"So do you wanna go out tonight, like to a lounge or something?" He tried his best to talk over the music.

"What did you say?" she asked, annoyed and decided to turn the radio off.

Mel looked at her, stunned. "Damn, calm down. I was only trying to make conversation."

His phone began to ring and without realizing it was still attached to the auxiliary cord in the radio, he accidentally clicked, "Answer."

"Babe, you there?" a female voice on the other end asked.

Sdia turned to him, astounded. Mel hurriedly grabbed his phone from the radio and tried to end the call.

"I don't know why my sista keeps calling me," he

complained.

Sdia smiled. "She can't wait to see her big brother," she said, nudging him on the shoulder. Inside, she was fuming. She could feel her stomach knotting, her heart racing, and her temples throbbing. She grabbed her cell from her purse and began to dial Charmaine's number. Mel quickly snatched the phone from her hand, accidentally scratching her on the wrist. "What the hell are you doing!" she shouted.

He looked at the screen on her phone. "Who you calling?" he asked defensively, before tossing it out the window.

For a quick moment, Sdia thought she was dreaming. It happened so fast. She reached for her phone, only to have Mel knock her hand into the dashboard. She looked at her index finger and noticed her nail had broken. In seconds, she was punching, smacking, and scratching while shouting and cursing at him. Mel forcefully tried to protect his face from the quick blows but had no luck.

"What the fuck you doing? Oh shit, bitch!"

The word, "bitch" was like a gunshot at a horse race. Sdia went nuts, pulling the back of his shirt with one hand, sending powerful blows to the side of his face with the other, and kicking him in the side.

"Motherfucker, who the fuck do you think you are!" she shouted in between hits.

Mel had managed to pull his car over onto the highway's shoulder. Huge trucks and cars sped by causing the ground to shake as the car came to a complete stop. He pulled the keys from the ignition, jumped out of the car, and rushed over to the passenger's side. He yanked the door open and snatched her out by her hair. Sdia screamed and kicked as she tried to hold onto the armrest. Tears poured from her eyes.

"What are you doing? Get the fuck off of me. Stop!"

Mel threw her to the ground. "Bitch, are you crazy?" he asked, gazing down at her. She looked up at him with fear in her eyes. Her body grew numb. She couldn't move. When she opened her mouth, nothing came out. Her head stung. She could tell that a lot of her hair had been pulled from her head.

"Get the fuck up!" he roared, snatching her up by the arm. His pupils had expanded to the point that the whites in his eyes were no longer visible.

Sdia stumbled to her feet as she wiped the snot from her nose with the back of her hand. *Oh, my God! I can't believe this just happened. What am I doing here?* Her hands shook uncontrollably. Her mind wondered, *Should I get back in his car? Should I flag down a car and hitch a ride?* She stood there with a blank expression. Her feet were cemented to the ground; she didn't budge.

"Come on, baby." Mel smiled. "Would you please get in the car?" he asked, wiping her tears with both of his thumbs. "Come here," he whispered as he pulled her close.

Sdia buried her face in his chest and sobbed. He was probably being so calm now because he feared other motorists seeing what had just escalated and calling the police.

"I'm sorry, Sdia. I don't know what came ova me. I promise to get you another phone," he explained as he stroked her back.

She continued to cry as her body jerked uncontrollably.

Mel gently escorted her into the car and closed the door.

He hurriedly walked around to the driver's side as he cursed himself. He jumped into the driver's side and put the key into the ignition. He leaned over and softly kissed her cheek.

"Sdia, I'm so sorry." She stared out the window. "Look at me, please!" he begged, pulling her by the chin to face him.

She gave in. He pulled her close and gently kissed her on the lips, slowly easing his tongue into her mouth. She pulled away shamefully, not wanting to face him. For some odd reason, she was feeling guilty.

"All right, it's cool!" Mel nodded in agreement. He fixed the rearview mirror, turned on the radio, and cautiously returned to the highway. Traffic had begun to move, and the police were clearing up the majority of the accident.

The two rode in silence before Mel made a stop at the rest area. Sdia rejected his offer to eat, but he insisted. He purchased a four-piece chicken dinner from Roy Rogers. Still devastated by the earlier events, she sat quietly and waited for him to finish his meal. The events from earlier continuously played in her mind. Never in her life had she experienced being treated in such a way. *I can't believe he did that. I can't believe he threw my phone out the window. This motherfucker put his hands on me after he was the one talking to a bitch!* The tears began to form once more, and she tried her best to hold them back but had succumbed to the burning sensation in her eyes.

Mel glanced over and shook his head in disbelief. "If you don't want your food, I'll take it." He reached over and grabbed the bag from her lap. She didn't have an appetite. All she wanted to do was see her mother, and she knew Sharon had probably tried to call her phone several times.

"Can I use your phone?" she asked in a raspy voice. Her throat burned from all the screaming and yelling.

"Oh, so now you want to use my phone?" he asked.

"I need to call my mother," she said as she stared out the window.

Mel tapped her on the shoulder with his phone. He smiled as he waited for her to turn and face him. "No problem, sweetheart. Here you go."

Sdia turned to take the phone, not looking him in the eyes. She reached for the phone, but he teasingly pulled away. "Nah, I'm just playing. Here you go," he replied, handing her the phone.

Once again she reached for the phone to have it quickly pulled away. Mel looked at her and laughed. He continued to taunt her with one hand while the other remained on the steering wheel. He glanced at the highway before looking back at her. He tried to lift her face with the hand that held the phone, but she sternly held her head down.

"You not getting the phone till you look at me!" he warned.

Sdia sniffled. *This motherfucker is crazy! What the hell did I get myself into?* She didn't want to play. She didn't want to be bothered. All she wanted was to be with her family. "Seriously, Mel. Can you please stop?" she replied, lifting her head and staring him in the eyes with her hand out.

The smile on his face quickly disappeared. He cleared his throat and dropped the phone into the palm of her hand. Sdia noticed his facial expression and quickly pulled the visor down to examine herself in the mirror. She gasped at the sight of her bloodshot, swollen eyes and the long scratch on the side of her temple.

"Oh, my God," she said in a calm, mellow tone. "Do you see this long ass scratch on my head?" She closed the visor and took a deep breath. "This is some bullshit. Aw man. Uh, uh, uh." She shook her head from side to side and laughed. "This shit is crazy."

Mel looked at her and sucked his teeth. Sdia dialed her mother's cellphone number.

Sdia hung up and dialed Charmaine. The phone went straight to voice mail and she left a message.

"Here you go," she said as she handed the phone to Mel.

He gently took the phone from her hand.

"You finished?" he asked.

Sdia nodded and turned back to face the window.

"Yo, you gonna sit like that for the rest of the ride?" he complained.

Sdia let out a loud sigh and looked at her broken fingernail. "Seriously, Mel, don't talk to me. I don't have anything to say to you." *Uh oh, I wonder if I should have said that. He may try to put me out his car!* Sdia didn't know what his reaction was going to be.

Mel laughed. "Oh, okay. Don't talk to you, right? Remember you said that," Mel replied as he leaned over and turned on the radio, turning the volume up to the max.

This type of shit doesn't happen to me. I don't get dragged out of cars and called bitch and shit! I swear after today I am never speaking to him again! All she could do was think about how he belittled and disrespected her and it made her furious. Sdia leaned over and turned down the radio.

"I don't believe this shit. Who the fuck do you think you are?" she shouted, turning to face him. "Do you see this long ass scratch on my face?" she repeated.

Mel looked at her and rolled his eyes as he continued to nod his head to the music. He pulled his half-smoked blunt from the blue plastic ashtray that sat in the cup holder, placed it in the corner of his mouth, and lit it.

"I said I was sorry. What more do you want? Besides, didn't you tell me not to talk to you?" He looked her up and down for a brief moment, before focusing his attention back on the highway.

Sdia sat speechless. Instead of responding and entertaining his actions, she leaned over, turned the radio up and pushed her seat back.

"God, I hope my eyes clear up before I get home."

Chapter 29

Lamar tossed his duffle bag in the back of his trunk. "Keys, wallet, cell phone," he repeated aloud as he counted on his fingers. He grabbed a Kleenex from the glove compartment and blew his nose. He dreaded the long ride ahead, but he looked forward to seeing his family. His mouth watered at the thought of his mother's homemade stuffing and yams. Two days had passed since he'd spoken to Natalya or Will, and he felt great. He was ready for a new beginning, and a new life. He figured once he was surrounded by his family, he'd be more relaxed and able to get his thoughts together. For now, he had to concentrate on the road. Lamar contemplated changing his cellphone number, but decided to wait until he was back home. He knew his mother would be calling him while he was on the road.

"Okay, let's get this show on the road." He smiled, adjusted his seat, and steadily pulled out of the garage.

Lamar knew Will and Natalya were worried about him, and not once did he consider calling them back. They had too much drama for him. He weighed his options with both of them and came to the conclusion that neither of them was a healthy choice as it pertained to a relationship, nor would they be beneficial to him. He let out a loud sigh. It felt as if a big load had been lifted off his chest. *How could I live a happy life with someone else's wife—my boss's wife? Why was I dealing with a man who was constantly pressuring me to make a commitment? Am I gay or bisexual? Now that it's over, Carl may find out about Natalya and me. That's how it usually works!* These were all of the questions that flooded his head. Lamar eased onto the crowded interstate. Cars sped past him, causing the concrete below to shake.

After driving for an hour, he stopped at the rest area and purchased a small cup of coffee and a chocolate donut. He made his way back onto the busy highway. "Damn, these people ain't playing. Everybody's trying to get home for the holiday!" he said.

His phone rang loudly, breaking his concentration. He reached behind to grab it from his jacket pocket and briefly took his eyes off the highway when suddenly, a Sunoco gas truck cut him off. Lamar's heart dropped to his feet as he frantically slammed on the brakes. His tires squealed, and his car went skidding across the highway.

"Oh God!" he screamed.

He could hear his heart pounding in his chest as he reached for the emergency brake. His hot coffee cup tilted into his lap.

"Aww shit!" he cried, as he tried to turn the steering wheel from left to right, hoping to hit the median instead.

Everything around him grew silent. The only sound that could be heard was the pounding of his heart and his heavy panting. Lamar removed his hands from the steering wheel as he fought to unleash his seatbelt. He broke from the seatbelt and reached for the door, pressing the unlock button.

He looked ahead at the truck, screaming as loud as he could with his eyes closed, "OH, JESUS, NO. PLEASE!"

A loud explosion boomed as broken glass flew into his lap and an orange light filled the car. Lamar could feel an extreme amount of heat and a burning sensation on his face. He screamed in agony as he was violently tossed from side to side, trying to douse the flames that quickly evolved around him.

"It's a boy, Mrs. Baldwin, a beautiful baby boy. Happy Birthday, Lamar. Blow out the candles. How was school today? I love you, Lamar; the graduating class of 2010 "Thank you, Mr. Adler. I love you Natalya. I'm ready for all of it, Will. Do you accept Christ as your Lord and savior?"

* * *

"Oh, shit! Did you just hear that?" Mel asked, turning to Sdia.

"What was that?" she asked, waking up from a deep sleep and wiping the slobber from the side of her mouth.

"It sounded like an explosion," he replied, stretching his neck to see the road ahead.

"Yeah, it was. I see the smoke."

She pointed to a thick cloud of smoke in the sky.

Mel looked at his watch. "Fuck. We're gonna be stuck here for a while."

Loud sirens could be heard behind as cars scattered on the opposite side of the highway to make room for the speeding ambulance. Mel looked over at her and nodded.

"You know, this puts like an extra three hours on the trip, right?"

She shrugged as she continued to look out the window. "There's nothing we can do about it, but sit."

Cars sat bumper to bumper without moving an inch.

"I smell smoke," Sdia said as she rolled the window down and stuck out her head. She could feel the heat from the fire ahead. Some people stood on the hoods of their cars, while others stood outside and conversed about the unknown accident ahead.

Mel rolled his window down and yelled to the driver ahead who was standing on the roof of his car. "What happened?"

The young white man turned with sadness in his eyes and said, "Man, bro. Looks like a car ran into a gas truck."

Sdia leaned forward and looked at the man, saying, "Oh, my God. Are you serious?"

Mel smirked. "Yeah, I know. This traffic isn't moving at all."

Sdia knew there were no chances of survivors in an accident like that. "I feel sorry for whoever that was," she sympathized.

Mel drummed his fingers on the steering wheel. "Babe, do me a favor and pass me that lighter," he said, pointing to the side door.

A lump grew in her stomach as she turned and looked at him, disgusted. *What a selfish bastard! He has no type of emotion. How in the hell did I hook up with a piece of shit like this?* She grabbed the lighter from the door and tossed it into his lap.

It took an hour and a half before traffic began to move. Sdia positioned her seat higher for a better view and peeked over the metal rail as they drove past the scene of the accident. A burnt tire, broken glass and other unrecognizable debris lay scattered in the middle of the highway. Police officers and firefighters collected burnt objects and stuffed them into garbage bags. Sdia had never seen the after effects of an explosion in real life,; only in movies. The gas truck was completely roofless. The driver had no chance of making it out in time. He probably wasn't even aware that the car behind him was going too fast. A black steel-toe boot lay on its side along with a piece of plaid cloth. Sdia assumed that was a piece of the truck driver's shirt. They always dressed the same, wearing lumberjack shirts. She shook her head in disbelief at the other dismantled vehicle. "Oh, shit. Do you see that?" she asked, turning to Mel.

The entire front of the car had been smashed in. It looked as if it had gone through a compactor. The driver had to have died on impact. If not, then they must have burnt to death. A black duffle bag, broken CDs and burnt papers lay on the ground.

"That was a Benz Coupe!" Mel blurted out excitedly. "I know my cars!"

Tears rolled down Sdia's cheek. "What a messed up way to go. I feel so bad for their families." Her voice cracked.

Mel looked at her and shook his head. "I know you ain't cryin. Why are you cryin?"

She wiped the tears from her eyes, and said, "Because I'm human, and I have feelings. That could've been us." She turned to face him.

"No, the fuck, it couldn't've been us. I'm not dumb enough to drive behind gas trucks. Anyway, you should be happy we're on the opposite side of traffic!" he replied, curling his lip. Sdia rolled her eyes.

"Can I please use your phone to call my mother? I'm sure she's worried."

She dialed the number and waited for Sharon to pick up, but instead, she got her voicemail.

"Hey, ma, it's Dia. There was a terrible accident on the road, so we running a little late, and we won't be there until late. Oh, you'll meet Mel tomorrow. Love you. Bye."

Mel turned and looked at her. "What you mean she won't meet me until tomorrow?" he asked.

"It's gonna to be too late by the time we get there," Sdia replied as she looked at herself in the rearview mirror.

Mel looked at his watch. "It's only five o'clock. What the hell you mean it's gonna be too late?" he pressed her.

I wish he would shut the hell up! Sdia wanted to turn around and bitch slap him. Mel was really starting to turn her off. Everything he said and did began to annoy her. She still couldn't figure out what she had seen in him in the first place. His phone continued to ring numerous times as they drove. Each time his phone rang, he would glance at the screen, send it to voice mail, and then look at Sdia. She pretended as if she were intrigued with the scenery or the song on the radio.

She focused her attention on everything but him. Before she knew it, they were coming across the Baltimore Washington Parkway. Sdia sat up and gazed out the window like a child on an airplane for the first time. Her face lit up with excitement and joy. She couldn't wait to see her family.

"You all right, baby?" he asked, stroking the back of her hair.

"Yes, I'm fine. Just glad to be back home," she replied, stretching.

"I'ma have to stop at the next exit. I need to pee," Mel said, lighting a cigarette.

Sdia sat back in the seat. "That's cool. I need to use the restroom, too."

Mel pulled into the next rest area and jumped from the

car, practically running to the entrance.

"Uh, uh, uh." Sdia shook her head. She already knew he was probably going to call the desperate bitch back who had been calling the whole time they were on the road. "Thank you, Lord!" She looked up at the sky and said, "Thank you for allowing me to see the light, and most of all, for not sleeping with this jerk. I know you love me!" She smiled to herself and didn't pay the group of girls who were staring at her any attention. "I know they must think I'm some kind of nut talking to myself and praying in the open, but who cares?"

She decided to use the entrance to the gift shop and use the restroom. To her surprise, Mel was standing by the key chains clutching his phone in the palm of his hand. Spit flew from his mouth as he yelled into the receiver. Sdia couldn't make out what he was saying, but she knew by his tone and appearance that it was a girl on the other end of his phone. She decided it would be best to leave the gift shop unnoticed and to add this event to her list of reasons why she wasn't going to deal with him anymore. After using the restroom, she freshened up in the foggy, full-length mirror that hung on the wall. She combed through her soft hair, pulling up pieces sporadically to give it a free-flowing effect. Her eyes were back to normal, and the scratch on the side of her forehead had shrunk. She was feeling somewhat back to regular self and had a good mind to tell Mel to drop her off at Charmaine's. She didn't want him to know where her parents lived, and there was no reason for him to meet them.

"I wonder if Charmaine is home," she said as she reached into her purse for her cell phone. "Shit!" she cursed, remembering Mel had thrown it out the window. She bit the inside of her jaw as she contemplated how to get rid of him. *Maybe he can drop me off at the mall, and I can have my mother come and pick me up. No, wait. That isn't going to work. The malls close early today, and by the time we get there, it's gonna be too late!* She applied a little Mac lip gloss and clear mascara before leaving the restroom. When she stepped out, Mel was standing to the side, holding a dozen roses.

"These are for you, babe," he said, handing them to her.

Sdia politely took the roses from him and smiled. "Thank you," she said as she proceeded to walk away.

Mel grabbed her wrist. "Thank you? That's all I get is a thank you?" He pulled her close and passionately kissed her. Sdia placed her hand in his chest and gently pulled away.

"Mel, you're embarrassing me," she said in between kisses.

He ignored her and continued to ease his tongue into her mouth. Sdia could feel herself becoming aroused and decided to follow his lead. His wet lips felt great against hers, and she could taste the strawberry flavor from the gum he was chewing.

A group of guys sat at a Roy Rogers table, staring at them, as if they were watching a movie, and this only made Mel act out more. He began to gently stroke Sdia's back and eased his hand down her shoulder blades.

"Okay, we have to get going," she said, and kindly pulled away.

Mel wiped his lips and smiled. "Come here." He held his thumb out and wiped the smudged lipstick from around her mouth.

"Yeah, I know. I don't want to keep moms waiting."

They held hands as they walked back to the car. Sdia's head grew foggy, and within seconds, she was on cloud nine again. Mel opened the passenger's side of the car for her and helped her inside. Once she was seated, he bent down and took her by the hand.

"I just want to tell you that I'm sorry for what happened earlier. I would never do anything to hurt you, and I'm so glad that you're allowing me to spend this holiday with you and your family." He softly kissed the back and palm of her hand. "You don't know how much I care for you."

Sdia took a deep breath and smelled the roses. *Maybe he isn't so bad after all, or should I wake up and smell the roses?* She sat there dumbfounded, until they reached her parent's house. Mel was familiar with the streets of Washington, D.C. Not once did she have to direct him about where to go.

"How often do you come out here?" she asked.

"Just to visit my sista. I can't wait for you to meet her." He turned and smiled, grabbing her hand to kiss it.

"Home sweet home!" she shouted as they pulled onto her block. "I don't see my father's car," she said, squirming in her seat. She wanted to break from out of the seatbelt and jump out of the moving car.

"Damn, you happy to be home," Mel said, noticing the excitement in her eyes. "I got you here safe and sound."

Sdia unfastened her seat belt. "Here, here, park right here," she said, pointing to her parent's driveway.

Mel parked the car and they walked to the front door.

"Hey, pumpkin!" Sharon snatched the door open.

Sdia hugged her mother tightly and almost knocked her down. "Hey, Ma!" she landed wet kisses all over her face.

"Okay, Dia, you're choking me," she said, patting her on the shoulder.

Sdia pulled away, embarrassed. "Oh, my bad. This is Mel." She stood back with her hand out, introducing him. Mel shook Sharon's hand and smiled. "How are you?" Sharon looked at him and smiled. "Nice to meet you, Mel. Come in." Sharon stood aside as the two entered the house. Sdia knew her mom was sizing Mel up, making mental notes of his flaws to discuss later on with her.

"I know you two are starving. I'ma fry y'all some chicken. Go ahead and have a seat in the living room," Sharon called from the kitchen.

"Your mom's is pretty. I see where you get your good looks from," Mel said.

"Do you want something to drink?"

"Yeah, a glass of water is fine."

Sdia walked into the kitchen where Sharon was cutting boiled eggs for potato salad. "Ma, you don't have to make potato salad and all that stuff. We got enough cooking to do tomorrow."

Sharon shrugged. "These are leftover potatoes. He's cute, Dia."

Sdia frowned. "You think so?" She knew Sharon was going to think Mel was a cutie, but she had to play it off, like she wasn't that into him.

"Yeah, Dia, he is definitely a nice looking guy, but you know that looks don't mean a thing!" she warned.

Sdia grabbed a glass from the cupboard. "Do you have any fresh water?" she asked.

"You know we keep spring water in the house," Sharon replied.

"I need to buy another cellphone. I know Charmaine must have called a thousand times," Sdia said. She was praying that Sharon didn't ask how she had lost her phone because she didn't feel like lying.

"Where's Daddy?" Sdia asked.

Sharon looked at the clock on the wall. "He should be home any minute. He had to run a few errands. Why don't you and Mel come in here and keep me company? You know I have to interview him," she said as she held up the butcher knife and winked.

"I bet!" Sdia replied, walking into the living room. She handed Mel the glass of water and sat down beside him.

"Have you spoken to your sister?"

Mel took a sip of his water and swallowed. "She ain't home, so I'ma just go to my man's house."

Sdia shook her head and looked around the living room. "Let's go in the kitchen, and keep my mother company."

"You have a nice house, Mrs. Mitchell," Mel said as he took a seat at the barstool.

"Thank you. So where are you from, Mel?" Sharon asked.

"I'm originally from Philadelphia, but my parents moved to Jersey when I was six," he replied.

"Do you live near your parents?"

Mel took a deep breath and looked down at his glass. "Unfortunately, my parents passed away when I was younger."

"I'm sorry to hear that," she replied, slightly embarrassed. "So what do you do for a living?"

"I own a small barbershop. Sdia's been there," he replied, turning to Sdia.

"Do you have any children?"

Mel laughed. "Nah, I'm definitely not ready to be a father.

"Do you want some chips or something?" Sdia interrupted.

"No thanks, sweetheart," Mel responded.

"So how many sisters and brothers do you have?" Sharon continued to drill him with questions.

"It's just me and my sister. She's a couple years younger than I am." His smile appeared almost forced.

"Does your sister live close to you?" Sharon asked, already knowing the answer.

"No, she lives out here," Mel replied.

Sdia sat on the barstool looking from Mel to Sharon. She enjoyed the interrogation that Sharon was putting him through. She knew Mel had to be nervous as hell. It made her smile at the thought of him feeling uncomfortable and under pressure. *Serves his ass right!*

Chapter 30

"Happy Thanksgiving!" Abby cheered as she swung the front door open.

Natalya smiled and said, "Happy Thanksgiving, sweetheart!" She hugged Abby tightly. Carl stood in the doorway clenching a bottle of Rosè and apple pie to his chest.

"Smelling good, Abby. Where's your hubby?" He turned and looked at the antique furnished living room.

"He's in the office. You know he can't stay away from work!" she replied, jokingly.

Carl handed her the bottle of Rosè and pie. "Gotta pay the bills; gotta pay the bills."

Natalya looked at Abby and frowned. "He would know."

Carl looked at the two women and said, "Yes, I would know. After all, someone has to pay the bills," he said, before walking away.

Abby looked at Natalya in shock. "Well, all right then."

Natalya fanned her hand. "His fat ass better pay the bills." She laughed. "I'm almost glad I have another yeast infection; it's the perfect excuse to not give him any."

"It's not like you would give him any if you didn't." Abby laughed.

"I know that's right," Natalya said, giving her a high five.

"I hope those same rules apply to Lamar," Abby whispered.

Natalya placed her hand over her mouth and smirked.

"Ugh, girl you are nasty." Abby burst into laughter.

"Lamar don't care about a damn yeast infection. He'll take it bloody, yeast infected, and all."

"Okay, end of subject, and you better get your ass to a GYN immediately," Abby teased.

"Yeah, I know. I've been meaning to make an appointment, but every time I get ready to, I get sidetracked. Seems like I'm getting a yeast infection every damn week."

"Yeah, it's probably from all that bread you eat," Abby said, playfully smacking Natalya on the behind.

* * *

When Carl first approached Abby's home he looked at Natalya and then at his watch. "Lord, please get me through the night," he had prayed. He'd taken a deep breath once he stepped inside. After he made small talk with Abby, heard Natalya's obnoxious comments, Carl headed straight to Paul's office.

"Hey, pal, how's it going?" He held his hand out.

"Happy Thanksgiving, Carl," he said, standing and looking up.

Paul was Carl's only black friend. He stood about six feet tall and had a slender build, with salt and pepper hair. He and Carl had met back in college. After graduating, Paul took over his father's contracting company while Carl went ahead and accepted a full-time position at the company he interned for. The two men hadn't seen each other in months, despite Paul's constant alibis about how he and Carl were out playing golf. Thinking about the situation brought a smile to Carl's face. He wished he had the balls to lie to Natalya the way Paul did with Abby.

"Looking good, Carl," Paul said as he patted him on the back. "Looks like you've lost a few pounds."

Carl pulled away and said, "You mean, looks like I've gained a few!"

The two men laughed.

"So how are things going back at the office?" Carl asked, knowing just last month Paul had to let his lover/secretary go.

Paul shrugged and whispered, "Can't win them all. It was really taking a toll on me trying to keep up with the mistress and wife, you know?"

Carl swallowed. *Should I tell him about Marina or what?* "Yeah, I know exactly what you mean," he replied, giving Paul a wink.

"So, you don't say, you old geezer you!" Paul's face lit up and he punched Carl in the arm.

"Who's the fox?" he asked.

"My secretary," he replied, turning away. Carl felt like a school boy revealing his crush to his friends. "Woo!" Paul roared, as if he were rooting for his favorite team.

Carl didn't regret sharing the news with him. He knew he could get a few pointers from Paul since he had been in the same situation a couple of months ago. Paul had to let his secretary go, but it cost him $50,000 with occasional shopping sprees and dinners. He had only been seeing his secretary for a total of eight months before things had gotten out of hand. Many rumors were surfacing about how he and she were seen after hours at bars and pool halls, and how he treated her differently from everyone else in the office. Paul didn't deny the fact he allowed

Terri to take three-hour lunch breaks and a vacation every month. When some of his employees started to complain, he simply told them, "Terri's going through personal issues." Things went well for a while; that is, until Terri showed up one morning hysterical and told him that her period hadn't arrived in a month. That's when Paul knew he had to think fast.

"Look Terri. I...I just want for you and the baby to be all right!"

"How is a child supposed to be all right without both of its parents, Paul?" Terri replied. Streams of tears flowed from her eyes.

"I promise you I'm going to be there every step of the way. I just need to get things in place at home."

"But if I quit, how are we supposed to survive?"

"Come on now. Why would you even ask a question like that? You and the baby will never want for anything as long as I am here!" Paul whined, trying to sound as compassionate and as sincere as possible.

"Promise?" Terri sniffled.

"I promise to God it's going to be about you, me, and the baby!"

"Paul, how'd you manage to . . ."

Carl's voice brought Paul to the present and he finished explaining the near disaster.

"Well, I didn't want to take any chances of my employees or Abby finding out. Yes, I was trying to save my own ass, but at the same time, I had to make Terri believe I was looking out for her and the baby. Hell, I couldn't help myself. I've always found younger women attractive and not for their physical attributes, but for their lack of experience and vulnerability."

"Sounds exciting in theory, but experience can be a really good thing sometimes. It all depends on the purpose," Carl said.

Paul went on to tell Carl on how reluctant Terri was about resigning, but after constant persuasion and a check, she agreed. In the beginning, Paul was a wreck, not knowing whether he was ready for a child at the age of forty-eight since he and Abby didn't have any of their own. Terri was only in her second trimester and already running him crazy with all types of weird requests and cravings for the most disgusting foods. She was away in Florida for the holiday visiting her mother, and for the first time in months, he could relax and spend time with his wife without the constant nagging of his mistress.

"I don't know how you do it, Brother," Carl said. He blew his breath on the face of his Rolex before wiping it with his sleeve.

"It definitely wasn't easy." Paul looked down and shook his head.

"I can't imagine having a sexy wife and a pregnant girlfriend. I don't think I'd be able to juggle the two. Forget about finances. I'm talking about stamina."

Paul laughed. "Let's just say that Viagra and I have grown to become the best of friends."

Carl's let out a deep belly laugh. "I bet!"

Paul shrugged. "I mean what can I say?"

"So do you know the gender of the baby yet?"

"I'd love a Paul junior, but Terri thinks it's a girl," Paul replied, pouring a shot of whisky. He handed it to Carl.

"You know, you and Natalya should try for one!"

Carl coughed, almost choking from the comment. "You've got to be kidding me. I couldn't get any even if I were the last man on earth."

Paul took a sip of his whiskey. "One of those, huh?" he asked, nodding in agreement.

Carl shook his head. "Yeah, I've been depending on Palm and his five daughters," he replied, giving his hand a little jerk. He told him about Marina—how they'd been fooling around, but had never been intimate.

"I suggest you don't become intimate with this woman, at least not while you're married," Paul said with sincerity and concern. "I would hate to see you in my position."

Carl appreciated the words of advice given. It only confirmed why he considered Paul such a good friend. "Let me ask you question."

"Shoot." Paul nodded.

"Do you think Abby is suspicious? I mean…don't you think she knows something. You know women have that intuition bullshit."

"Not a clue." Paul said smugly.

"How do you know for sure?"

"Like I said…Viagra and I have become very well acquainted." Paul laughed.

"Are you guys done in there?" Abby asked as she slowly opened the door.

"Come in, sweetheart," Paul replied. "We were just finishing up."

Abby walked in carrying a silver tray filled with hors d'oeuvres. He could see why Paul had married her. Although she and Natalya were the same age, they were so different. Abby had southern hospitality and knew how to take care of her man, or at least it appeared so. Carl often wondered why Paul started cheating in the first place. *If I had a woman like Abby, I'd be home every night.* According to Paul, Abby just didn't have that extra oomph he was used to. Carl wished he had met Abby first. He didn't have a preference when it came to women. Black, White, Hispanic, it didn't matter. All he knew was that he loved women, and he truly believed that he and Abby would've been great together. Abby wasn't as attractive as Natalya, but she definitely was a nice looking black woman with lots of sex appeal. Carl learned a long time ago that beauty was only skin deep, and Natalya taught him that.

Abby stood in front of Carl holding the tray. "Here you go, Carl."

He grabbed a spinach quiche and stuffed it into his mouth. She stood back and smiled.

"I'd better hurry up in the kitchen. I've got some hungry men back here!" She placed the tray on the desk and headed for the door. Carl watched her as she swayed both hips from side to side. He admired the way her black slacks hugged her petite frame. He glanced over at Paul, who was busy pouring another glass of whiskey. He wanted to make sure he hadn't noticed him lusting over his wife.

"Here you go, Carl. You'll need another one before dinner. I know how Natalya can be," Paul teased, handing him the glass.

Carl tilted his head and in one gulp, the liquid was gone. "Thanks, man. I am definitely going to need that to get me through the night." He patted Paul on the arm before leaving the office. Paul guzzled down his drink and followed Carl.

I sure miss Marina, Carl thought. *I need to hear her voice!* "Hey buddy. I'm going to use the restroom really quickly. Tell Natalya I'll be down in second," he called out to a stumbling Paul. He anxiously pulled his phone from his pocket and dialed Marina's number.

Chapter 31

"Will, you ain't gonna sit up here and waste that damn food!" his mother shouted from across the table.

"I know he ain't tripping off that dude!" his sister, Tay said.

"Would y'all please stop? Ain't nobody thinking about Lamar," Will replied as he poked at the slice of turkey on his plate.

"If I would have known you was gonna be moping around, I would have stayed my black ass home!" his mother said.

"I'm just a little tired, Ma, that's all!" Will replied, trying to sound as normal as possible.

"Good, I'm glad that's all it is because wherever Lamar is, he ain't worried about your ass. I bet he's enjoying Thanksgiving with his family."

"Yeah, something you need to be doing!" his sister added.

Getta grip, Will. Getta fucking grip! he told himself as he forced a forkful of collard greens into his mouth, even though his appetite was nonexistent. He hadn't eaten in a total of three days. He wasn't the type of person who could eat when he was depressed, and when he did, the food would run through him. Will looked forward to going to the doctor on Monday. Every night he was waking up in a cold sweat.

"You need to eat as much as you can, Will. It looks like you've lost a few pounds." His mother continued to taunt him.

He looked up from his plate and rolled his eyes. "I know, Ma."

The last thing he wanted to hear was how much weight he had lost, or how he needed to do this and do that. Will was starting to regret that he had invited them. His mother rose from the table and took her plate and glass.

"I'm stuffed. Will, go ahead and lay down. Me and Tay will clean off the table."

Will didn't have the strength to debate the suggestion. He was hoping she'd say that.

Tay looked at him and blew her breath. "You need to savor moments like this, Will. This could be our last Thanksgiving together!" She looked at her mother for confirmation.

"Here you go with that scary crap, Tay. Ain't nothing gonna happen to nobody. Damn!" Will replied, frustrated.

Tay was nineteen years old going on thirty. She thought she knew everything and was always looking for her mother to agree with her. Will couldn't get to his room quick enough. He pulled off his shirt, turned off the lights, and fell backwards onto the bed. He didn't expect to be in the bedroom, but rather in the restroom with diarrhea. This was the first time in weeks he was able to have a bite of solid food without it sending him to the toilet. "Maybe I don't need to go to the doctor after all!" He wanted to get up so badly and join his mother and sister in the kitchen. They had driven all the way from North Carolina just to spend Thanksgiving with him, and this was the gratitude he showed them. Will tried to pull himself up from the bed, but was unable to sit up. He was extremely dizzy.

"Damn!" he said. "What the fuck is going on?"

The last time he felt lightheaded was when he drank a

fifth of Bacardi. He prayed that tomorrow he'd be in a better mood. He wanted to spend at least one day with his mother and sister. Will removed his cellphone from his drawer.

"Hey, Will," his mom said. "Do you want a Tylenol?"

Tay burst into the room.

"Damn, Tay. Next time knock!" he shouted.

"Whatever, do you want one or not?"

Will shook his head yes, still angry with her for barging in on him. He was just about to call Lamar, despite his mother's advice about waiting for Lamar to contact him first. *He's my man. I have a right to know why I haven't heard from him in days!* He began to get angry at the thought of Lamar being with another man. Will dialed his number.

Lamar's voicemail immediately picked up.

"Shit!" he whispered. He didn't bother trying his home number because he knew he wouldn't get an answer there either. "Why didn't I ask him for his mother's number?" he said. "Damn, how stupid could I have been?" He rolled over on his side and clutched his stomach. He had to move his bowels, but he didn't have the strength to get out of bed. "I bet he's with another nigga!" He turned his phone off on purpose. "I wonder if he'll ever call again." Will couldn't focus. He tried his best to fall asleep, but he couldn't. He rolled over on his back and stared at the dark ceiling.

"Lord, please ease my mind and give me peace!" he said.

A stream of tears rolled down his cheek. His heart, mind, and every part of his body ached. It was agonizing not knowing why Lamar would just cut off all ties.

* * *

Sdia awoke to the soulful scent of collard greens, yams, stuffing, and turkey.

"Yes!" she said as she hopped out of bed, grabbing her satin robe from the chair next to her. She looked in her vanity mirror, and said, "Happy Thanksgiving, Sdia!"

Mel had only left the house a few hours ago. She couldn't deny that she had a wonderful time chatting with him and her mother. Mel definitely knew how to put on an act for his elders. Sdia couldn't wait to hear how Sharon felt about him. She was beginning to have second thoughts about whether she wanted to see him, although the episode that took place on the road was serious. She reasoned, *Maybe I was being a smart ass by taking out my phone. I shouldn't have been so disrespectful!* She couldn't get over how well Mel had gotten along with her mother, and she couldn't wait to have him over this evening for dinner. Sdia silently prayed for Thomas's approval of Mel, but unfortunately, by the time he got home last night, Mel was gone.

When Sdia got downstairs, Sharon was on the phone chatting with her friend Loretta and going over what she had cooked and how much further she had to go.

"Good morning, pumpkin," Sharon called out, pulling the phone away from her ear.

Sdia blew her a kiss as she walked to the living room to turn on the television. It was 8:30 in the morning and Jerry Springer was on. Today there were black people on the show, which was right up her alley. She went into the kitchen to snoop around. She wanted to sample everything Sharon had prepared for dinner. Sdia stuck her finger in a large aluminum pan of candied yams.

"Oh, my favorite," she said as she sucked the marshmallow from her finger.

"Hold on, Loretta," Sharon said as she leaned over and pinched Sdia on the shoulder.

"Ouch, Ma!" Sdia shouted, rubbing the injured area.

Sharon waved her hands, directing her to the boxes of cereal that sat in the open cabinet. Sdia rolled her eyes and grabbed a box of Frosted Flakes. She sat at the table and listened to Sharon converse on the phone with Loretta. *That's right, I gotta call Charmaine!* She definitely needed help around the kitchen with the remainder of things Sharon needed done. As she sat at the table eating her breakfast, she thought about what to wear. She packed smart this time around. The last time she forgot to pack an outfit for the club. *I wonder if the club is poppin' tonight. Do people go out on Thanksgiving Day?*

Sharon hung up the phone and poured herself a cup of coffee. She shook her head and smiled. "Loretta is a trip. She wants to bring her new boyfriend ova for dinner. She even bragged about him baking a sweet potato pie," she said with her face frowned.

"Are you serious?" Sdia asked, almost choking off of her milk.

After eating, Sdia called Charmaine to see what time she was going to be over. They joked around for twenty minutes before Charmaine agreed to come over by one o'clock. Sdia wondered why Mel hadn't called. She hated feeling like this. She contemplated whether to call him. As always, he was supposed to call her when he got to his friend's house, which of course never happened. Sdia pulled a pair of jeans from her suitcase and a brown sweater. It was forty degrees outside, and her mother hadn't turned on the fireplace, so it was perfect to lounge around the house in. Sharon walked past the room and noticed Sdia looking through her luggage.

"Uh-uh, honey, I know you aren't going to cook in that!" She stood with her hands on her hips. "We can't sit around and wait for Loretta and Charmaine. I still have to do the stuffing, green beans, roast beef and baked macaroni and cheese. As a matter of fact, you can cut the vegetables and cheese."

"Damn!" Sdia said to herself. She was not in the mood to cook. She had important things to do, like try to figure out where Mel was.

Chapter 32

Mel looked at the time on his watch. "Shit, I gotta go!" He jumped to his feet and grabbed his jeans from the night stand.

"Where are you going?" Niki asked as she sat up in bed.

"What?" Mel asked, wrinkling his nose.

Niki swallowed, realizing what she had asked.

"What did I tell you about that?" he scolded her.

"I'm sorry, boo," she replied, sitting with her knees in her chest.

"I'm not spending Thanksgiving with you. I got shit to do!" He took a seat on the edge of the bed and placed his Timbs on his feet. Niki looked around the room.

"Can I see you later?" she asked nervously.

Mel turned and looked at her with his lip curled. He was so turned off. Niki was a beautiful girl, but she was too desperate for him, and that's why he would never take her seriously. Maybe it was because she was three years younger, and he'd met her in the typical spot, the club. For her to be so pretty, insecurity screamed through too many of her actions. She was the total opposite of what he wanted in a woman. He laughed and stood to his feet. "I'll call you later or something!" He walked out of the room and headed for the front door. "Don't call me a thousand times, either. I'll call you!" he reiterated, before leaving her apartment.

Mel rushed down the crowded streets of DC. He was on the go. It was already going on noon, and he hadn't spoken to Sdia. He wanted to get to Jasmine's so that he could

234

take a shower and call Sdia from the house phone. His cellphone had been turned off all night, and he didn't want her to be suspicious.

"I'll just tell her that the battery died, and I left my charger in the car. When she asks why I didn't charge it, I'll tell her that my sister borrowed the car." Mel looked in his rearview mirror and smiled. He had it all figured out. He knew Jasmine was home. She never did much. She was a homebody and he loved it. The last thing he wanted was to catch another murder charge for some clown disrespecting or trying to hurt his baby sister. He knew how stupid and disrespectful niggas could be to women; he was one of them! He cracked his window as he finished the rest of his blunt. Mel slowly pulled in front of Jasmine's apartment complex. He parallel parked and walked up the steps leading to her building.

"Damn, it's cold!" he said as he placed both hands in the pockets of his mink. Before he could knock on the door, Jasmine swung it open.

"Hiiiii, Mel!" she yelled, smiling from ear to ear.

"Damn, Jaz, . Calm down!" he said, chuckling.

Jasmine snatched him by the arm and pulled him into her small apartment. Mel removed his coat and looked around at the small living room. "Where's your furniture?" he asked, dissatisfied.

Jasmine looked down at her feet. "I had a lot of things to do, Mel!" she explained.

Mel placed his coat on the back of the doorknob to her living room closet. "Come on now, Jaz. I sent you over $15,000 and you mean to tell me you didn't buy once piece of furniture?" Mel grew angry. "You know that's fucked up, right?" He knew Jasmine probably spent the money on clothes. She was a compulsive shopper. Mel smiled at her. He could see her eyes beginning to well up with tears.

"Come here," he demanded as he held his arms open for a hug.

Jasmine wiped her eyes and walked toward her brother. She placed her head on his shoulder.

"I'm proud of you, Jaz. You just gotta learn how to be more responsible. Here," he said, kissing her on the forehead and handing her a wad of money.

"What's this for?" she asked, amazed.

Mel walked over to her kitchen table and sat down. "For all of your troubles this weekend."

Jasmine shook her head and smiled. "Who do you want me to lie to now?" She already knew how her brother operated.

"Just go with the flow," he replied, winking his eye.

"I gotcha, Mel," she reassured.

"Where you gonna eat at?" he asked as he walked into the kitchen to check the refrigerator for something cold to drink. "Damn, Jaz. Where the fuck is ya food?" he complained.

"I ain't go shopping yet," she replied as she sat on the floor counting the money.

"I'ma take you to the grocery store, and I'ma buy you a living room set before I leave," he called out from the kitchen.

"Thanks," she responded, uninterested.

He continued to examine the kitchen, looking through the cabinets, pantries, and oven. He wanted to see what her living conditions were. "Yo, Jaz, do you be eating?" he asked, after finding a box of baking soda and Kraft Mac and Cheese in the cabinet.

"What you eat wit'? Ya fingers? Where are all ya utensils?" Mel shook his head in disbelief. This was unacceptable. He didn't bother to look in her bedroom or bathroom. He already knew the conditions weren't going to be any better.

"Where you eating at?" Jasmine called out after counting over $4,000.

"My girl's parent's house. Where are you eating?" He took a seat at the table.

"My friend from school. At her house," Jasmine replied as she walked over and pulled a chair to join him.

Mel quickly looked up. "What friend?" he asked suspiciously.

Jasmine smiled. "Don't worry. It's a girl!"

Mel raised his eyebrows. "Oh, yeah?"

"Listen to you, I know that's right up your alley. You always asking to be introduced to some of my college friends. But the answer is nope. Don't even think about it, Mel. She is not that type of girl. She's got class!"

Mel didn't try to pursue the topic. He wasn't in the mood. Mel removed his charger from his duffle bag and plugged it into Jasmine's bedroom wall. He looked at the collage that hung on her wall and smiled. Pictures of Jasmine and her college friends were everywhere. Mel wished he could have gone to college instead of prison. Although he was grateful for God's blessings, he wished he would have taken the college route.

"Damn!" he said aloud, remembering he hadn't stopped by the barbershop to collect the rent from the barbers.

"Yo, Jaz!" he shouted at the top of his lungs. "Where's ya cordless phone?"

Jasmine rushed into the room holding a black cordless phone in one hand and her cellphone in the other. Mel took the phone and called Ty, one of the barbers. Ty's voicemail came on.

"Yo, Ty, call me when you get this message. Oh yeah, Happy Thanksgiving, man." Mel ended the call, and then he called Sdia.

"Hello?" she answered, aggravated.

"Happy Thanksgiving, baby," Mel cheered.

"Whose number is this?" she asked.

"It's my sister's house number."

"Oh, okay."

"The battery on my cellphone died. My phone is charging."

"Oh, yeah?" she asked, surprised.

"Yeah, didn't you try to call me?" Mel asked.

"Actually, no."

Mel's blood began to boil. He balled his fist. If she were standing in front of him, he would've punch her in the face for not being concerned about his whereabouts.

"What time are y'all eating?" he asked, trying to brush off his frustration.

"Hmmm, I'm not sure. I guess at about 7:30."

"All right, baby. I'ma call you before I get there, okay?"

"Okay, babes," she replied, hanging up the phone.

Mel had a good mind to not show up. "Let's see how she likes that. Trying to be a smart ass, acting like she don't care if I call or not!" He pulled out a pair of jeans and button-up shirt from his bag.

"I need some ass," he said aloud, looking down at his erect penis. He debated whether he should stop back at Niki's for a quickie before heading to Sdia's for dinner. "Nah, that's too much running around, and then I'ma have to take another shower and be extra late. I'll just call her after I leave Sdia's."

Mel really wanted to have sex with Sdia, but he knew that wasn't going to happen anytime soon. He had to be tactful when it came to her. He had already messed up by hitting her, and he knew she was going to hold a grudge about that for a while. He estimated how much more money he would have to spend and how many more lies he would have to tell in order to gain her complete trust. He couldn't deny the fact that she was beautiful, intelligent, and most of all, a challenge. The feelings he had for her were the total opposite of what he had ever felt for a woman. It was like he loved her, but he hated her. Sometimes he couldn't understand his own emotions. He had thoughts of hurting her, and then he thought of making passionate love to her. Mel stared at the iron as he imagined himself inside of her. He was going to do anything and everything to keep her close to him, just as his father did with his mother.

"It's over, Glenda? Are you threatening to leave? I swear if you take any of your clothes from out of that closet I'm going to break your fucking neck!" Mel's father shouted. "If you even think about leaving this house, I'll set this whole shit on fire and kill those little fuckers sleeping in the next room!"

"Please don't say that, Marvin," Glenda rushed over from the closet to her husband as he sat on the edge of the

239

bed shirtless in a pair of beige khakis.

"Keep on fucking with me, bitch, and I'll kill Mel and Jasmine. I don't give a fuck if they're my kids or not."

Glenda sobbed hysterically as she kneeled in front of her husband. "You're sleeping with my sister. What you expect me to do?" Saliva slowly fell from her mouth as she continued to wail. "How could you?"

Marvin quickly jumped to his feet and shoved her backward. He walked over to the closet and grabbed the can of gasoline. His mother watched in terror as he approached her with the can in his hand. "Take off your clothes," he ordered.

"No, Marvin. Don't!" she begged as he pulled and tugged on the white nightgown she wore. He unscrewed the top and began to slowly empty the contents over her head. Glenda sat on the floor with her hands raised over her head.

"Put your fucking hands down!" he shouted, smacking her hands away.

Mel discreetly hid in the dark hallway, peeking around the corner. Tears spilled from his eyes as he watched his mother beg and plead for her and her children's lives.

Glenda placed her hands over her eyes as gasoline dripped from her head onto her forehead. "Open your fucking eyes!" Marvin, commanded. He removed a book of matches from his pocket and lit one. "Look at me!" he shouted. Glenda continued to hold her head down. "I said look at me!" he roared, grabbing her by the back of her hair and pulling her head back. He held the lit match to her face. "If you ever think about leaving me, I will kill you and the kids. Do you hear me?" he asked, staring her coldly in the eyes. Glenda shook her head yes. "You fucking bitch!" Marvin concluded, hawking spit in her face. He blew out the match and violently tossed her backward. Glenda fell backward and into a fetal position. She lay on the floor naked and crying. Marvin walked past her and fell backward onto the bed.

"Now get over here and suck my dick!"

Chapter 33

"Hey, girl?" Charmaine said as she entered Sdia's room after conversing with Sdia's parents.

Sdia sat on the edge of the bed putting on costume jewelry. "I see you still love football!" She laughed.

"Oh you heard me and pops?"

"Did I? Your loud talking ass," Sdia teased.

"Whatever. Oooh, that bracelet is nice!" Charmaine said, as she rushed over and lifted Sdia's arm.

"Thank you. Mel bought it for me," Sdia replied proudly.

"Oh," Charmaine said, no longer interested. "You look nice." She complimented Sdia, looking her up and down. Sdia modeled her outfit, spinning around and striking poses.

"I heard Mel is coming," Charmaine yawned.

"Ugh! Why you gotta do all that?" she crossed her arms.

Charmaine shrugged. "Say it like what?" she asked, realizing she had started something.

"Like you don't like him or something!" Sdia replied defensively.

"I didn't mean to say it like that. I like Mel. I think he's cool. He just seems a little off. And don't get all defensive like I never mentioned this before!"

"Whatever, Charmaine. I'm telling you he's a good dude. Watch, you'll see when you meet him. Do you think I should wear my black boots or flats?" She held a black knee-high Saint Laurent suede boot in one hand and a black leather classic Tory Burch flat in the other.

Charmaine pointed to the flats. "I like those, Dia."

Sdia tossed the boots under her bed and walked into the bathroom to remove her scarf from her head. She frowned at the ugly scratch Mel had caused on her head the day before. *Fucking bastard! He's lucky this damn scarf covered it. All hell would break loose if anyone saw my face.* She opened the medicine cabinet and removed some foundation. She quickly dabbed the scarred area.

"Do you know what I was thinking?" Charmaine burst into the bathroom.

Startled Sdia jumped, dropping the foundation onto the floor.

"Shit!" She rolled her eyes as she bent down to pick up the shattered glass.

Charmaine buried her face in her hands. "My bad." She quickly rushed over.

"No. Don't worry about it." Sdia replied turning away to avoid eye contact.

"What the hell happened to your face?" She gently grabbed her by the chin and titled Sdia's face towards hers.

Sdia frowned.

"Hello?" She ran her finger across the scratch.

Sdia inhaled a sharp breath. "It's nothing. I accidentally scratched myself while I was putting on mascara!"

"Mascara?" Charmaine replied narrowed eyed.

"Yeah. Mascara!"

Charmaine rose to her feet and held both hands up. "Okay, okay. Don't shoot me. So who else is coming besides Meeeel?" she sang his name. She grabbed a comb from Sdia's dresser and began to comb her hair.

"Loretta's coming, and I think her new boyfriend may be coming," Sdia replied, heading for the door.

"You look really nice, Dia!" Charmaine complimented her.

"Thanks, Maine, so do you!"

* * *

Downstairs, the two helped Sharon prepare the rest of the meal, and then they sat on the couch with Thomas watching the game. Sdia looked at the clock. It was going on 6:30. She went upstairs to call Mel, and then she thought about how desperate she would look. *Chill out, Sdia, and stop acting so goddamn pressed. You told him 7:30!* She shook her head back to reality and returned to the living room.

"You want something to drink?" She looked at her father.

"Yeah, bring me a beer," he replied.

"You ain't gotta ask me!" Charmaine growled.

"Shut up, Charmaine. I was getting to you!"

Sdia got up and went into the kitchen. Sharon sat at the table chatting on the phone.

"Dia, we gonna eat as soon as Loretta gets here. She should be here in a few. Is your friend still coming?" she asked, pulling the phone away from her mouth.

"Yeah, I'ma call him in a minute," Sdia replied as she fished through the refrigerator for a beer.

After bringing Charmaine and her father their drinks, she ran upstairs to call Mel. Sdia removed the house phone from the dresser and saw that Mel had called twice.

"I called you about four times!" Mel shouted.

Sdia's eyes widened, stunned by his tone. "I know. My mother was on the phone. She probably didn't hear you calling." An uneasy rumble turned her stomach, almost as if she had to make a bowel movement. "You can come ova now. We're waiting for you."

"All right, I'll be there in a few," Mel replied.

Sdia hung up the phone and walked over to her dresser. She stared at herself in the mirror as her eyes filled with tears.

* * *

"Let me get a dozen red roses and a dozen yellow roses," Mel ordered the clerk.

The Ethiopian woman grabbed the roses from the fridge and smiled. "That'll be $100.26!" she replied in a thick accent.

Mel paid her and exited the store. "What did I tell you?" he said as he answered his phone. It was Niki calling.

"I, I just thought that maybe . . ."

Mel quickly hung up before she could finish. He switched his phone off and continued to drive until he reached his destination. Mel got out of the car and rang the doorbell. He could hear chatter through the front door.

"Just a second," a female voice called out.

Mel straightened out his jeans and shirt as he waited for her to come to the door. Charmaine snatched the door open and looked Mel up and down. He smiled.

"Happy Thanksgiving," he said, extending his hand.

Charmaine looked at his hand. "Come in, I'll get Sdia. She's in the kitchen," she said, as she walked toward the kitchen.

Mel stood in the living room holding the roses in both hands. He looked around at the expensive portraits that hung on the wall that he hadn't paid attention to the night before. *It's all money in here!* he thought.

"Hello, Mel. How are you?" Sharon said, surprised. She removed her apron and tossed it on the couch. "Have a seat."

"Happy Thanksgiving, Mrs. Mitchell. These are for you." Mel placed the yellow roses in her hand.

"Thank you, Mel. These are gorgeous," Sharon replied and took a seat on the couch across from him. "Where's your sister?" she asked.

"Oh, she's at a friend's house," he replied with a smile.

"Thomas?" she called aloud. "You haven't met my husband, have you?" She stood and turned on the television. "Here, make yourself comfortable while I see what's keeping everyone." She handed Mel the remote control and went into the kitchen.

"He is? Charmaine didn't tell me!"

He could hear Sdia's voice in the kitchen.

"Hey, Mel!" Sdia said as she quickly emerged from the kitchen with her arms wide.

He looked at her and smiled. "Happy Thanksgiving, beautiful!" He held her in his arms and softly kissed her on the lips.

"Hah!" Charmaine said, as she slammed the plates onto the dining room table.

Sdia jumped, wiping her lips.

"Oh, my bad. This is my best friend, Charmaine," she said as she walked over and placed her hand on Charmaine's shoulder.

"I already met him," she angrily replied and pulled away.

Sdia looked at Mel and shrugged. "Anyway, babe. You thirsty?" she asked, rolling her eyes at Charmaine.

"Nah, I'm good," he replied, picking up the roses from the coffee table.

"Babe, they're beautiful." She took the roses from his hand and smelled them; maybe Mel wasn't so bad after all. She looked at Charmaine who pretended not to notice the romantic moment. Instead she continued to slam the plates on the table.

"Thank you," Sdia said as she leaned over and kissed him on the cheek.

"She's on her way, just calm down!" Sharon yelled as she walked into the dining room holding an aluminum pan.

"Shit, I'm hungry!" a male voice called from behind.

Mel straightened up his posture and looked toward Sharon.

Thomas slowly followed behind as he balanced two glass dishes—one filled with candied yams and the other filled with cornbread stuffing. The scent of candied yams filled the air. Mel rushed over and grabbed the dish from Thomas.

"Let me help you with that, sir."

Thomas looked at him, impressed. "Thank you, young man," he replied as he placed the dish he carried onto the table.

"No problem," Mel replied.

Sdia nudged Charmaine, who stood with her arms crossed. "Pahlease," she said, blowing her breath.

"By the way, my name is Mel," he said, turning to face

Thomas.

Thomas shook his hand and said, "Nice to meet you, Mel. My name is Thomas."

Sharon smiled and announced, "Well, why don't we all have a seat?" She motioned Sdia and Charmaine to come into the dining room.

"Let me put these in some water," Sdia said as she walked into the kitchen with her roses. Charmaine followed. "What the hell is wrong with you?" Sdia asked angrily, gazing at Charmaine.

"What? What's wrong with me? No, the question is what's wrong with you?" she replied, with her hands on her hips.

"Maine, what are you talking about?" Sdia looked at her, confused.

Charmaine laughed. "That nigga is a phony, a fake, a damn conman. Can't you see that, Dia?"

"I don't know what you're talkin' 'bout." Sdia turned her back to fill a vase with water.

"You know damn well what I'm talking about." Charmaine grabbed her by the shoulders. "That nigga is a psycho!"

Sharon burst into the kitchen. "I don't know what the hell is taking Loretta so long. Her ass needs to hurry up!" She grabbed the phone from the receiver and dialed her number.

Sdia took the opportunity and rushed past Charmaine and into the dining room where her father and Mel were conversing about bikes.

"Yeah, that Harley is nice, Mr. Mitchell."

Mel looked at Sdia and smiled. She had already told him what held her father's interest, and he was playing on it.

"Thanks, and call me Thomas. But, yeah, man, I got that Harley about two months ago, and let me tell you, it hugs the road. You see, the thing about Harleys is that you have to know how to control the power of such a huge bike."

Mel nodded and smiled. "Yeah, I know. I've been riding for about five years now and I love it."

Sdia left the two at the table and sat on the couch. She didn't want to impose on their one-on-one time, and she was hoping her parents would give a good review on Mel. *He has a couple of flaws that can be fixed. All he needs is someone to love him and understand him,"* she thought as she flipped through the channels.

"Okay, y'all. Loretta and her boyfriend are on their way," Sharon said excitedly, as she came from the kitchen carrying four champagne glasses in one hand while Charmaine held a bottle of Moet & Chandon Imperial with two champagne glasses in hers.

"Mel, do you drink?" Sharon asked.

"Yes, I do occasionally," he replied with a smile.

Sharon looked at Thomas and raised her eyebrows. She was definitely impressed. Thomas poured everyone a glass. "Dia, come on over here with us," he commanded.

Sdia went over and joined them. Sharon brought out a tray of hors d'oeuvres and they all sat at the table and talked about politics, history, and religion. Sdia had no idea how much of an intellectual Mel was. Not once did he stumble upon the topics that were discussed. He was mature and had a lot of experience for his age. Thomas seemed particularly interested in Mel's barbershop. He had thought about starting his own business as a DJ, but he never went about doing it. Mel shared with him how he got a loan from the bank and how every businessman encounters financial hardship. Thomas shook his head in agreement with everything Mel talked about. Sdia could tell that he was just as impressed as she was.

The doorbell rang and Sdia could hear Loretta's voice outside.

"Oh, Lord, my girlfriend is here," Sharon said jokingly, as she walked to the front door.

"Hey, Tom Tom!" a husky voice called out.

Mel looked up at the full-figured woman dressed in Fendi from head to toe.

"This is Sdia's friend, Mel," Sharon said, pointing at him.

"Hey, boo-boo bear," Loretta shouted. She pulled Mel by his arms and pressed his face into her bosom. Charmaine burst into laughter.

"Aunt Loretta!" Sdia shouted, pulling Mel by the arm.

"You're smothering him!" She rolled her eyes at Charmaine.

"Anyway, who's your friend?" Sharon asked, trying to take the focus off of what had just happened.

"Oooh, sookie sookie now!" Loretta shouted. "This is my new man, Raheem."

The light-complexioned man stood with his hands in both pockets. "Hello," he replied, nodding to everyone.

Sharon motioned for him to have a seat on the couch and handed him a glass of champagne. He stood about five feet seven, 135 pounds, way smaller than Loretta, and he had curly black hair with a thin trimmed mustache.

"How you doing, man?" Thomas asked, walking over and shaking his hand.

"Fine and yourself?" Raheem replied.

Thomas made conversation while the ladies and Mel stood in the dining room. Mel wished he had joined the men, but it was too late. Like a predator in the sea with a hold of its prey, Loretta was not about to let him go. Sdia tried her best to save him from embarrassment, but there was little she could do.

"So Mel, how much money do you make?" Loretta asked, seductively sucking and biting on a piece of cheese.

"Enough," Mel replied, forcefully putting a smile on his face.

Loretta licked her cherry red lip. "How much is enough?"

She walked closer and smiled. Mel backed up so far he was nearly sitting on the table. "You are so damn fine!" she said. "You don't have any kids?"

Sdia quickly intervened. "No, he doesn't have any kids, and he owns a barbershop." She walked over and gently moved Loretta out of the way.

"Dia, you ain't give this man no ass yet?" Loretta asked. Her question caused Thomas and Raheem to look up.

Mel looked down at his feet, shamefully.

Charmaine looked at Sdia with a smirk, enjoying every minute of it. Sharon grabbed the champagne glass from Loretta's hand.

"Okay, I think you've had enough to drink!" she said, trying to blame her friend's outburst on the liquor.

However, if anyone knew Loretta, they would know that was just her personality. Catching a clue, Loretta walked over to the couch and plopped down on Raheem's lap. He blew air into his cheeks, causing his eyes to water and his face to turn red.

"She must have forgotten her man was skin and bones," Sdia whispered to Mel in an attempt to comfort him.

"Thomas and Charmaine, help me bring the rest of the food out," Sharon commanded as she walked into the kitchen.

"So, what are you going to do after this?" Sdia asked Mel.

He looked at his watch. "I'm not sure. Why?"

Sdia shrugged. "I was just asking. I was thinking about going to a lounge with Charmaine."

Mel looked at her and nodded. "Yeah, that sounds like a plan. What lounge y'all going to?" he asked, contemptuously. "Don't forget, we have to hit the road a little early. You know there's going to be a lot of traffic," he added.

The three returned from the kitchen with the rest of the food. "It's about time," Sdia said, trying to evade the topic. "I don't know about you, but I'm starved."

After dinner, the seven of them sat in the family room and chatted. Raheem intrigued everyone with his stories of the ER. Sdia was impressed that he was a doctor. He didn't give off that professional aura when she first met him. Come to find out, Raheem had performed an emergency operation on one of Thomas's employees when he was in a car accident last May. Sdia could tell that her father had taken more interest in Raheem. Once in a while during the conversation, Mel would add his two cents worth; that's if

Loretta wasn't harassing him. Loretta had no problem with giving her opinion, and she didn't care who was around. If she was attracted to someone of the opposite sex, she was going to let them know, and she didn't care what anyone thought about it.

Mel leaned over and whispered in Sdia's ear, "It's getting late, baby, and we gotta hit the road kind of early."

Sdia looked at the clock on the wall and yawned. "Yeah, I know, but we aren't hitting any road until we hit the mall. You owe me a cellphone," she replied sarcastically.

Mel curled his lip. "That's fine." He stood and announced, "Thank you all for such a wonderful evening." Mel began to shake everyone's hand individually.

"You're welcome, honey, and thanks for the beautiful flowers," Sharon said with a smile.

Charmaine walked into the kitchen before Mel could shake her hand.

"Nice meeting you, Charmaine," he called out as she disappeared behind the swinging doors.

Sdia walked Mel to the door. Mel reached out and grabbed her by the hand "So what time do you—" His phone began to ring. He grabbed it from his pocket, looked at the caller ID, and smiled. "I gotta take this call, but I will call you in the morning," he said, quickly giving her a peck on the lips before rushing to his car.

Chapter 34

Will parked his car in the hooded garage and walked into the medical building. "Suite 204," he said, holding a scrap piece of paper.

It was his first time out of the house after dropping his mother and sister off at the airport. He didn't know what he would have done if it weren't for them taking care of him the whole weekend. Will promised his mother that he'd come down to see her within the next couple of weeks. Hopefully, he'd be back to his normal self.

"Here we go, 204," he said as he pushed the heavy door open. Will hated the smell of a doctor's office. It reminded him of needles.

"Good morning, how can I help you?" a chubby white woman said, as she sat behind the desk.

"Hello, I have a ten o'clock appointment with Dr. Skalvoski," he said nervously.

"And your name?" she asked, revealing a set of coffee stained teeth.

"Edwards," he replied.

The woman looked in the appointment book. "Yes, I see. May I have your insurance card and ID, please?"

Will pulled out his wallet and handed her his card and ID.

"Please have a seat and complete these forms for me, Mr. Edwards."

Will took the forms from her hand and looked around the half-filled room for a seat. Sick faces stared at him blankly as he made his way to a seat near the window. He removed his leather jacket and began to fill out the forms. After completing the forms, Will returned them to the receptionist.

"Thank you, Mr. Edwards. Have a seat. A nurse will be with you shortly."

Will walked to the water fountain and took a sip. He grabbed a magazine from the rack before returning to his seat.

Knowing is caring. Have you and your partner been tested?

Every page Will turned to in the magazine stressed the importance of safe sex. Will began to read an article about an Aids activist who had been infected with the disease for five years.

"Mr. Edwards?" a young black nurse called as she held a chart in her hand.

Will stood and placed the magazine back on the shelf.

"How are you?" she asked.

"I'm okay," he replied, as he followed her through the narrow hall.

"Remove your shoes and stand on the scale, please," she said.

Will complied and removed his boots.

"One-thirty-five," she said, jotting it down on an information sheet.

"Wow! I lost a lot of weight," Will replied, concerned.

"It happens sometimes when your eating habits change," the nurse reasoned.

She took his height and asked him to have a seat so that she could check his blood pressure. "So what brings you in today?" she asked.

Will looked down at his feet. "Well, you see, I've had diarrhea for over four weeks, and this white film covers my tongue and jaw. No matter how much I brush my teeth, it doesn't seem to disappear. I also noticed this lump under my arm," he said, reaching under his left arm. The nurse nodded as she wrote down his symptoms.

"Okay, Mr. Edwards, remove your clothes and place this gown on. The doctor will be with you momentarily." She left the room and closed the door behind her. Will removed his clothes and sat on top of the exam table clicking his heels. He looked around at the medical instruments inside of the metal jars and swallowed. He felt like a child again. He remembered how his mother would have to drag him into the doctor's office and hold his hand when it was time for his needle. "I guess that would explain why I don't have any tattoos." He smiled. Just then, the door opened and in stepped a middle-aged Jewish man.

"Hello, Mr. Edwards. My name is Mr. Skalvoski. How are you?" the gray-haired Jewish man asked.

"I've been better," Will replied.

"So, you're having some diarrhea accompanied with white build-up in your mouth along with a few other things?" he asked, looking at the nurse's notes.

Will looked at him and shook his head.

"Can I have you open wide?" he asked as he held a small flashlight to Will's mouth and a culture stick.

The doctor cleared his throat and said, "It looks like that could be thrush, Mr. Edwards."

Will looked at him, confused. "Thrush? What is

thrush?"

The doctor took a seat on his stool. "It's what babies get inside of their mouths. It's basically an overgrowth of yeast. The medical terminology is Candidosis." The doctor washed his hands and placed a pair of examining gloves on.

"I'm going to exam you a little further. Tell me about this lump under your arm," he said as he untied Will's gown.

"Well, yeah, it's been there for quite some time. At first, I thought it was from my deodorant because I remember having this problem when I switched deodorants, but that usually cleared up within a week or so, and this hasn't."

The doctor felt under Will's arm and shook his head in agreement. "Yes, that feels like a boil." He examined the sides of Will's neck. "It seems as if your adenoids are a bit swollen as well."

Will frowned. "So what does this mean?"

The doctor returned to his stool. "Well, I would like to run a line of tests on you, Mr. Edwards, just to make sure everything is okay. It could be a number of things, one including allergies."

Will placed his gown back on. "So does this mean you need to draw blood? I have to get a needle?" he asked, insuperably.

The doctor smiled. He found Will's reaction obscure for a grown man. "Mr. Edwards, I want to do a complete physical on you. I want to test you for everything including STD's."

"Do you think I've been burnt? It doesn't hurt when I

pee. I mean, I don't have any penile discharge," he said.

"Have you ever been tested for HIV?" the doctor interrupted.

Will's face dropped. "What?" he asked fretfully.

"Are you sexually active, Mr. Edwards?" the doctor reiterated.

"Yeah, but is it necessary to be tested? I've been with my partner for a while now. I haven't heard from him. I mean, her, in few days, but he's pretty clean," Will reasoned.

"I understand, Mr. Edwards, but if you're having unprotected sex, I would strongly recommend you be tested for hepatitis and other sexually transmitted diseases. It's clearly up to you, but let me add that we will test you for pylori, just to be on the safe side, Mr. Edwards. We want to make sure you're 100 percent healthy!"

Will fidgeted with his fingers. "Well, you know best, doc." He managed to force a smile on his face.

The doctor reached over and removed a consent form for an H.I.V. test from a folder. "Here you are, Mr. Edwards. Just fill out this form, and I'll be back with your order form."

Gently, Will took the form from his hand and carefully read it. His heart pounded at the thought of being stuck with a needle, but it had been years since he'd been tested for HIV. Suddenly, he began to feel himself become depressed as Lamar crossed his mind. It had been almost a week, and he still had not heard from him. He even blocked his number and called his job phone, but it just rang. *This must be God trying to tell me something. Maybe he sees that Lamar wasn't good enough for me.* He looked around at the posters on the wall discussing diabetes and the seriousness of lung cancer. "Never know what you've got until your health fails," he said, mocking his grandmother. He wished he'd come in sooner, but instead, he was busy chasing behind Lamar, who was probably lying up with the next man. Will looked up at the ceiling.

Please put peace in my heart, Lord, because I need strength.

Suddenly, he felt a flutter in his chest and the need to cough. *Maybe that's God lifting all of my burdens.* He smiled to himself and continued to pray silently as he thought about what he'd do once he was 100 percent back to normal as Dr. Skavolski said. *The first thing I'm going to do is get back into church. The second thing I'm going to do is change my number, and the third thing I'm going to do is start spending alone time with myself and my family.*

Just thinking about what he wanted to do excited him. He wanted to jump to his feet and shout, "Hallelujah!" He looked at his reflection in the mirror and smiled.

"Today is a new beginning."

Chapter 35

"Has anyone seen Lamar?" Carl asked as he hurriedly walked from his office to Marina's desk.

"No, I haven't heard from him this morning, Mr. Adler," she replied, smiling.

Carl bit the top of his pen. "He may have said he was returning tomorrow. I can't remember," he said, looking up at the ceiling.

"Yeah, I think he did mention something like that," Marina added.

Carl returned to his office and turned on his computer. "Work, work, work," he said as he looked at his busy schedule. If he had to choose, he'd be at work all the time just so that he wouldn't have to deal with Natalya. He was surprised the holiday went by smoothly between them. It could have been because he stayed in his office half of the time e-mailing and instant messaging Marina.

"Marina," he said aloud, smiling, "You just don't know what you do to me!"

Carl hadn't felt this way in years; probably, ever since he was in high school. He considered Marina's suggestion about him and Natalya separating for a while, and it didn't seem like such a bad idea. He weighed the advantages and disadvantages of being away from her, and he could only come up with one disadvantage—he'd miss his home-office, which had nothing to do with her. *Wow!* he thought. "Technically, we are separated." Carl winced at the thought of Natalya getting half of what he owned. He knew how conniving and selfish she could be. He grabbed a Chinese take-out menu from his drawer. It was only 10:30 in the morning, and he was already thinking about lunch. All he had to eat the night before was a peanut butter and jelly sandwich; Natalya stopped cooking years ago.

"Maybe I'll order Marina something," he said. Carl knew how much she loved Chinese, and he wanted to surprise her, but he didn't want to raise any suspicion in the office. Especially after listening to Paul's calamity with his employee.

* * *

Natalya pressed *67 and dialed Lamar's number. "Shit!" she hollered at the top of her lungs. "That motherfucker still has his phone off!" she said as she walked into the bathroom. "I'll have Abby call."

"You can block your number and ask for him," she pleaded.

Abby blew her breath into the receiver. "Girl, you're acting like a damn fool calling that little boy."

Natalya sulked. "No, I'm not. I'm just a little concerned, that's all."

"What's the number?" Abby asked, then Natalya spouted off the numbers.

"Hello, Micro Media, can I help you?" Marina answered.

"Yes, may I please speak to Lamar Baldwin?" Abby asked.

"I'm sorry, but Lamar isn't in today. Can I take a message?"

"No thanks. I'll try tomorrow." Abby quickly hung up. "Happy now?" she asked.

"Yeah. Thanks, girl. I guess he's still in Connecticut," Natalya replied, sadly.

"He's going to call, girl. No one would think you're married the way you're behaving right now. The boy is young. He's probably partying with his friends."

"Partying on a Monday, Abby? Let's be serious here," Natalya argued.

"Look, who cares? You have the perfect life, Natalya, and the perfect husband."

"A fat ass slob for a husband with a two-inch —" Natalya laughed.

"This could be a sign from God, Natalya. Let it go."

"Do you want to go shopping in about an hour? Neiman's is having a big sale," Natalya asked, shifting the topic.

"Sure. I need to do a little tidying up around here, so I'll call you when I'm on my way."

Natalya went into the living room and sat on the couch. She clinched her coffee cup to her chest as she took long, deep slurps.

"Lamar, Lamar, Lamar," she said aloud, shaking her head in disbelief by his actions. "I can't believe he hasn't called me!" She sat and thought about the last conversation they had and wondered if she had done something wrong to trigger his actions.

* * *

"Ibtihaj, can you please tell John that I won't be in today? I have really bad cramps," Sdia said in a raspy voice.

It was 8:15 in the morning, and she was due for work in fifteen minutes, but there was no way in hell she was

262

going. She and Mel had just gotten in a couple of hours ago. It had taken them five hours to get home from DC. They had expected a lot of traffic.

"The earlier we leave, the less traffic we'll run into," Mel had said, confident.

Mel had told Sdia that he wanted to run a couple of errands with his sister before hitting the road, and this put them three hours behind schedule.

"Okay, Sdia. I hope you feel better," Ibtihaj said, before hanging up.

Sdia turned the ringer off on her phone, rolled over, and went back to bed. After sleeping for hours , Sdia was awakened by the doorbell. She jumped to her feet and almost stumbled over a pair of boots as she ran into the living room. She grabbed her robe from the couch and looked through the peephole. It was Mel. Sdia rubbed her eyes as he shoved his way inside. Bewildered, she turned and looked at him.

"What are you doing here?" she asked.

"Who do you have in here?" he shouted, rushing into her bedroom.

Sdia ran behind him and grabbed the sleeve of his leather jacket. The coldness from the leather gave her chill bumps. "Are you insane?" she yelled.

Mel continued to her bedroom. "I called you for two hours straight. Then I called your job, and they said you were out sick!" He snatched opened the closet door.

Sdia stood there in disbelief. She wanted to smack him in the back of his head for behaving so foolishly. Instead, she crossed her arms and tried to maintain her poise.

"I'm talking to you. Why didn't you answer my calls?"

Mel turned and looked at her.

Sdia slowly walked past him and grabbed her cellphone and house phone from her dresser. She held the cellphone in front of his face and pulled on the cord to the charger.

"Because my phone is charging. Call my house phone!" she ordered.

"What?" he asked, puzzled.

"Call my house phone since you know so fuckin' much!" she shouted. Sdia held her phone in front of his face. Mel removed his cellphone from his pocket and dialed her home number. The light on the phone came on, but it didn't ring. Mel rolled his eyes.

"Well, you need to turn on ya ringer!" He turned the other way, attempting to hide his embarrassment. Sdia placed the phone on the receiver and began to make her bed. Mel stood there and watched.

"Are you hungry?" he asked.

Sdia shook her head yes.

"What do you feel like eating?" he asked, walking to the opposite side of her bed and fluffing her pillow.

"I got a taste for some Belgian waffles with strawberries!" she said excitedly, licking her lips.

"Oooh, baby, that sounds good." Mel smiled. "Go ahead and get dressed while I finish up in here," she suggested.

Sdia rushed to her closet and pulled out a pair of jeans and a sweater. Mel shook his head, astonished. Sdia turned from the closet to catch him staring at her. "What's wrong?" she asked as she tossed her clothes onto the bed.

"Nothing. I was just thinking, that's all," he immediately replied.

"Are you sure?" she probed.

Mel ignored her, walked into the living room, and took a seat on the couch.

"Go ahead and get ready. I'll be out here!" he said.

Why does he want me to take a shower so bad? Oh hell, no! That nigga is tryna snoop around my damn house! Sdia's stomach flipped at the thought of him invading her privacy. She locked her bedroom door and went into the bathroom to shower.

Chapter 36

"What do you mean he isn't picking up?" Carl yelled, banging his fist on the desk.

"Like I said, it goes straight to his voice mail," Marina explained.

Carl shook his head. "Lamar should have called. This is so irresponsible!" Carl flipped through the Rolodex on her desk. "Are these the only numbers you have for him?"

"Yeah, basically, although we can call human resources to get his emergency contacts."

Carl placed his hand under his chin.

"Thanks, Marina. I think that's what we should do."

Marina placed her hand on top of his. "Carl, I mean, Mr. Adler, you don't think we're overreacting?"

Carl snatched his hand away. "Overreacting? Marina, it's been two days, and I haven't heard from one of my best employees. He's my assistant, . I depend on him, and I can't do all of this work alone. Are you kidding me?" He stared at her as if she'd lost her mind.

"Okay, okay, Mr. Adler. I apologize." She picked up the phone and contacted human resources. Marina was put on hold for ten minutes before she was given Lamar's emergency contact information. "I knew I should have created that list!" she scorned herself.

Every office she had worked in kept a list of all emergency contacts for their employees on site. She jotted down Lamar's mother's telephone number and requested a faxed copy. Marina hung up the phone and went into Carl's office. She softly tapped on the door with her fingernails.

"I have the list, Mr. Adler. Would you like me to call, or do you want to call?" she asked with a slight grin on her face.

Carl glanced up at her and smiled. "You're something else, Marina," he replied as he noticed her sensually rubbing the paper up and down her bosoms. "That's fine. You can call."

Marina did a seductive spin, and she returned to her desk to dial the number.

"Hello?" the voice of a troubled woman answered.

"Good morning, may I speak to Mrs. Baldwin?"

"This is she," the woman replied.

"Hello, Mrs. Baldwin, my name is Marina with Micro Media. I work with Lamar. I'm calling to find out if you've heard from him. He hasn't been to work since the break."

There was a long pause on the phone before it went dead. Marina looked at the phone.

"Hello? Hello?" she said. "No, this bitch didn't hang up on me!" She pressed the re-dial button. The phone rang for a while before an older man picked up.

"Hello?" he answered sternly.

"I just called, and I think we were cut off," Marina replied. She could hear what sounded like crying in the background.

"I'm sorry ... but ... Lamar passed away," the older man replied.

Marina placed her hand over her mouth and dropped the phone. Then she burst into tears. "Mr. Adler!" she screamed, running into Carl's office.

Carl jumped to his feet. "What's wrong, Marina?" he asked, grabbing her by the shoulders.

"Lamar! Lamar!" she cried as she pointed to the phone.

Carl pushed her aside and ran over to her desk as others from the office ran to her side. They hugged and patted her on the back as they compassionately interrogated her.

"Hello?" he said, out of breath. "This is Mr. Adler, Lamariel's boss."

The man on the other end of the phone could be heard trying to calm down a crying woman in the background. "Hello?" Carl said, slightly raising his tone.

"Lamar's dead. Marina said that Lamar died," they whispered to one another. Faces dropped, people gasped with hands over their mouth and others clutched their chest as the news began to quickly spread throughout the office.

The man returned to the phone and introduced himself as Lamar's uncle. Carl's mouth slowly widened as the man gave chilling details of his nephew's death.

"Oh, my God! Oh, my God! I am so sorry to hear that," Carl replied as he placed his head in his hand. His eyes began to fill with tears. "Lamariel was like the son I never had. Oh, my Lord, dear God. If there's anything, anything we can do here at Micro Media, please let me know," he replied, staring at Lamar's desk where a couple of his employees were kneeling down sobbing.

Carl swallowed as he placed the phone on the receiver. He looked around at the bewildered faces of those who knew Lamar well and lowered his head. Carl tried to pull himself together as he stood to his feet wiping his eyes and clearing his throat.

"Can I have everyone's attention?" he said in between

sniffles. "For those of you who haven't heard, Lamariel Baldwin was killed in a car crash last Wednesday evening on his way to Connecticut. He was going to spend the holiday with his family when he ran into a gas truck." There were loud gasp. Marina softly cried as she hugged a co-worker. "His body was burnt beyond recognition and there was no way of identifying him, except through dental records. His mother is quite distraught. That's the reason we are just finding out about this in such a manner."

"Well, when is his funeral?" someone called out.

"There will be no funeral. Lamar is going to be cremated."

The entire office gathered in a circle with their heads bowed as Carl led them in prayer.

"Heavenly Father, I ask you to bless the Baldwins right now in their time of need. May you ease their hearts, minds, and spirits, as you walk with them through this time of grief and despair. In Jesus' name we pray. Amen. You all may take off for the rest of the day, and I will arrange to send flowers from the office."

He kept his head bowed as he walked into his office and slammed the door behind him. Everyone stood around the office discussing the incident, exchanging information about their relationship with Lamar, and about their last conversation with him.

"I can't believe he's gone. He was so young, and so handsome." The comments were endless.

Marina quickly gathered her belongings and headed toward Carl's office. She proceeded to knock.

"I don't think he wants to be bothered right now. You know that he and Lamar were pretty close," Patty, her co-worker called from behind.

Marina swiftly turned and looked at her. "I know that, Patty. I'm just checking on him!" she furiously replied.

"Well, excuse me. I didn't know you two were so close," she said, astounded. She turned and walked away without giving Marina a chance to reply.

"That nosy white bitch!" She exploded in tears and ran for the exit.

* * *

"Would you like anything else?" the bartender asked.

Carl sat at the bar gazing down at the shot of Scotch, but then he looked up in a daze. "No, no, I'm fine. I'm fine," he replied. The bartender shook his head and walked to the other end of the bar.

Carl removed his cellphone from his suit pocket and looked at the time. It was 11:30 at night, and Natalya hadn't even made one attempt to phone him. For a split second, he wished he could have traded places with Lamar.

"Life is full of shit!" he slurred, turning to look at the older man sitting beside him.

"I'll drink to that!" the man replied, raising his glass.

Carl reached behind the stool and grabbed his suit jacket. He stumbled as he stood to his feet, fumbling for his car keys.

"Are you okay, sir?" the bartender asked, rushing over to assist him.

"I'm fine. I'm okay. I can drive," he replied, pulling out a fifty-dollar bill, trying to persuade him.

"Okay," he said, gladly snatching the money.

"Dammit, Lamar!" Carl cursed as he staggered to his car.

His head began to spin, and he didn't know how he was going to make it home, but he didn't mind taking his chances.

"If I'm lucky, I may be joining you," he said, looking up at the dark sky as if Lamar was peering down at him.

Carl got into the car and slowly drove home. By the time he reached his house, it was 12:45 a.m. Normally, it only took him fifteen minutes to get from the bar to his place. He didn't know how he made it home safely with as many drinks as he had. He slowly pulled into the driveway and looked up at his bedroom window. Carl hoped that Natalya was asleep and had forgotten to turn off the lights. The last face he wanted to see was hers. He knew she wasn't going to cause any ruckus about him coming home late like a normal wife, so he preferred for her to not say anything. It took him five minutes to reach his porch. Before he could put the key in the keyhole, the door flew open.

"Your fat ass is lucky I was up. I was just about to put the top lock on!" she said as she stood in the doorway wearing a satin nightgown.

She rubbed her eyes and waited for Carl to come inside. He squirmed through the small opening she left between her and the doorway, and tossed his briefcase and jacket on the floor. She looked at him skeptically, but didn't say a word. He turned and slowly dragged himself up the stairs. She walked to the bottom of the stairs and looked up.

"Out drinking, huh?"

Carl continued up the stairs, ignoring her existence. Natalya grew irritated and rushed up behind him. "What, you can't open your mouth?" she said, grabbing him by the arm.

271

Carl turned and looked at her. "My assistant is dead," he said blankly.

Natalya clutched her chest and fell backward into the wall. "What assistant?" she shrieked.

"My only assistant. Lamar." Carl's voice trembled.

Natalya's body went limp as she collapsed to the floor. "Oh, oh, oh, my Lord. Oh, my God. Jesus, please!" she screamed, cried, and wildly kicked the floor.

Carl looked at her curiously. "Natalya, Natalya, calm down," he said, caressing her hair. He dropped to his knees and pulled her close. "It's all right, Natalya. It's going to be all right," he said, as he looked at her puzzled.

His mind continued to investigate his wife's unusual behavior until he came up with a legitimate reason. *Instead of me savoring this moment where she's actually in my arms allowing me to console her, I'm being an asshole. She's sensitive. That's why she's so emotional!* Carl soothingly rocked her back and forth in his arms until she dozed off. He was stunned by the whole situation. Years had passed since he shared an intimate moment with his wife. Carl looked down at her nightgown that had risen, exposing her thick, cocoa-brown thighs. He reached down and adjusted her gown, being careful not to wake her.

"Up you go," he said, gently cradling her in his arms and carrying her into the bedroom where he delicately placed her in bed.

Why in the hell was she crying like this? She barely knew him. Carl didn't want to seem insensitive, but her behavior interested him; something just didn't seem right.

After tucking Natalya into bed he went downstairs to call Paul.

Paul answered on the first ring.

"What's up buddy? Abby told me what happened to your assistant. How are you holding up?"

"I'm okay. I just got finished putting Talya to bed."

"Oh. You finally gotta piece of ass huh?" Paul tried to make light of the tension.

"No!" Carl replied defensively. "She's taking Lamar's death pretty hard."

Paul hurriedly gulped down his cognac and cleared his throat. "Come again?"

"Yeah. She's taking this really hard. She damn near passed out."

"What the fuck?" Paul whispered into the receiver fearful his wife would hear him from room across the hall. "Give me a second pal." Paul got up from his office desk and closed the door. "Now come again. What the fuck do you mean she's taking it hard?"

"Yeah. I know it sounds strange because I'm in shock too. But...

"Sorry to bust your balls old man, but it sounds like they were fucking! Paul interrupted. "And if I were you... the last thing I'd be doing is tucking her in."

Chapter 37

"Where is he?" she asked, looking at her watch. It was already Friday and Sdia was exhausted. It was the second week that she had been arrived to work early.

It was 5:15 and Mel hadn't arrived. He offered to get her car detailed and had been her source of transportation for the entire week. Sdia figured that it was his way of keeping tabs on her, but she didn't care. It was less wear and tear on her car, and she was getting it detailed for free.

"I want to do something special for my baby. Let me be your personal chauffeur?" she recalled him saying, before taking her car to get serviced.

She clutched the left side of her jacket and brought it across her chest for warmth. She was too lazy to button it. People entered and exited the building, greeting her each time. She decided to wait in the lobby of the building. Just as she was about to open the door, she heard tires screeching behind her.

"It's about time!" she said, before turning around. Sdia flung the passenger's side of the door open. "It's 5:30. Where were you?" she asked, flopping down into her seat.

Mel looked at his watch. "I'm sorry, baby. I got kind of tied up," he replied, stroking her hair and neck.

Sdia pulled away and stared out of the window. *Damn, he looks good!* If he only knew how much she fantasized about making love to him every night. *What's wrong with me? He's almost as bad as Sean!* Sdia looked over at Mel, who was focused on the road. She stared at his jet-black wavy hair and wet lips.

"Your hair looks nice. Did you just get it cut?" she asked, breaking the silence.

Mel looked at her and smiled. "And you're beautiful." He grabbed her hand and kissed it. "I've got a surprise for you."

Looking up at him, Sdia smiled. "What now? It's not that I'm complaining. It's just that you haven't given me a chance to do something nice for you," she explained.

"Just being your man is enough," he said, looking over at her. "I love you so much!" he said, leaning over and kissing her on the cheek.

There he goes again with that "love" word. She wanted to say it back, but her mouth couldn't form the words. *Maybe he really does love me.*

"We're going out of town this weekend. I wanna take you to my cabin in the mountains."

Holy shit! Her heart skipped a beat. *No, not a cabin. I can't sleep in the same room with him let alone the same bed. Alone in a cabin with a bed means sex!* She looked at him in shock.

"Really?" she asked.

That was the only word she could scramble up. She didn't want to reject the offer, but she didn't want to put herself in an uncomfortable situation. It had only been six months since they had been dating, and she hadn't even spent the night with him, let alone a whole weekend. Mel looked at her, confused.

"What's wrong?" he asked, rubbing her hand.

Sdia looked down. "Nothing," she quickly replied, flashing him a Kool-Aid smile.

"Cool. Do you wanna stop home to pick up anything, or

do you just wanna buy everything you need when we get there?" he asked, satisfied with her response.

She could tell he was glowing. "I would like to stop home first."

Sdia prayed that Sharon hadn't called. She was the last person she wanted to speak to. She could hear her now: "You barely know him. How can you spend the night with him? If you sleep with him, you're a damn fool. Men don't like women who give it up fast." Sdia became nauseous just thinking about how Sharon always spoke the truth.

"You all right?" he asked, quickly glancing at her and placing his hand on her thigh.

Sdia placed her hand on top of his. *What the hell am I doing?*

"Yes, Mel. I'm fine."

Mel waited in the car while Sdia went upstairs to pack.

"Thank goodness I got a wax last week," she said as she pulled out two brand new pairs of lingerie she'd bought from Victoria's Secret. She had been stocking up on sexy sleepwear for a while. She knew it would come in handy someday, but she just didn't think it would be this soon. Sdia wondered if she was wrong for going on the trip, assuming they were going to have sex. She felt as if she was doubting herself, as if she didn't have the willpower to reject her desires. She was telling herself, *You aren't strong enough to go on this trip with him and share the same room. You're gonna have sex!* which she knew she was capable of doing, and she couldn't deny that she wanted him. She grabbed her Louis Vuitton luggage from under her bed that her mother had bought her last Christmas. Sdia couldn't believe what she was about to do. She looked around at her messy bedroom.

"I don't need to be anywhere but here cleaning up this dirty ass house!" Sdia went into the bathroom to get her toothbrush and looked at the ring around the tub.

"God is really trying to talk to me." She hadn't noticed how dirty the tub was until now. "Oh, shit," she shouted, shaking her head in disbelief as she examined the tile in the tub.

She snatched open the medicine cabinet and grabbed her bikini cream. The last thing she wanted was her inner thighs filled with razor bumps. She would die if Mel saw that. "There I go again. He's not going to see my inner thighs because I'm not going to take off my pajama pants!" she persuaded herself. Sdia did a dry run of her place and checked her bag to make sure she had everything she needed. She rushed back to the car, pushing her warnings aside.

"Are you hungry?" Mel asked, pulling out of her apartment complex.

"Kind of, are you?" Sdia asked, glancing over at him.

"A little; what you feel like eating?"

"It doesn't matter."

"I can go for some Popeye's," he said, licking his lips.

"All right, Popeye's is good."

Mel drove through the drive-thru and placed his order. Sdia sat back and closed her eyes. *Lord, please give me the strength I need in order to maintain my self-respect and dignity; in other words, help me keep my legs closed!* She opened her eyes and smiled.

"What's so funny?" Mel asked, playfully poking her in the side.

"Nothing," she replied, slapping his hand.

He leaned over and laid a wet kiss on her cheek. "I love your crazy ass."

Sdia's phone began to ring. She looked at the caller ID and sucked her teeth. "It's my mother!" She thought about ignoring the call, but she knew that would only worry Sharon. She placed her finger over her lips and signaled Mel not to talk. After taking a deep breath she answered the phone.

"Hi, Ma!" She tried to sound excited.

"Hey, pumpkin. I tried calling your house phone. Where are you?" she asked, concerned.

"Me and Mel are on our way to the movies, and then we're going out to dinner," she lied.

"What are y'all going to see?"

"We don't know yet. We have to see what's playing." She looked over at Mel who was busy putting the car in park before stepping out. He grabbed his phone from his hip and began to angrily push the buttons.

"Oh, okay. How was work?" Sharon asked, fishing to chat.

"Boring and long. How was your day?" she asked in a bubbly tone.

"It was okay. I did a little shopping. Girl, I found this gorgeous bag in Neiman's for only $500!" Sharon replied, energized.

Sdia tilted her head from side to side impatiently as Sharon continued. "They had a really, really nice sale, Dia. I wish you were here!"

As Sdia looked out the window, Mel was sitting on the hood of his car talking on his cellphone. He pointed his finger as he spoke. Sdia could tell by his body language that he was arguing with the person on the other end. Sharon continued to boast about the items she purchased.

"Hey, Ma. Can I call you back in a few?" She kept the phone positioned between her shoulder and ear.

"I'm sorry, pumpkin. Just call me when the movie is over," Sharon replied, slightly embarrassed.

"I love you, Ma, and I'll give you a call a little later on." Sdia smiled. Sometimes her mother reminded her of a little girl.

The phone remained glued to her ear as if she were still talking. She studied Mel's body language and facial expressions as he continued to argue. She tried to make out what he was saying, but the passing cars made it impossible. After holding this position for five minutes, she gave up. Sdia closed her phone. "Well, whoever it is he's arguing with must not be important. I'm the one he's with and taking to the mountains!"

Chapter 38

Will closed his Bible and placed it back under his pillow. He felt as if he had a ton lifted off of his shoulders. The Bible always had that effect on him. He'd been reading the Bible for the past week and praying every day. Will got up from the dining room table and opened the refrigerator. He became queasy at the sight of a half-filled bottle of Alizé' that Lamar had bought a few weeks ago. "It's so funny how I never noticed that bottle until now, after I've read the Bible and am feeling so full of faith. The devil is always testing God's children." He reached inside, grabbed the bottle, and emptied its contents down the drain.

"The devil is a liar!"

Will stood back as if he were shooting a three-pointer and tossed the bottle into the trash can. "I'm a changed man!" he said aloud, looking up at the ceiling as if he were speaking to God.

It was a Friday evening and he was in the house. Normally on Friday nights, he was at the gay bar drinking and dancing to the beat, but not tonight. Tonight he was home alone, and it was fine with him. "It isn't so bad after all," he recalled telling one of his friends. For the most part, his mother and sister kept him strong on the days he thought about Lamar, which was quite often. Will had to keep on reminding himself that Lamar wasn't worth his time and that he deserved better. However, the unanswered questions haunted his head concerning his whereabouts. The alarm on Will's phone went off.

"Medicine time," he said as he went into the bathroom

and opened the medicine cabinet.

He hated taking the lozenge his doctor had given him for the thrush. He always had a problem with swallowing pills. "I guess that's why I never took ecstasy," he deliberated as he popped the tablet into his mouth and waited for it to dissolve. Will considered going to church on Sunday since he wouldn't be going out on Saturday night. He smiled as he anticipated the members of the congregation hugging him and inquiring about his absence. "At least I know they love me!" He sat on his black leather couch Indian style, cutting his toenails. "I remember when I used to cut Lamar's toenails," he reminisced.

"Lamar, Lamar, Lamar," he said aloud. His eyes filled with tears. Just when he thought he was taking a step forward. He couldn't believe that the man he loved so dearly had just fallen off the face of the earth without a trace. "Damn!" he shouted, after accidentally clipping a piece of skin. Will's toe began to bleed. He tossed the nail clipper on the floor and stormed into the bathroom. As he opened the medicine cabinet, he caught a glimpse of himself in the mirror. He examined the dark circles under his eyes and frowned.

"I look terrible!" He looked closer at himself in the mirror. The beautiful complexion he once had was replaced with gray.

"Oh, shit!" he yelled as he slightly held his head down to get a closer view of his hair.

He could see his scalp through his cornrows. Will jumped back startled, and turned away. He couldn't look. He didn't want to look. "What's happening to me? Am I going bald?" Without a second thought, he dropped down to his knees and began to pray.

* * *

Natalya cried as she held her pillow tight. She hadn't been out of bed in days and she wasn't accepting any calls. Carl had been catering to her every need, calling every hour, coming home for lunch, and preparing dinner every night. He didn't appear to be suspicious about her behavior. In fact, he seemed delighted to be at her beck and call. She reached for the nightstand and grabbed the bottle of Vicodin her dentist had prescribed to her months ago when she had her tooth pulled. She popped a pill into her mouth, took a sip of water, and lay back.

"Ohh," she moaned from the soreness in her eyes.

Every time she blinked, her eyes burned. She placed her fingers over her eyes, and could feel the swelling. All she could think about was Lamar. She felt as if she was dreaming. Natalya never inquired about the circumstances surrounding his death. However, she did hear Carl telling Paul on the phone. Each time she thought about him burning and suffering, she broke down in tears.

"Lamar. God, why?" she cried out. She continued to cry until she cried herself to sleep.

* * *

Carl sat as his office desk and shuffled through paperwork. His heart dropped each time he saw a document with Lamar's signature. He had everyone in the office sign a sympathy card and sent four dozen roses to Lamar's mother's house. The office was silent except for the sound of the cleaning lady vacuuming the carpet. Carl looked at Marina's desk. He missed talking to her. She had taken the week off and was returning that Monday. He attempted to call, but each time he was forwarded to voice mail. Marina had taken it the hardest out of everyone in the office. She and Lamar were close. He looked at the clock on the wall. It was almost time for him to head home and prepare dinner. Because he had been cooking for the past few days, he had a good mind of ordering out since it was Friday. He licked his lips as he thought about Chinese food, particularly chicken egg fu young. He hadn't eaten that in a while. Natalya probably wouldn't complain since she was in a state of depression. Carl sat there trying to figure out why Lamar's death had such an impact on her. He tried to remember play-by-play all of the times Natalya and Lamar had met.

"I don't understand," he told Paul. "It's crazy how she's behaving. I don't get it. Do you think she's just upset because she met him? What do you think it is?"

Paul laughed. "I wish I could tell you, but I can't. Maybe they were secret lovers!" he teased.

"Yeah, right! Not by a long shot. Lamar wouldn't stand a chance with her!" Carl had said with certainty.

He shut off his computer and stood, stretching both arms. He wanted to have a drink just to take his mind off the situation. Carl didn't have the nerve to ask Natalya why Lamar's death had affected her so much, although he thought of ways to approach her. He knew he couldn't put it into action because he feared the outcome. In his mind, things were mediocre between the two of them, and he didn't want to risk that. He still wasn't able to have sex with her because he didn't want to put her in an uncomfortable situation, nor did he want to embarrass himself. "Nine times out of ten, she is going to push me away!" he repeatedly told himself every time the thought surfaced.

Carl walked outside of his office and over to Lamar's

desk. He touched the nameplate that sat on his desk and shook his head. "Lamariel Baldwin." He wondered how Lamar's family was holding up. Carl came up with the idea of having a plaque made in honor of Lamar, and he'd put it by the front entrance; he felt that would be a way to keep his memory alive.

"May I have some extra duck sauce?" Carl asked as he held out his hand. He hated how stingy some Chinese restaurants were with their condiments. He liked the fact that this particular restaurant was only minutes away from both the office and home so he never made a big fuss about going. The Chinese lady let out a sigh and tossed a couple of duck sauce packets onto the countertop.

"Here goa ya ducka sauce!" she said, irritated.

Carl took the duck sauce and smiled. "Have a wonderful evening." He knew that whatever her problem was, he was not the cause of it and that she had some serious issues. "Some people are just miserable with themselves," his grandmother used to tell him when he would come home from school upset after being teased and tormented. If he didn't understand what she meant then, he most definitely understood now.

When Carl got home, Natalya was taking a bubble bath. "Hey, Talya?" he called out as he poked his head into the bathroom.

Natalya looked up with swollen eyes. "Hi!" she replied in a scratchy voice.

"Are you okay? Do you need anything?"

She shook her head no. He closed the door and sat on the edge of the bed to remove his shoes. His stomach growled loudly. He hadn't eaten since last night. Carl pulled his robe from the closet, his deodorant from the dresser, a clean pair of boxers and went into the guest room to shower. *What if Paul is right? What if Natalya and Lamar were secret lovers?*

* * *

Natalya sat on the bed in her towel. She recalled how Lamar would put lotion on her body after showering. Her eyes began to well. She yearned for the touch of his soft hands. Natalya visualized the last time they had made love in the very bed she sat on. She swallowed as she tried to suppress memories that filled her mind. The scent of Lamar's cologne filled the air. Was she dreaming? Where was the smell coming from? An uncanny presence entered the room. Natalya shivered as she rubbed her chill-bumped arms. Something was happening that she couldn't explain. *Is Lamar's spirit in this room? Is he watching me?* She was unsure whether God would have allowed him to visit her after death. *What we did was wrong. Does God forgive those things?* As much as she wanted to, she couldn't mentally conceal the fact that she was committing adultery with her husband's assistant. Physically it wasn't noticeable, but mentally it haunted her. The last thing she wanted was for Carl to find out. Natalya lay back on the bed and closed her eyes. *Carl will never find out. I would never tell. It's impossible for Lamar to tell, and I know that Abby's lips are sealed!* In a sense she felt relieved. She thought about trying to make her marriage work and toyed with the idea that maybe, just maybe, Lamar's death symbolized the biggest sin in her life that God had put to an end.

Chapter 39

Sdia entered the cabin and removed her shoes and socks. Her mother always taught her to remove her shoes when entering a home with carpet. She placed her bags down and looked around the living room in awe; the country-style cabin was beautiful.

"This is really nice, Mel. Who designed it?" she asked.

He walked past her and placed his duffle bag on the coffee table. "My sister. Why don't you go ahead and make yourself at home?" he recommended.

Sdia had never stayed in a cabin, but it was always something she dreamed of owning one day. She walked over to the fireplace and kneeled down.

"When was the last time you were here?" she asked, referring to the cobwebs that covered some of the half-burned wood.

"Last year. I only come here once in a blue moon, especially when I need to clear my mind."

For him to have only been there just the year before, she had to acknowledge that he did keep the place clean. She took a seat on the couch and took a deep breath.

"It smells like maple syrup in here." It really reminded her of the country. She inspected the kitchen area; everything was baby blue and wood. The color scheme was definitely inviting. Mel opened the kitchen cabinet and shook his head.

"I don't even know why I'm checking in here like there's something to eat." Sdia laughed. "Come on, let me give you a little tour," he said with his hand out.

Sdia stood to her feet and followed him. Mel gave her a brief tour showing off his stylish taste in furniture. Sdia knew that a woman with an appetite for design had decorated his place, and she didn't think it was his sister. Instead of trying to feed her suspicions, she left the unanswered query alone and focused her attention on the beautiful crème and brown decorated bathroom that sat across the hall from his bedroom. Alongside the whirlpool tub lay small crème candles that sat in small, shiny candle holders.

"Brown must be your favorite color," she said as she entered his bedroom. Mel followed her. "A little dusting wouldn't hurt," she kidded as she ran her fingers across the cherry oak dresser.

Mel said, "It wouldn't, and that's just why you're gonna dust."

A soft beige comforter rested on the cherry oak King-size bed. Sdia took a seat on the King bed's bench that rested at the foot of the bed. She sank her toes into the soft mink rug. The soft fur between her toes sent chills up her spine. If she could, she would have lay flat out.

"Are you hungry?" Mel asked, as he emptied his duffle bag.

"Sure," Sdia replied.

"I'm going to run to the grocery store. I want to cook something special for you!" Mel chimed.

Excitement took over Sdia as she sat and grasped where she was and whom she was with. Her stomach began to flip. "That would be nice," she replied coolly, struggling to hide her thrill. She looked around the room.

"What are you gonna cook?" she asked.

"I was thinking a butter-herb salmon, dill potatoes, and garlic-butter asparagus."

Sdia's mouth watered at the thought. Small crème lamps sat atop the bedside tables. "I see you're a Doza fan, huh?" she asked.

"I'm also a Sdia fan," he said, squatting down and adoringly kissing her lips.

"I'm cold," she quickly replied the moment she felt her nipples getting hard. She didn't want Mel to see how excited he had gotten her. He walked over to the furnace and turned on the heat.

"I'm gonna bring your bags in here," he said, leaving the room.

"Oh, my God!" Sdia placed her hands on her head. Once again she was scuffling with her emotions.

Mel returned to the room with Sdia's Louis Vuitton bags. "Do you want to put your things in the drawer?"

"No, thanks. I'll be fine." She wanted so desperately to call Charmaine and get some advice, but she knew that would be the worst thing she could do. All she would hear was how stupid she was and how she was playing herself going away with him. What was the use?

* * *

"Just my luck; this must be a sign from God," Sdia said after she'd cruised the aisles of the small grocery store and stumbled across a pack of condoms. Just then, her phone began to ring.

"Hey, Ma!" she answered, trying to sound as normal as possible.

"I thought you were gonna call me back, big head," Sharon replied.

"Oh, my bad. We're about to go into this movie theater," Sdia said, gritting her teeth. *Why did I say that?* She knew Sharon was about to ask what movie she was going to see.

"What movie?" Sharon asked.

"The new one that just came out with that black actress. I forgot her name, but the one where—" Sdia danced around the question.

"So you don't know the movie you're about to see?" Sharon giggled. "You must be talking about the one with Halle Berry."

"Yeah, that's her name." Sdia felt bad for lying, but if Sharon knew where she was, she would be upset, and Sdia didn't feel like being criticized for something she wanted to do.

"Well, all righty then. Call me when the movie is over. Love ya!"

Sdia's heart sank. She felt so bad. Sometimes her mother could be such an angel. "Love you, too," she sadly replied. She looked at the condoms and shook her head, confused.

"July, August, September, October, November, December—six months." Sdia counted on her fingers how long she had known Mel. She sighed. "I guess that's long enough!" Her body tingled at the thought of having sex. It had been so long. *Sean. Boy oh boy!* she thought. She hadn't spoken to him in months, and she hadn't thought about him as much since Mel occupied ninety percent of her brain. When they first broke up, all she would do was think about him and the times they had shared. It made her depressed, but since Mel came into her life, she hadn't had time to reminisce about the past. She couldn't care less if she ever spoke to Sean again.

"Great, now I'm thinking about Sean!" She sucked her teeth. She often found herself comparing other men to Sean, but with Mel, there was no comparison. He had Sean beat. Thinking about Mel gave her chill bumps. *What if Sean calls my mother for Mother's Day? He usually never misses Mother's Day! He can call her; it's not as if they're beefing. He didn't do anything to her! Wow! Wouldn't that be something? Then I could rub it in his face that I got a new man!* She chuckled at the thought of running into him with Mel on her arm. *Here I go again with my random what ifs. I'm always thinking way ahead!*

"Sean would be so jealous!" she said under her breath. As she stared at the box of *Magnum* condoms, she tried to imagine what Mel's penis looked like. "God, I'm such a pervert!" She shook her head.

"Do you see something you want?" a voice called from behind.

Sdia jumped and turned around. Her heart skipped a beat. *Busted!* an inner voice taunted her.

"Do you need some help?" Mel smiled.

Sdia placed her hand on her hip. "What? Please! I was only looking," she replied, walking away. Mel ran behind her with the shopping cart.

"Let me know if this is cool?" he asked, pointing to the contents in the cart. Although he had gotten some of her favorite snacks, Sdia rolled her eyes and looked in the cart as if she was displeased.

"That's cool," she replied, slowly looking away. Mel smirked.

"Go ahead and get what you want, Sdia."

Sdia walked ahead, down the aisle containing the ice cream. "What kind of ice cream do you like?" she asked.

Mel looked into the freezers at all of the different flavors. "I like strawberry, but get what you want," he insisted.

"I love French vanilla!" she expressed, grabbing a pint of Breyer's French Vanilla.

"Is that all you want?" he asked.

Sdia shrugged. "Yeah, I guess so. Oh, I know what I want!" she said, thrilled. "I want a banana so that I can make a milkshake." She rushed to the fruit stand and grabbed five bananas. "Do you have a blender?" she called out.

"Yeah, I think so." Mel yawned.

She continued dashing up and down the aisles, pulling all kinds of junk foods and juices from the shelves. "Do you have anything in the house to drink?" Sdia asked, looking over her shoulder.

"Something like what—liquor?" Mel replied.

"Yeah, it wouldn't hurt to have a little drink."

That idea seemed to brighten his entire mood.

Within ten minutes, they made it out of the checkout line and headed to the car. They spoke very little as they returned back to the cabin and brought the groceries directly to the kitchen.

"I'll empty out the bags. You can get comfortable if you like," Mel said as he put the groceries away.

Sdia walked into the bedroom and removed her new bra and panty set from Victoria's Secret. "Perfect!" she said, holding the set against her body. She deliberated whether she wanted to have a drink or wait until dinner. "I can't believe I'm here," she murmured. She looked around the room and took a deep breath.

"Where are your towels and washcloths?" she asked, walking into the kitchen where Mel was seasoning the salmon.

He looked up at her, and replied, "Give me just a second, baby." He grabbed a paper towel and wiped his hands. Sdia leaned up against the wall and watched him as he made his way around the kitchen.

"Where's the liquor? I need a drink," she stated.

"My bad, sweetheart. I'll get it for you," he replied. He walked over to the cabinet and pulled out a bottle of Chardonnay.

"You don't have anything else?" Sdia frowned.

Mel reached into the back of the cabinet and pulled out a bottle of coconut rum. "How's this?"

"That's exactly what I wanted." Sdia smiled and walked over and took the bottle from his hand. "I'm glad I bought that pineapple juice. That's the only way I'll drink this," she said, yanking the refrigerator door open and removing the juice. She filled her glass halfway with the liquor and added a small amount of juice.

"I hear that!" Mel said, inspired. He removed a bottle of Hennessey Privilege from the cabinet and poured himself a glass. "Here, we need to toast." He held his glass to hers.

Sdia jokingly rolled her eyes and raised her glass. "Cheers to us!" she snickered, and within two minutes her glass was empty. "Wheeew!" she said, softly hitting her chest.

Mel looked at her and twisted his lips. "You can't be serious. That shit is weak. Here, take a sip of this." He handed her his glass.

"No, thanks. I hate Hennessy." Sdia shoved the glass away. "My father drinks that shit, and just the smell of it makes me nauseous." She had a low tolerance for alcohol, something she inherited from her mother. Sdia knew her limit and had vowed to never get drunk again after passing out in the bathroom of Charmaine's house after breaking up with Sean.

Sdia went into the bathroom to shower. She was beginning to feel tranquil and wondered what the rest of the night had to offer. She double-checked the bathroom door to make sure it was locked before she removed her clothes. She pulled down her panties and to her amazement, she didn't have any discharge. "Wow! This is out of the norm." Usually she would have a sufficient amount in her underwear by the end of the day. She reckoned, since she was on vacation, her vagina was, too, and with that thought, she let out a giggle.

"It's a self-cleansing organ." At least that's what her gynecologist said. "Damn!" she said in a low tone.

Some of the polish on her toenail was beginning to chip. She continued to bathe, making certain she cleaned every crevice, nook, and cranny. Sdia habitually showered for long periods of time. Her mother and father always complained about the amount of time she took in the bathroom, essentially because they had a water bill to pay. "You can never be too clean!" she told her mother, but only Sdia knew the real reason for that. Self-consciously, she was hoping to wash away the contaminated feeling her uncle had scarred her with. She stepped out of the shower and slowly dried off. Her head began to spin. The liquor was beginning to take more and more of an effect.

"Talk about low tolerance," she said, grabbing her robe from the hook behind the door. It was a satin purple robe framed with lace that stopped above her knees. Sdia went into the kitchen where Mel was preparing the table.

"Hey!" she said, walking up to the table.

"Hey, babe. How was the shower?" he asked.

"It was wonderful." She waited for Mel to pull out a chair for her. Mel hurried over and pulled a chair from under the table.

"I'm happy to hear that," he said, as he walked over to the stove and began to make their plates.

He's such a gentleman and so damn fine! She watched with admiration.

Mel placed the piping hot plate in front of her. "Here you are, sweetheart," he said, bending down and kissing her on the forehead.

"Thank you." Sdia looked up and smiled.

They sat at the table and chatted while enjoying their feast. Sdia was astounded by his cooking skills. She would have never guessed his capabilities in the kitchen. Sdia slid her half-empty plate across the table.

"I'm stuffed," she said, leaning back in the chair.

Mel shoved the last asparagus into his mouth. "You still have food on your plate!"

She looked at her plate and sighed. "I know. I think I waited too long to eat."

"Do you feel like some ice cream?" he asked as he started to clean off the table.

"No, thank you!" she replied, holding her stomach. "Why don't you go ahead and freshen up. I can take care of this."

One of Sdia's pet peeves was to be the only person relaxed and refreshed in a house after dark, while others were still fully clothed. It made her feel edgy.

"I'm okay, baby. You don't have to help," Mel replied.

"Seriously, Mel, I want you to unwind."

Mel swept the trash into the dustpan and emptied it into the trash. "All right, if you insist." He walked behind her and placed his hands inside the small pockets on her robe. "I love you," he said, avidly kissing her on the neck.

"Go on, Mel. I can take care of this," she replied nervously, while pushing him away. His kisses made her stomach flutter.

Mel backed away, catching a clue. He wasn't offended by her actions, only motivated. He had plans on wearing her out before the night was over.

When Mel finished showering, he walked into the kitchen expecting to see Sdia. To his amazement, she was in the room watching television. Mel walked in with a towel wrapped around his waist. He wore boxers underneath. Water trickled down his muscular chest.

"Damn, baby, you fast," he said as he grabbed a bottle of lotion from the dresser.

Sdia continued to put her focus on the television, pretending to be interested. Mel looked at the television and laughed. "What the hell are you watching?"

"I don't know. It looked interesting," she replied with a shrug, staring at the screen.

"Can you lotion my back?" he asked as he held out the bottle of lotion.

"You don't need any lotion. It's time for bed." At first she had looked up at him, but then quickly turned away.

Mel chuckled. "I won't feel right going to bed ashy," he said convincingly, placing the bottle in her hand.

"Turn around." She took the lotion from his hand and squirted a small amount into her palm.

Mel turned his back to Sdia, exposing several tattoos. She could only make out the hand that held a gun with the words, "press your luck," and money dispensing as bullets. The tattoos that one would call art that covered the upper right corner of his back were distorted past the point of appreciation. *But he doesn't think so*, she thought. Sdia lightly placed her hand on his back and began to rub the lotion in a circular motion.

"Damn, baby. That feels good!" he said, bending his head.

She placed her hands higher on his back and began to massage the lotion into his shoulders. Mel slowly rotated his neck. Sdia could feel the heat from his body on her fingertips.

"Thanks, baby," he said, slightly turning to face her.

"No problem," she replied, walking away while rubbing the remaining lotion into her hands.

He grabbed his white tank top from the bed and threw it on. "Let's see what's on." He picked up the remote and changed the channel. Her brooding was disturbed by Mel briefly looking up from the television and in her direction. "Aren't you going to lay down, babe?" he asked with a slight sneer.

"Yeah, I am. I was just trying to figure out if I wanted anything to snack on," she replied, trying to persuade even herself.

Mel slid back onto the bed. He grabbed a pillow and

propped it. "Can you do me a favor and hit that light?"

Sdia flipped the light with her index finger and slowly walked toward the bed, gripping the front of her robe.

"It's all right. Your robe looks pretty secure to me," Mel mocked.

She rolled her eyes as she took a seat on the edge of the bed. "Whatever." Sdia sat through two episodes of *Martin* without changing positions or leaving for the restroom. Her back was killing her.

"Come here," Mel called as he leaned forward and grabbed her arm. She obeyed as she slid her body across the bed and positioned herself next to him at the head of the bed. Her back felt much better as she tried to make herself comfortable. Mel looked at her and smiled.

"Here, baby. Take this," he said, placing a pillow behind her back.

"Thank you," she replied, batting her eyes.

He placed his hand on her back and soothingly stroked up and down. Sdia sat stiff and emotionless. Her heart thumped in her chest and her hands began to tremble.

"Are you all right?" Mel asked, taking her hand and kissing it.

"Yes. Just a little tired from that ride," she replied, rubbing her sinuses.

Mel continued to lay passionate kisses on her hand and eventually moved to her arm. Chills ran up her spine, as her nipples grew hard. *Damn his lips are soft!* Every kiss stimulated her. Sdia sank her body into the pillow and closed her eyes as he made his way to her neck, kissing, licking, and sucking it fervently. Sdia placed her hand on his head and delicately stroked the back of his neck. Mel made circles around her ears with the tip of his tongue before affectionately grabbing her face and kissing her in the mouth. He placed his body between her legs and removed her robe, all while sucking and licking her bottom lip and chin. Sdia could feel his erect penis through his boxers. She opened her incredulous eyes, feeling the big knot that rested on her vagina. *Oh my God! What am I about to do?* She could feel the liquor beginning to wear off. Mel pulled one strap to her nightgown down and tickled her nipple with his tongue. He stopped and looked down at the wet spot on his boxers.

"Damn, baby!" he whispered, as he reached down and ran his fingers across her wet panties. He reached beneath her gown to expose her perfect breasts. Embarrassed, Sdia slightly turned away. Mel licked the inside of her navel before moving to the left and gently biting her side. His wet tongue sent her on a high. She arched her back and prepared herself for what was to come. Mel's heart throbbed as he approached the prize he had worked six long months for. He gazed up at Sdia as he removed her panties with his teeth. She lay there gripping the sheets with her eyes closed, biting down on her bottom lip. Mel kissed and nibbled on her inner thighs, occasionally brushing his nose across her vagina.

"You feel so soft," he whispered between kisses.

Sdia lay there frozen and wordless with mixed emotions. *I'm not ready for this. What am I doing? What would my mother say?*

Without notice, he placed her clit between his lips and passionately sucked. A chill shot up her spine, and she immediately clutched the sheets, moaning loudly as he skillfully tasted her love. His penis grew harder from the combination of two sounds—her moans and his tongue smacking against her wet womanhood. She rotated her hips slowly. She was in ecstasy.

"You taste so good!" he said, as he continued to dine.

Mel's chin and lips glistened as he rose from the foot of the bed. He looked down and kissed her on the mouth. Her first reaction was to turn her face, but instead, she returned the act. She was never one to kiss after receiving oral sex. "It's your shit," Sean would say. "You're basically calling yourself dirty!"

Before returning between her legs, Mel removed his boxers and wife beater. Sdia raised her head from the pillow and looked down at the anaconda that was prepared to strike.

"Uh . . . I . . ." she said, trying to catch his attention, but he was busy playing peek-a-boo, rubbing and poking her vagina with the head of his penis. Her stomach did flips as she began to breathe heavily. Finally, he tried to insert his penis, but months of celibacy made it impossible.

"Damn, babe. It's so tight!" he exclaimed as he tried once more to enter.

She squirmed from the pain, realizing how long it had really been. "I think we should—" she said, in between moans and her internal thoughts. *Stop him, Sdia. Make him stop!*

Mel kneeled forward, took one of her breasts into his mouth, and continued to play with her vagina. He could feel her juices beginning to overflow. Conquered by anticipation and with one push, he was inside. Sdia gasped, almost jumping from the bed. Mel immediately grabbed her face and kissed her.

"I'm sorry," he explained, as he passionately began to thrust against her. He looked down at her, cross-eyed.

"You fit like a glove. Shit!"

Sdia moaned softly, wrapping her hands around his waist while slowing winding on him. Mel sucked her neck and ears and he continued to move in and out of her slowly and carefully, being sure not to hurt her. Sdia could feel herself about to climax. Her moans became louder, and she began to call his name.

"Mel, I'm . . . oh!" And before she knew it, she was leaking and trembling under his body.

Mel continued to plow her until he could feel the head of his penis throbbing inside of her. He didn't have the energy to remove himself. He continued until the warm liquid erupted from his penis and slowly leaked inside of her. Sdia pushed his chest with the palm of her hands.

"Oh, my God! Did you?"

He didn't give her a chance to finish. He placed his finger over her lips.

"Don't worry, I'm safe."

Chapter 40

"Hello. Mr. Will Edwards, please."

"Yes, this is Will. Who's speaking?" he asked, hesitantly.

"Good morning. This is Donna from Doctor Skavolski's office. He would like you to come in."

"Is everything okay?" Will asked uneasily. "Are my test results in?"

"Yes, your results are in," she replied without emotion.

"Well, why can't I just get the results over the phone?"

"I don't know your test results, Mr. Edwards. This is just a routine follow-up. Besides, even if I did know your results, we aren't allowed to give them over the phone."

Will sighed. "Oh, I see."

"Are you available to come in tomorrow morning?" she asked.

"Sure. Around what time?"

"We have an 8:30 and a 10:15. Which one would you like?"

"Ten-fifteen is fine," he replied, uptight.

"You'll be fine, Mr. Edwards," she reassured. "See you tomorrow."

Will hung up the phone and took a deep breath. "I'll be glad when all of this is over." The anticipation was killing him. "Never, ever again will I put myself in this predicament." He knew he was clean. He just hated being on edge. He thought about Lamar for a brief moment. That only intensified his feelings of agony.

"Bastard!" he said.

It had been a month and still no sign of him. Will wondered if they had even really had a relationship. How was it that he had absolutely no type of contact from his man? He obsessed over the same question every day and presumed he'd ask himself that same question for the rest of his life.

"Get it together, man. It's time to move on!" he drilled himself. Once again, he was alone on a Friday night. His luck with men became nonexistent. The last time he went to the club, no one approached him, and he had put on his best. You couldn't tell him he wasn't giving it to "trade." He rationalized with himself as he sat at the bar. He came up with several reasons, and one being, maybe he looked unapproachable. Nevertheless, he did just get out of an intense relationship, so maybe it was too early to get into another. Will thought about calling his mother to talk, but he knew she would castigate his decisions like she continuously did when he made bad choices. He wished he had someone to talk to. For years, he kept to himself. Even in high school, he was a loner. Most of the gay boys he knew hung around women, but not him. He was always alone, and it didn't bother him until now. *What's wrong with me? I must be worthless. That's why Lamar left me, and that's why I don't have any friends.* He began to beat himself up once again. That was his favorite thing to do when things were looking bleak for him.

Will went into the bathroom to shower. He decided that spending the rest of the evening watching movies and stuffing his face with ice cream would be the best resolution. After showering, he slipped into his Adidas sweat suit, and decided to walk to the grocery store to see what Redbox movies were available. He placed his iPhone in his pocket and headed for the stairs. Once outside, he took a deep breath. The crisp air filled his lungs, triggering a cough. He cleared his throat, opened iTunes on his phone, and placed his headphones in each ear. He walked on beat to the sound of "Shackles," by Mary Mary, pretending that with each step he took, a link was being broken.

* * *

"Are you sure you're okay, Talya?" Carl asked with sincerity. He felt at fault for telling her he was going to meet a couple of his co-workers for a drink; in reality, he was meeting Marina.

Natalya nodded. "I'll be fine, Carl," she said, genuinely smiling.

"Really?" he asked, looking at her, disbelievingly.

"Yes." She sighed. looking down at her nails.

It had been almost a month, and she hadn't gotten a manicure. Her reaction was an indicator for him to get out of dodge while he still had the chance. He had a bigger chance of winning the lotto than getting on her good side.

"Okay, call me if you need me," he said, cautiously leaning in to kiss her on the cheek.

Unexpectedly, she turned her face, instigating a kiss on the lips. Carl was astonished, and he didn't know what to do. Natalya slowly pulled away and smiled.

"You don't want to keep your friends waiting."

Carl's lips remained in the air.

"Carl!" she shouted. "You're going to be late!"

Carl opened his eyes and swallowed. For a split second he thought about canceling and staying home.

Natalya turned away and grabbed the remote from the

nightstand. "Have fun!" she stated, kindly dismissing him.

Is this short-term? Will she be like this when I get home? Maybe I should cancel my plans. Carl looked at his watch. "Well, I guess I'm going to be heading out." He looked from the corner of his eye to see her reaction. Natalya yawned, aiming the remote at the TV. Carl stretched and glanced over at her one last time before exiting the room.

* * *

"Hi, sweetie!" Marina said, excitedly. She held her arms out for a hug. Carl hugged her tightly, nearly lifting her from the ground.

"I've missed you so much!" he said.

"I've missed you, too, baby," she replied, kissing him all over the face. "It's been pure agony being away from the man I love for so long." She had been on vacation in Columbia for two weeks visiting her family. Carl stood back and looked at her from head to toe.

"You look beautiful," he said, referring to her bronze tan.

"Thank you." She blushed.

Carl sniffed the air. "It smells wonderful."

She closed the door behind him. "Have a seat and make yourself at home. Dinner will be ready in a minute," she said, returning to the kitchen.

He removed his shoes and slowly sat back in the leather recliner. "Go ahead and make yourself a drink," she suggested, referring to the mini bar.

Carl couldn't wait to get his lips on the meal she was preparing. The aroma made his mouth water. "Do you need some help?" He was trying to be modest. God knows he didn't feel like messing around in some kitchen.

"No thanks, sweetie."

Marina frowned. "The last place I need help is with cooking!"

"Oh, my!" Carl said, looking down at the beans and rice, pastilles, and garden salad she placed in front of him on the table.

"Looks good, doesn't it?" she asked as she pulled out a chair with her left hand and her plate in the other.

"It looks and smells wonderful." Carl stared at his plate.

"Thanks, sweetheart."

"What's this?" he asked, poking at the pastilles with his fork.

"Those are pastilles; they're ground up plantains stuffed with pork and vegetables. It took me hours to make them. You have to boil them."

"Uh huh." Carl broke off a small piece and placed it into his mouth. "Not bad, not bad at all." He continued to eat as she watched him.

"I'm glad you like it."

"The last time I had a decent meal was on Thanksgiving. Other than that, Natalya and I dine on fast food; that's if she can stomach eating with me!" he shamefully admitted. "She never cooks. I can't recall ever seeing her pick up a pot or pan, but she makes a mean cup of coffee." He chuckled, looking up at Marina.

"You do it to yourself, Carl. I don't understand why you put up with her shit," she replied, stuffing a forkful of salad into her mouth.

Carl shrugged. "I know, Marina, and I'm sorry to have to put you through this, but you have to understand."

"What? What do I need to understand? Go ahead and finish."

"Nothing. You're right. I can do something about it. Let's just drop it," he said, returning to his meal.

"No, I will not drop it. We need to talk about this. I want to know where we are taking this."

"We can talk about it later, Marina. I don't want to spoil the night. What type of dressing is this?" He tried his best to evade the issue, but she was adamant.

"No. I want to know!" she shouted.

Me and my big ass mouth. I talk too much! he scorned himself.

"Okay, let's talk," he said, standing with his hand out for her to join him in the living room.

Marina removed the napkin from her lap, wiped her hands, and tossed it onto the table as he led the way. Carl waited for her to sit down before he took his seat.

"Marina, Marina, Marina." He sighed, taking her by the hand and kissing it. "What am I going to do with you?"

"Tell me the truth," she replied.

Carl had no choice but to be honest with her. He couldn't lie. She deserved to be loved. She was a good woman, and he knew he didn't want to lose her. "I don't want to be with Natalya, but I do love her. If we get a divorce, she's going to try to get me for everything I have, babe, and I've worked too hard to get where I am!"

"So you'd rather be disrespected, emotionally abused, and basically treated like shit because you don't want her to take you to court? Does that make sense to you, Carl? I mean, seriously, you're a pretty smart man. You're placing your self-worth on the level of materialistic things!"

Carl sat dumbfounded. She had a good point.

"She's playing the hell out of you," she concluded, before getting up to clear the kitchen table.

Carl followed her to the kitchen. "I don't want to jump into anything with you until I get everything in order with my marriage. That's why I'm not going to sleep with you. As much as I want to, I can't," he said, suddenly becoming emotional. "You deserve the best, and if I can't give you all of me, then I don't want to give you anything!"

A stream of tears fell from her eyes. "I love you so much," she said, walking toward him with her arms extended.

Carl held her in his arms and whispered in her ear, "I promise you by the beginning of next year, my divorce papers will be filed."

Chapter 41

Sdia felt sick to her stomach. Since her and Mel's trip back from Pennsylvania, he had become increasingly obsessive. Everything she did and everywhere she went, he had to be informed. It was as if he owned her. Repeatedly, she questioned her actions, wondering if she had made a huge mistake by sleeping with him. She wanted to talk to someone so badly, but she knew that if she told her mother or Charmaine, she would feel worse.

"Shit!" she cursed, picking up her telephone.

It was Mel. This was his fifth time calling within two hours. Sdia lowered the volume until it was on silent and continued to watch television. "I'll call him back in a few minutes. He won't die if he doesn't speak to me now. I'm watching television," she said. Her home phone rang loudly.

She banged her fist onto the coffee table.

"Fuck!" She jumped up from the sofa. "Hello!" she answered, exposing her frustration.

"What's up with your phone?" Mel asked.

Sdia looked at her fingernails. "Nothing."

There was a silent pause.

"Come and open the door," he replied.

She sighed and hung up the phone.

"Hi, beautiful," Mel said as he walked into the house and kissed her on the cheek. He went straight to the coffee table and picked up her cellphone, scrolling through the missed call log.

"You didn't see me calling?" he asked.

"No, I didn't hear you calling," she sarcastically corrected him.

"Next time turn up the fucking volume," he said, tossing the phone at her.

Sdia's reflexes were too slow. The phone fell to the floor.

"Why would you do that?" she asked angrily.

"Because I bought it, and I pay the bill."

Sdia rolled her eyes and walked away. He ran behind her, grabbed her by the waist, and kissed the back of her neck.

"Stop it, Mel," she said, closing her eyes, but he continued to kiss her neck before turning her around to face him. *Goddamn he's fine!*

"I love you," he said, kissing her forehead.

"I love you, too."

"What's wrong?" he asked warily as he took a step back.

Sdia twisted her lips. Mel rolled his eyes and walked away, taking a seat on the sofa.

"Come here," he ordered.

She slowly walked over and sat down without saying a word.

"Are you still bugging out about what happened?" he asked, playing in her hair.

She fidgeted with her fingers. "No, I'm fine."

He looked at her with disbelief. "Babe, I love you, and I'm not going anywhere."

Sdia looked up momentarily. "That's not what's wrong.

I'm just a little nervous," she said, shrugging.

"About?" he asked sarcastically.

". . . We had unprotected sex."

"Okay, and your point is?" he replied, removing the blunt he had smoked earlier from his pocket and turning up the television as loud as it could go.

"What the fuck do you mean what's my point?" she shouted.

Mel laughed. "Calm down and stop fucking yelling." He lit his blunt.

"I should be the one who's nervous. You're the one who said that lame ass nigga you was fucking with cheated on you." He began choking on the smoke.

"Bullshit!" she shouted. "I haven't had sex in a year, and I got tested right after I broke up with Sean," she explained.

Mel took a long pull of the blunt. "Yeah, okay," he said, trying to keep the smoke in his lungs. He removed his vibrating phone from his pocket and looked at it.

"You too funny," he said, ignoring the call and placing it on his lap. "I could see if you thought you were pregnant or something!"

Sdia could feel her anger boiling over. *Who the fuck does he think he is? He's tryna play me like I'm some fucking whore!*

Mel's ring tone sounded off, indicating that he had a new text message, and without a sound or fair warning Sdia snatched the phone from this lap and leaped off of the couch. She quickly looked at the screen. "Baby, are you still coming ova?" She read aloud.

Mel leaped for the phone, dropping the blunt from his

hand and onto the sofa. "Oh, shit!" he said, hurriedly picking it up, but it was too late. It had already burned a small hole.

"Oh, hell no!" Sdia shouted, walking toward the house door. "Who the fuck is this? Get the fuck out!" she said, her voice beginning to tremble.

Mel snatched the phone from her hand, powered it off, and shoved it into his pocket. "Nobody," he replied, nervously.

Sdia snatched her hand back and smacked him across the face. Mel's head jerked to the left, almost knocking him off of his feet. She held her hand over her mouth, shocked by her strength. In an attempt to make a run for the bedroom, she spun around. She would have made it if she hadn't tripped over the coffee table and fallen face first.

"Are you fucking crazy?" he yelled, snatching her up by the top of her head and dragging her down the hall. He wiped his lip with the back of his hand and noticed blood, which only made him angrier. He violently yanked her head like a ragdoll.

"Stop! Please, Mel. I'm sorry!" she screamed while kicking her legs as she tried to break away, but it was no use. His grip was too tight, and she knew that if she pulled away, she would lose a lock of hair. Sdia closed her eyes and cried loudly, hoping that her neighbors would hear. Mel dragged her into the bedroom and shut the door behind, locking it. Sdia jumped to her feet and ran toward the closet, but he was on her heels.

"Where the fuck you going?" he yelled, grabbing her by the back of her neck and tossing her onto the bed. Sdia covered her face with her hands as he threw hard blows.

He stood between her legs cursing and talking between hits.

"Bitch, are you out of ya fucking mind? I will fucking kill you!"

Sdia tried to fight back with all of her might, but she had no wins; he was too strong. Sdia could taste the warm blood in her mouth. She looked up into his cold eyes. There were no whites. His eyes were completely black. She gasped. It was as if he didn't have a soul. Mel ripped off her T-shirt.

"You gonna try to fucking play me like I'm some bitch-ass nigga?" He snatched her bra off and stared down at her as she cried out in sorrow. Mel licked his lips as his penis began to harden. "Say you sorry!" he ordered, pulling his hand imitating a backhand.

"I'm sorry. Please don't!" Sdia cried, trying to free her arms from under his grip.

Mel leaned down and stared her in the eyes. "Tell me you love me!" he said, gritting his teeth.

She didn't want to look at him and turned her face. *God help me! Please God, help me!*

He snatched her face forward until they were face to face once more. "Tell me you love me, and that you'll never leave me!" he shouted.

Sdia sniffled as she abided his order. Mel began to slowly and soothingly suck her breast while looking up at her to see if she was reacting. Sdia squirmed like a fish without water, jerking and twitching her body, trying to break free.

"Let me go!" she said, out of breath and slightly turned on. *What's wrong with me?* Her movements slowly began to transform to a halt.

"I love you," he sang in her ear. "I don't want anybody else." He began to unzip his pants and reached into his boxers.

"Mel, please. Don't!" Her voice trembled. Sdia's heart raced. She didn't know what to do.

He bit his bottom lip and looked at her. "Shut up."

The thought of having sex made her stomach churn and at the same time, it aroused her. He loosened his grip on her arm, and she immediately grabbed the loop of her jeans in an attempt to keep them on.

"No. Don't!" Her mouth ordered him to stop, but her body wanted him to continue. *What am I thinking? What the fuck is wrong with me? Am I crazy? This man just beat the shit out of me, and he's sleeping with other women. Am I actually turned on right now?*

Mel looked down at her with a smirk. "I'm sorry," he said, stroking her cheek. He leaned forward and gently ran his tongue across her busted lip. "I love you so much, Dia. I swear to God I do. I would never leave you!" he said, as he began to suck her lip. He stopped momentarily and looked at her lip as if he were trying to accomplish something. He caressed her back as he continued to suck on her injured lip until a blood clot formed.

Turned off by his rage, but turned on by the feeling of his soft, wet lips and hard penis between her legs, she closed her eyes and gave into temptation as he began to orally please her from head to toe.

Chapter 42

"Hello, Mr. Edwards. How are you?" the nurse asked, smiling from ear to ear.

"I'm fine and you?" he replied.

"Great, thanks. Have a seat, and Dr. Skavolski will be with you shortly."

Will walked over to the waiting area and took a seat by the magazine rack. He looked around at everyone in the office and tried to guess their reason for visiting the doctor. He soon focused his attention on a young white man who sat alone in the corner. He looked as if he could have been in his early twenties. He wore a thin navy blue windbreaker with nothing underneath, a pair of faded black jeans, and green flip flops . Will stared at his caved-in chest.

If he studied hard enough, he could have counted each bone in his chest. The young man sat blankly staring down at the floor. Will knew he noticed him staring, but he didn't care. Open sores sporadically covered his forehead, cheeks, and the back of his hands as white residue seeped from the corner of his mouth. Will felt his stomach turning. He had never seen anyone look so bad. He reached for the magazine rack. He felt he had stared at the young man long enough and didn't think he could stomach him much longer. He grabbed the first magazine in sight and knocked over the rack.

"Damn!" he whispered as the cheap rack tilted over. He looked around in embarrassment as everyone stared at him. The young man rose to his feet and walked over to help.

"Don't you hate when that happens?" he said jokingly, as he handed Will a small stack of magazines.

Will looked up as he forced a smile on his face. "Who are you telling?" Will replied.

The young man continued to hold the magazines out for Will to take. *Shit. Why is he putting me on the spot?* Will thought as he glanced down at the man's hand. *I know I'm fucked up right now, but there is no way in hell I'm touching those magazines!* It didn't take long for the man to perceive how Will was feeling. He looked down at his hands as his face slowly transformed to hurt.

"Mr. Edwards," the nurse called.

Thank you, God! Will thought as he stood. "Excuse me," he said, brushing past the man who continued to pick up the magazines.

"Hello. We're going to room three," she said as she smiled and led the way.

He wanted to turn around badly to see if the young man was watching him, but he didn't have the nerve. The nurse took his temperature, checked his pressure, and asked a few routine questions before leaving. He sat in the room nervously awaiting the doctor's arrival.

The doctor entered the office to find Will fumbling through the drawers.

"Looking for something, Mr. Edwards?" he asked with a smirk. "Have a seat," he said as he pulled out a chair.

Will turned, mortified. "Uh, oh, hello, Dr. Skavolski. I was just—" he tried to explain.

The doctor fanned his hand. "It's all right. Happens all the time."

Will walked over and took a seat. He wiped his

forehead with the back of his hand anxiously.

"So is everything okay?" he asked, fearfully.

The doctor pulled a stool from under the desk and sat down. "So, how have you been feeling?" he asked, evading the question.

Will looked up at the ceiling. "I've been okay."

The doctor glanced down at his clipboard and swallowed. "Mr. Edwards, a couple of weeks ago we ran a series of tests on you, and well . . . you tested positive for HIV. Now, it doesn't mean—"

Will's heart dropped to his stomach. He clutched his chest as he tried to catch his breath. He couldn't speak. The doctor leaned forward and grabbed his hand. "Listen, Mr. Edwards. Having HIV isn't a death sentence. It clearly means that ..."

Will didn't hear a word he was saying. The doctor's voice drifted into thin air. He sat there as if frozen stiff. *Am I dreaming? This can't be true! He must have gotten my test mixed up with someone else's!*

Will swallowed the lump in his throat. "There must be a mistake." His voice trembled.

The doctor shook his head and looked down. "I'm afraid not, Mr. Edwards. These are your results. Listen, we're going to help you get through this, but I need you to work with me." He stood to his feet and placed his hand on Will's shoulder. "Mr. Edwards, I need to know everyone you've been intimate with."

Will couldn't think. He didn't want to think. All he wanted was his mother. He fell to his knees and began to sob hysterically. "Oh, my God! God, no, no, no!" he shouted as his body jerked with each cry.

The nurse tapped on the door before entering. She sat down in front of Will, extended her arms and held him as he cried.

"Everything is going to be all right!"

* * *

Will's head pounded. He could feel his temples pulsating. "Oh, Jesus!" he moaned as he pulled himself from bed; he had been crying all morning and afternoon. It was now 5:30, and he was finally home. The nurse and doctor held him in the office for over four hours as he recapped the names of all forty-seven men he had unprotected sex with. He knew he had at least six one-night stands, but he couldn't remember their names, or if they even used a condom.

Later on, they provided him with a counselor with whom he had to meet with the next day.

After a couple of weeks, he'd be able to find out how long he'd been living with the infection. The thought of him dying popped into his head, and he began to weep loudly, not caring who heard. His life was basically over. "How do I tell my mother? How can I enjoy life? What do I tell everyone? I'm going to die!" Many thoughts manifested as he lay in a fetal position on the cold wooden floor in his underwear. He could never forgive himself for being so naive and callous with his life. "All of the commercials, the ads on the train, and the articles in magazines; it was all there for me to take heed to; how did I ignore the signs?" he asked himself as his right cheek lay in a pool of slob and tears. He couldn't think of a single reason why he should be living. It wasn't like he actually had a life. Every day was the same routine—work, home, home, work and occasionally he'd hit the bar. *I can't believe I'm sick! I bet I got infected when I went to Cancun two years ago. I bet it was the guy I slept with the first night I got there; he looked kind of sick now when I think back on it. No wait! I slept with him my third night there. Ohhh, I know! It was probably the dude from the gas station. He was really thin. FUCK! Why God, why?*

He began to mentally run through the negative aspects of his life from beginning to end until he was on his feet reaching in the medicine cabinet and pulling out a full pack of Tylenol PM. His hands trembled as he held an empty glass under the faucet, allowing the cool water to spill over onto his hand. Will took a long glance at himself in the mirror. His bloodshot, swollen eyes gazed back. Tears oozed from his eyes until the vision of himself became blurry. He floated into his room with the cup of water in one hand and the packet of pills in the other. He was completely congested and hardly able to breathe from his nose. He gasped for air in between cries as he imagined his mother and sister's reaction to the self-centered infliction he was about to cause.

He took a seat on the edge of his bed and looked around the room for his Bible. He gently placed the cup of water and pack of pills onto the floor, walked over to his window sill, and grabbed his small Bible. He returned to the bed and fumbled through the pages until he got to Psalms 23. Will placed the Bible face down onto his bed and took baby steps into each room of his apartment, focusing on any and every little thing that he saw, self-consciously he was saying goodbye. He had never noticed the small crack in the bathroom commode until now, nor had he ever recognized that the kitchen tiles weren't all the same size. After almost a half hour of exploring, he returned to his bed with his cell phone in hand. *Now, for the hardest part,* he thought as he slowly dialed his voicemail. He couldn't bear the thought of calling his mother and hearing her voice. So he decided to forward a message to her to share with his sister. Will waited for the operator's prompt to leave a message, and then he began to speak:

"Hey, Ma," his voice began to crack as he took a deep breath. "Don't think that you missed my call because you didn't!" He let out a fake chuckle. "Anyway, I was just calling to say hello and to tell you that I love you and miss you and Tay so much. Today has been a long day for me, Ma, extremely long. I was sitting thinking about how it used to be when the three of us lived together." There was a long pause as he pulled the phone away from his mouth and cried into the pillow.

"I used to always say I couldn't wait until I turned eighteen so that I could move. I always thought you and Tay stayed in my business and never gave me my privacy. Now I would give anything to go back to those days. Ma, I've been going through so much, and a lot of times I keep what I go through to myself because I don't want to burden you, but believe me, it's hard trying to deal with this much. I can't explain how much you and Tay mean to me and how grateful I am to have y'all in my life. God is good, Ma, and I am truly blessed. I know you're probably saying, 'Why is this boy leaving me this message?' All I can say is that I have my reasons. I love you, Ma, more than you'll ever know, and please let Tay know the same. I want to apologize for any and everything I have ever done to disrespect or hurt the two of you, and I mean it from the bottom of my heart. I love you, Ma. I love you so much, and I know as a single parent you did the best you could raising us and I want to thank you! Please try to understand why I did what I am about to do. Please, Ma. I can't stand facing you with this horrible, horrible disease that has taken over my mind, body, and soul. I love you, Ma!"

Then he broke down and cried softly into the phone before hanging up and placing his cellphone beside him. He grabbed his Bible and began to calmly read Psalm 23 aloud. After reading the verses, he reached down and slowly picked up his glass of water. The condensation from the water rolled off of his hand as he tightly gripped the glass. Will reached over to his side and opened up the box of medication, slowly popping each capsule from the package. By the time he was done, he had twenty-four pills lying beside him. He turned the pages of his Bible until he got to Psalm 51. He placed two pills in his mouth and took a long sip of water.

"Have mercy upon me, Oh God," he recited, placing two more pills in his mouth as he continued to read. Will pulled himself up to the head of his bed and placed his head on his pillow. He had taken thirteen pills and hadn't felt anything, so he continued to place them in his mouth until they were all gone. Will set the empty glass on his nightstand, lay back onto his pillow, and for the next hour and a half he continuously read Psalm 51 until he could feel himself becoming dizzy. He breathed slowly, clutching the Bible in his hand. He realized his heart was slowing down. He tried to finish reading, but his vision was hazy. He tried to take his mind off the passage by envisioning his mother's beautiful smile.

"Wait!" he shouted, as he thought of jumping up and going to the neighbor's house for help. *I can't leave my mother and Tay alone. They need me! God, help me! Please, Lord Jesus, help me.* He placed his hand on the nightstand as he tried to pull himself up, but his efforts were futile. "I'm not ready to die!" he mumbled softly.

Will's lips grew cold as his body trembled uncontrollably. He felt himself breaking out in a cold sweat as his breathing slowly altered to light wheezes. He could feel his life slowly drifting away.

"God, forgive me, please!" he wheezed, before closing his eyes.

Chapter 43

"This is my fourth time calling you, Mel. You need to call me when you get this message!" Sdia slammed the phone down. Once again, she had been trying to contact him relentlessly for the past hour. The last time she had spoken to him was the day before, when he had told her he would call her back as soon as he was finished eating. That was sixteen hours ago, and his phone was off. Her stomach did flips as she walked through her apartment spot cleaning, something she often did when she couldn't get in contact with him. Her home phone began to ring. She dropped the magazine from her hand and ran over to answer it.

"This better be his ass!" she said as she snatched the phone from the receiver.

She looked at the caller ID and sighed. It was Sharon. Sdia strained a smile onto her face.

"Hello, Mother. How are you?" she answered in a British accent.

"Quite fine, my dear," Sharon replied in an accent of her own.

The two laughed out loud. Sharon proceeded to ask Sdia how her day was going and whether she had decided if she was coming down for the weekend.

"It's not like you can't come out here, Ma," Sdia replied.

Sharon hadn't been up north to see Sdia in months. She was always using Thomas as an excuse.

"Daddy's a grown man, Ma!" Sdia always had to

remind her.

She cut the conversation short by telling her mother that the maintenance man had come to fix her closet door and that she needed to keep an eye on him.

At first, Sharon was a little hesitant to hang up, but eventually she caught on. Sdia went into her bedroom and fell face first onto the bed. Her face became hot as she cried as hard as she could into the pillow. *This is it. It's over. I can't do this anymore. I hate him!* She made the hundredth promise to never call him again or answer his calls. *I got played. He used me. He doesn't care. I played myself by messing with him. Charmaine was right.* So many thoughts came in and out of her head until she found herself with the worst migraine ever. She slowly sat up sniffing and wiping her eyes.

"I need a drink!" She went into the kitchen and removed a half-full bottle of Hennessey Privilege that Mel had purchased a couple of weeks ago. She opened the bottle and sniffed the contents.

"Ewww!" she said, frowning. It definitely wasn't her choice of liquor, but it would have to do. It was either that or one of the Xanax bars Ibtihaj had given her. *God I hate the thought of taking pills, but what's worse drinking or popping a Xan?* Sdia bit her bottom lip and contemplated how she was going to get fucked up. She had only taken the Xanax bar once and that was to calm her nerves for a big article she had due. "This shit feels amazing!" She recalled telling her co-worker within ten minutes of taking the pill. Ibtihaj was reluctant about giving it to her, but with a few crocodile tears, fake tremors and pretending to have a nervous breakdown, Ibtihaj eventually gave in. It was unfortunate that Ibtihaj's brother-in-law was killed in a car accident and that her sister was prescribed the medication, but for Sdia they definitely came in handy. Sdia walked into the kitchen and grabbed one of the five Xanax bars from her stash behind the toaster and popped it in her mouth. "Fuck!" The bitter taste was nauseating. *Henny is definitely is out of the picture tonight!* She quickly ran to the refrigerator and grabbed a bottled water and TV dinner. She placed the frozen meal into the microwave and decided to take a shower while it cooked. She wanted to be relaxed before she passed out.

Before taking a shower, she checked her cellphone for missed calls and turned the ringer off on her house phone. She felt like calling Charmaine, but their friendship had changed over the past few months, particularly after Thanksgiving ; they were already into the New Year.

"That bitch is jealous of you. She's just mad that nobody wants her hating ass!" Mel would say.

Sdia couldn't mention Charmaine's name around him without him flipping the handle. If Charmaine called and Mel was around, she wasn't allowed to answer. He'd go berserk. She felt miserable and wanted to know why she was always getting the raw end of the deal.

Sdia sat down on the couch and took a sip of water. "Oh, my God!" The bitter taste of the pill remained glued to her taste buds. "I should be working on my article about the homeless shelter instead of sitting here stressing over some nigga!" She placed her hand on her forehead. *Why can't I get it together?* She took another sip of water. *FUCK!* She had actually forgotten how bad the pill really taste. *I should take another one.* She knew she'd be on her ass if she took another pill and that it would only prolong the submission of her article that was due in two days. *Fuck it!* She walked back over to her stash, grabbed another pill and popped it in her mouth. She glanced over at her chicken pot pie that was still cooking in the microwave. *Why didn't I take this shit after I ate something?* She shook her head. *Guess I gotta grin and bear this one out!* All she wanted to do was get high. "I can't believe this asshole has me popping pills!" She guzzled down the bottle of water until it was gone. Her heart wanted to race as she tried to imagine him having sex with another woman, but the emotions she wanted to feel didn't fester; she felt numb to that harsh reality. Their relationship had changed tremendously within the past month, particularly after he violated her. *Was it rape or consensual? I could have tried harder to stop him; I must have enjoyed it, which makes me a freak. What's wrong with me?* Sdia couldn't determine whether she enjoyed it or despised it.

Is it the same as what Uncle George did to me? No, it can't be. I'm older now. I've had sex with Mel before. He's my boyfriend and I love him! I wonder if Uncle George molested my mother. I've got to tell someone what he did to me...anyone! Maybe if I told Mel he'd love me and stop treating me this way. I wonder what my parents would say if they knew what Uncle George did to me. Mel's probably eating another bitch ass \ as we speak. He loves to eat ass. Although her thoughts were scrambled; they still made sense.

She had her suspicions of Mel seeing other women; constantly going into another room to talk on the phone, the late night text messaging, coming over with the scent of sex and perfume clinging to his clothes and disappearing for days at a time. Those were all the signs of a cheating spouse, but she knew he would never confess. Every time she confronted him, he'd simply reply, "Babe, it's all in your head. Stop being so insecure, Sdia!" But no matter how much she tried, she couldn't suppress the feeling that he was being untrue. She began to replay every incident in her mind to support her beliefs. The last time she had seen Mel, he had taken her out for dinner and a movie. During dinner, he was extremely panicky and left his seat more than three times to use the restroom, or so he said. When they got to the movie theater, he sat uninterested for a half-hour before pulling out his cellphone and texting.

"You could at least watch the ending!" she had grumbled.

"Why you worried about me?" he asked, bothered.

Sdia stood, then grabbed her coat from the seat and walked out of the movie theater.

"Aww, you mad?" He laughed, following behind her.

Tears fell from her eyes as she silently cried. *Why is God punishing me? Why can't I find a good man?* She tilted her head back as the effect of the pills kicked in. *Ok. No more thinking Sdia. Just rest. Just close you eyes and rest.* She placed her head back onto the couch and closed her eyes. Sdia could feel her head spinning nonstop. She could smell her TV dinner burning, but she didn't have the energy to get up.

By the time she opened her eyes it was 6:30 in the evening. "Really? Six hours later and I still haven't heard from this nigga? Sdia sighed. She didn't know how much more she could take of Mel's disrespectful ways. She considered calling him once more, but she knew he probably wouldn't answer. Her skin grew clammy and hot. She fanned her face with her hand as she removed her boxers with the other. She lay there in a wife beater and panties, half-awake. She couldn't take her mind off of

Mel's whereabouts, and she started getting choked up. As her eyes began to burn, she tried her best to fight back the tears.

"Fucking bastard!" she said, wiping her eyes.

Tears spilled down the side of her temples as she stared at the ceiling. She could hear her cellphone ringing in the other room, but she didn't budge. With her luck, it would just be her mother since no one else ever called.

"Where are all of your friends, Dia?" Sharon would ask. "Don't you talk to other guys on the phone?"

She hated when her mother asked her that. She used to ask the same questions when she and Sean were together. Sdia tried having male friends, but it only brought problems. She learned that early on with Sean, and she didn't even bother trying it with Mel. He just wasn't having it. There were times like these that she wished she had someone to fall back on. She looked at the cordless phone.

"I should call his ass again!" She reached for the house phone and dialed his number once more, but to no avail. She got his voicemail. "I swear to my mother, I'm never speaking to his ass again. He better not ever call me *again*. I should change my number," she pondered, clutching the phone in her fist so tight that the vein in her forearm protruded. If Mel were standing in front of her right then, she knew she would have bashed him in the face with the phone. He was really trying to play her. Her mind kept shifting from Mel to Charmaine. Sharon always told her never to give up her friends for a man.

Sdia went into her bedroom to get her cellphone. She was going to take her chances and call Charmaine. The Xanax had built up some courage, and she knew that she wouldn't have been able to call if she was sober. She slowly dialed the numbers as she thought of how to start the conversation.

"Hello?" Charmaine answered, slightly irritated.

"Hey!" Sdia replied, impersonating her sober self.

There was a long pause before Charmaine responded, "What's up, Dia?"

Sdia let out a sigh of relief. "Nothing much, I was just calling to—"

Charmaine cut her off. "Having problems with ya man?" she asked, sarcastically.

Sdia sucked her teeth and slurred, "Maine, now you know that's not even true."

"So why haven't I heard from you?"

"So much has been going on. I mean with work and—"

"Work and what?" she interrupted. "It's not like you're in school or have kids. You wrong, and you know you are. How are you going to cut me off for a man? We're supposed to be friends. I would never do that to you. That's some real fucked up shit. I would never put a man before you, and I bet his bitch ass was happy we weren't speaking. Anything I told you was always for your own good ... always!" As she raised her voice, her words began to crack.

Sdia sat there silent. *What can I say? Everything she's saying is true.* She tried to hold back the tears, but she just couldn't. "Sorry," she answered.

Charmaine sucked her teeth.

"Look . . ." Her voice trembled. "I have to go. I'ma have to call you back some other time," she said, quickly hanging up.

Sdia burst into tears. *What have I done? How could I have let this happen?* She could hear her mother's words replaying in her mind: *The last thing you ever want to do is turn your back on your friends, Dia. Remember, men come and go, but true friends are forever!*

Chapter 44

"Is there something wrong with the food?" Natalya asked.

Carl looked up from his plate.

"No, Talya. Everything looks great. You know I've always loved your veal." He took his fork and broke off a small corner, placing it in his mouth.

"Good, so what do you have planned this evening?" she asked, lifting the glass of wine to her lips.

Carl shrugged. "I don't know."

Natalya grunted. *Here I am trying to play wife, and his fat ass doesn't even appreciate that. Damn, Lamar!* She could feel the tears beginning to well from the thought of him. She quickly rose to her feet and began to clear the table, sniffing as she tried to suppress her pain.

"What's wrong, Talya?" Carl asked, concerned.

"Nothing, I'm fine," she replied, turning to the sink.

Carl continued to gather large portions of mixed vegetables, mashed potatoes, and veal on his fork and crammed it into his mouth. "What do you have planned for the evening?" he asked, with a mouthful of food.

"I'm not sure. I was hoping that maybe we could—" Carl's cell rang.

"Hold on, babe," he said, removing it from his hip.

Natalya shook her head. "Oh, no, he didn't!"

"Oh, I have to take this call. Excuse me," he said as he walked out of the kitchen.

Natalya stood there in dismay. She couldn't believe her

eyes. "Who does he think he is? Is he crazy or what?"

* * *

"That's fine. How's 6:30?" Carl asked.

"Perfect," Marina replied.

"Okay, I'll see you then," he said before disconnecting the call. Carl entered the kitchen to find Natalya standing there infuriated.

"What was that all about?" she asked, staring at him.

Carl took a seat and continued with his meal. "Nothing, just a couple of the guys from the job. They want to shoot some pool. What were you saying before I stepped out?" he asked.

Natalya fanned her hand. "Nothing. I wasn't saying anything." Natalya sucked her teeth. "Just leave me your credit card before you head out. I need to pick up some more Monistat 7 she said, tossing the dishrag onto the table and walking out.

"Oh okay," he said, shrugging and stuffing the remainder of food into his mouth. He looked up at the ceiling and smiled. *I really don't care what she has to say. My only concern is an outfit to wear and seeing Marina. It's time for me to start taking care of me. From now on, we're playing by my rules; it's a new day, new game, and new season and guess what, Natalya? You got traded!*

* * *

"She got a fat ass!" Roc said excitedly, making a reckless U-turn.

"Come on, son!" Mel snapped and looked at his watch.

"I told this dude I was going to be there in fifteen minutes, and you want to look at bitches. I knew I should have driven."

"Calm down. He can wait. Did you see that bitch? That bitch was bad!" Roc replied, putting the car in park.

"I gotta be back in Jersey by midnight," Mel said, annoyed.

"Give me a minute, son. Two minutes," Roc replied, holding up two fingers as he jumped from the car.

Mel huffed and glanced at his watch. "Hurry up!"

"Thirsty ass. I ain't neva chasing no female down. With Sdia it was different; I was returning her wallet." He justified his actions.

There was no shame in Roc's game; when he saw something he wanted, he went after it. He was one of those guys who hung out of the passenger's side of their friend's car yelling, "Yo, ma!" And if a female didn't respond, she was sure to hear, "Fuck you, you bum ass bitch!" Mel smiled as he thought about his friend's savage behavior.

"Damn!" he said, looking at his phone; it was Niki.

"Yo?" he said, flipping the phone open.

"Hey, babe. What's up?" she asked cautiously, trying not to intrude on his whereabouts.

"Ain't shit. What's up wit' you?" He figured he'd chat with her to kill time.

"Nothing. I miss you, baby," she said, in a low sexy tone.

"Didn't you get enough last night? I just left you not even an hour ago!" he bragged.

Niki laughed. "I know, but I want some more. I miss you."

"Yeah?" He chuckled. "I'ma come through and bless that before I head back home. I promise."

"Hmmm, okay, Daddy," she purred.

Mel heard the alert of a new voicemail in his ear. "Niki, let me call you right back," he said, before switching over. Mel listened to his voicemail:

This is my fourth time calling you, Mel. You need to call me when you get this message! Sdia's voice played loudly into the receiver.

Mel sucked his teeth and deleted the message. "Damn, here we go with this bullshit!" He hung up and called her house and cellphone. He didn't feel like arguing with her, so he was grateful when he got her answering machine.

"Babe, it's me. I had to rush out of town last night for an emergency. My battery died, and I just charged my phone. I'ma be heading back home in the next few hours after I take Jaz grocery shopping. Make sure you call me when you get this message. I'ma stop by when I get back. I got a surprise for you. I love you. Bye." Mel hung up the phone and recalled the message he just left. *Perfect. I know she ain't gonna question that!* He looked at his watch. "Roc has been in there for almost ten fucking minutes. He needs to hurry up. I got shit to do!" He grabbed the keys from the ignition and got out the car.

"Where did his thirsty ass go?" he mumbled as he walked toward the end of the block toward *La Elite* boutique.

"Yo!" Roc stuck his head out the door of the boutique. "I'm in here," he said with a smirk.

Mel knew what that meant. Whoever the female was he hunted down must be the shit. Roc always kept at least two fly bitches. His baby's mother was beautiful, and he wasn't a bad looking dude himself. He stayed fresh, rocking the latest and driving the hottest cars. Half the time women were approaching him. Their only complaint was his hostile attitude and wild behavior. He was definitely a thug.

From the moment Mel walked into the boutique, his eyes widened from what he saw. She was short, chocolate-complexioned, with long, jet-black hair and her body was amazing. Her waist looked at least twenty-four inches, her hips looked to be about thirty-four and her ass was like a bubble.

"Oh shit!" he muttered. Roc had definitely picked a winner.

The female looked up briefly before returning her attention to the dress she held. Her girlfriend stood beside her smiling, as Roc continued to flirt with the two.

"You want that dress? If you want it, it's yours," he said, slowly removing it from her hand and turning toward the register.

Mel couldn't help but laugh out loud. "I hear that!" he said, interrupting.

The dress had to be at least $300, but money wasn't an issue for Roc. If he had it, then he would spend it. Mel carefully examined the two women. They both had to be in their early to mid-thirties. The short, dark-skinned one returned the stares with a slight smile on her face. *Damn, she's bad!* he thought, wishing he had seen her first. She quickly turned and joined Roc at the register.

"Excuse me," she said, taking the dress from the counter. "I can pay for this myself." She pulled out her wallet, turned and looked at Mel and smiled. Roc rolled his eyes. He caught the hint. Mel motioned him to come over.

"You ready, son? That bitch is wack," Roc said, walking over.

"Yeah, I got a lot of shit to do." Mel laughed. He knew Roc had hard feelings, so he emphasized the importance of his agenda.

"Those bitches look old anyway!" Roc added, turning and giving the two women one last glance.

Mel nodded in agreement. In the back of his mind, he wanted so badly to get the dark-skinned woman's number. She was stunning. For the first time in his life, he was willing to go after the same girl his best friend had wanted. The two men briskly walked to the car, with Roc leading the way.

"That bitch is dumb!" he said as he took the keys from Mel.

Mel waited for Roc to unlock the door. *Damn!* he thought to himself as his male instincts began to kick in. Mel had to get her number, and he knew she was feeling him; her eyes said it all.

"Yo. Wait right here, son. I think I left my phone in the store," he said as he patted his pockets.

"Yeah, all right!" Roc laughed.

Mel jogged away toward the boutique, in hopes of finding the beautiful lady inside. He slowly pulled the door open and coolly walked in.

"Hello, can I help you?" a saleswoman called from behind the counter, causing everyone in the store to look at him.

"Nah, just looking," he replied with a fake smile. He looked around until he spotted his prey. She was by the jewelry counter trying on necklaces. Mel smiled as he approached her from behind. Her girlfriend gestured to help fasten the necklace, but before she could reach out,

Mel stepped in front of her, being careful to stay out of view of the target. He placed his index finger over his lips, signaling for her to keep quiet. She looked at him and smiled, complying with his demand. He could smell the sweet scent of her perfume as he gently assisted her with fastening the latch. She quickly turned around. The scent of his cologne had exposed his presence.

"Oh!" she said, startled, staring up at him.

Mel smiled and said, "I'm sorry. Your friend was having trouble, so I offered a hand."

She turned and looked at her friend for confirmation. "Yeah, girl. That latch was too small," her girlfriend said.

The woman turned to face Mel and smiled. "Well, thank you."

Mel took a step back and looked her up and down before replying, "You're quite welcome." He extended his hand for a handshake. The woman placed her hand in his, revealing a large diamond wedding ring. *Wow, just my luck! I knew someone that fine wasn't walking around single.*

"My name is Natalya, and this is my best friend, Abby," she said, turning to her friend.

"Mel," he said, extending his hand to Abby. "Well, it was nice meeting you two," he said, handing Natalya the necklace. He proceeded to the door, and Natalya quickly nudged Abby.

"Should I?" she asked.

"Hell yeah! He is absolutely delicious," Abby replied, wishing that it had been her that he approached.

"I don't want to seem desperate," she whispered and frowned.

"Uh, hello! Can't you see he came back in here for you? So really, who's the desperate one?" she asked, trying to ease Natalya's mind.

"Right," Natalya replied. She ran behind Mel, stopping him before he could open the door.

"Excuse me, Mel?" she said, tapping him on the shoulder. "I'd like to give you my number. Maybe we can go out for a latte or something," she said, batting her eyes.

"A latte?" he mocked, looking down at her wedding ring and letting out a low whistle. *Got-damn, that rock is huge! That's gotta be at least five karats.*

Natalya blushed in embarrassment. "Oh, I see. Is this a problem for you?" she asked, looking down at her finger and then at him.

Mel placed his hands in his pocket and laughed. "Nah, that's your problem."

"Trust me, it's a long story." She laughed along with him. She couldn't believe her determination. It was so out of her character.

Mel retrieved his phone to enter her number. "Natalya, right?"

To be continued...

Dear Reader,

I hope that you enjoyed, *Lust Now, Cry Later.* Although the characters in *Lust Now, Cry Later* are fictional, HIV/AIDS is real. When all is said, you have control over your actions and who you choose to allow into your life. I hope that through the lives of my characters you were able to learn, find the strength and confidence to take control over the situations in your life that you might be facing. May we all continue to love, respect, and protect ourselves and each other!

Peace & Blessings,

Tahanee

For more information on testing centers in your area please call CDC National Hotline: **1-800-CDC-INFO (1-800-232-4636).**

A Sneak Peek Inside
Lust Now, Cry Later
Part 2

~

Dying For Love

(Lust Now, Cry Later 2)

Chapter 1

Mel stood sideways on the opposite side of the glass door smoking a cigarette. He leaned forward and peered through the glass until he spotted his target. "Have a great weekend," Sdia called out to the staff from the other departments as they stood around in the lobby conversing. She smiled and nodded as she made her way to the exit. *Fucking bitch is always flirting!* His blood was beginning to boil. He clenched his fist as he continued to study her every move.

Sdia casually walked through the lobby, swaying her body from side to side. She bowed her head and reached into her purse for her keys. As she approached the glass door, she slowly raised her head. Abruptly she stopped in her tracks. Mel's familiar dark brown eyes coldly stared into hers. She frantically looked around at the familiar faces. She took a deep breath and quickly pushed the glass doors open.

"Why the fuck you ain't answering my calls?" he

shouted, as he grabbed her by the arm, ripping her from the entrance.

"Mel, please. Not here!" she pleaded, staring at him with fear.

"No, fuck that!" His voice grew louder. "Who the fuck do you think you're playing with?" he asked, shoving her forward.

"Let's talk," she said as she nervously looked around in search of anyone who may have noticed the run in.

"Yeah, let's talk," he mocked, directing her toward the parking lot.

"Have a good weekend," the short, Hispanic maintenance man called out as they walked past him."

Sdia smiled, forcing her eyes to squint and leak the welled up tears that had formed. "You too." Her voice shook.

Mel sucked his teeth as he made his way in front of her, grabbing her by the wrist, transforming his shove into a pull. He pressed the automatic lock on his car key.

"Get in," he demanded, jerking the door open and forcing her inside.

Sdia climbed into the car and quickly wiped the tears from her eyes. Mel rushed over to the driver's side and slid in. He fastened his seatbelt before reaching over and grabbing a handful of her hair. "Why the fuck do I have to keep on going through this with you." He snarled through gritted teeth. "What's wrong with you?" he asked, releasing her hair and violently shoving her head forward. Her long black hair bounced, falling forward, and then latched onto the tears and snot that rested on her face. "I'm fucking talking to you, dummy!" Mel grabbed her by the

340

back of her neck and clawed away the hair from her face. "You look so fucking stupid!" He pushed her head down toward her lap. "I fucking hate you! You know that? Look at me when I'm talking to you, bitch!" he demanded, grabbing her by the hair once more and pulling her head backward. He wiggled her head up and down like a ragdoll. "Do you hear me talking to you? You don't want to be with me anymore?" Sdia stared at him blankly. "Bitch, I'm talking to you!" He grabbed her by the face and squeezed her cheeks. Sdia tried to squirm away, but her attempts only caused him to apply more pressure. "Where do you think you're going, huh? You ain't going no fucking where!" She could feel her teeth pressing against the inside of her jaws. "I should squeeze your face until your fucking eyeballs pop out of your motherfucking head!" he threatened.

"You're hurting me," she managed to blurb through fish-like lips.

"Shut the fuck up and put that seatbelt on. Mel violently shoved her face away. "You're coming home with me!"

~

Will Sdia's actions of courage lead to her own demise?

Will Lamar's secret be enough for Carl to end his marriage with Natalya?

Is Mel going to finally meet his match when he becomes involved with Natalya?

Stay tuned to find out the mind-blowing drama that unfolds in "Dying For Love" (A Lust Now, Cry Later sequel)

*****

341

Wahida Clark Presents: Tahanee Sayyid

Tahanee Sayyid is an Author & Relationship Columnist who offers women logical resolutions, methods and suggestions to accomplish a positive outcome in their relationship.

Although Tahanee understands the human needs and desires regarding the way we interact, communicate have with ourselves and others; she does not believe that one needs companionship in-order to attain happiness and thrive in life.

Tahanee's passion for writing landed her a position as a writer for Yandy Smith (of VH1's Love In Hip Hop) Everything Girls Love magazine. She is also the Host and creator of the new show, Bedroom Busters and Bites.

Tahanee's desire and ability to connect with the public has garnered her speaking engagements at Gaudette College, Howard University and University of Maryland University College to name a few. She has also made public appearances at churches, fundraisers and Aids Awareness Events. Whether it is through her books, cooking show or articles the importance of, self-love and having standards is always the message behind her work.

Tahanee has over fifteen years in the Education field and is a Computer Operations Technician.

For more excerpts, book release dates, appearances, and more visit: Tahanee.org

Stay Connected!!!
Instagram: @Totallytahanee
Facebook: Tahaneezarinah
Twitter: Totallytahanee
YouTube: Bedroom Busters and Bites

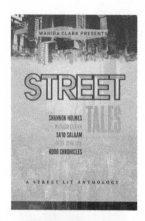

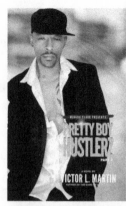
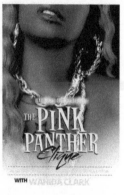